THE HOUSE OF LAST RESORT

THE HOUSE OF LAST RESORT

A NOVEL

CHRISTOPHER GOLDEN

ST. MARTIN'S PRESS
NEW YORK

First published in the United States by St. Martin's Press, an imprint of St. Martin's Publishing Group

Design by James Sinclair

www.stmartins.com

Library of Congress Cataloging-in-Publication Data

Names: Golden, Christopher, author.
Title: The house of last resort : a novel / Christopher Golden.
Description: First edition. | New York : St. Martin's Press, 2024.
Identifiers: LCCN 2023036034 | ISBN 9781250285898
    (hardcover) | ISBN 9781250285904 (ebook)
Subjects: LCGFT: Paranormal fiction. | Horror fiction. | Novels.
Classification: LCC PS3557.O35927 H68 2024 | DDC 813/.54—
    dc23/eng/20230817
LC record available at https://lccn.loc.gov/2023036034

Our books may be purchased in bulk for promotional, educational, or business use. Please contact your local bookseller or the Macmillan Corporate and Premium Sales Department at 1-800-221-7945, extension 5442, or by email at MacmillanSpecialMarkets@macmillan.com.

First Edition: 2024

10 9 8 7 6 5 4 3 2 1

For Nicholas and Danielle

Only you and your darkness know who you are.
—Amber Tamblyn

BOOK ONE

SEPTEMBER ABOVE

1

The rats are like fingers.

No. That's not right. Fingers can reach out, can grasp and extend. The rats are not like fingers at all. They are periscopes, like those on submarines, each able to give its captain only a limited view of the world above. From their place below, among the dead, the lost ones can see only as far as the rats can see. But they are patient, and so they wait. And they let the rats run.

2

Tommy fought the urge to jump from the car and run all the way home. Kate would murder him, of course, and his grandparents—who awaited their arrival—would be less than pleased. The fact that he'd sold his childhood home and given up the apartment he and Kate had shared in Boston would also be a problem. They'd put the Mediterranean Sea and thousands of miles of Atlantic Ocean between themselves and everything they knew to start this new adventure together in Sicily.

This was home now.

The tiny Fiat wound its way up through the narrow streets of Becchina. The engine whined in protest at having to pull the small trailer up the twisty road that was the heart of this hill town.

"Hey," Kate said, reaching over to put a hand on his thigh. "It's going to be perfect."

"Your Tommy-sense kicking in again?"

"I don't need superpowers. You think I can't just look at you and see how tense you are?" Kate took his right hand off the wheel and kissed his knuckles. "I told you. It's going to be perfect. Trust me."

She squeezed his hand to ground him, let him know she was with him all the way.

Tommy pulled back his hand. "I need both to steer. Last thing I want to do is crash into one of these old buildings. Not the first impression I want to make on the locals."

Kate scoffed. "It wouldn't exactly be your first impression. You're like royalty around here."

"That's a slight exaggeration."

"Is it, though?"

She was overstating a bit, but it was true he wasn't exactly a stranger to Becchina. The population had dwindled over the past few decades, but many of the people had met him before. He had been here five times in his twenty-eight years, visiting his grandparents first with his mom and dad, and later just with his mother. Then, four months ago, he had come to Becchina with Kate, and that had changed everything.

In many ways, it had become a ghost town. There were many of them in Sicily—places too distant from the island's coast or from the few business hubs, places abandoned by the young in favor of Palermo, or more likely Rome or Milan on the mainland. The more adventurous departed for other European nations or for the United States. Some of the hill towns in the vast island's interior managed to use tourism to keep their communities alive, if not exactly vibrant, but Becchina didn't have the castles of Erice, or the cathedral of Monreale. It didn't have fifth-century temples with a view of the Mediterranean like Agrigento.

Becchina did have a few things going for it. An ancient set of stone steps wove down through the town—two hundred twenty-seven steps, more than the famous stairs in Ragusa. The town also boasted a church with a blue neoclassical dome older than the one on the basilica in Ragusa, but church and dome were both in desperate need of restoration. The town had breathtaking views of the valley and quiet streets that were clean and colorful. Yet somehow it had never made it onto the radar of the travel sites.

A forty-minute drive from the volcanic Mount Etna, Becchina should have been alive.

Instead, it was the corpse of a town that didn't even realize it was already dead.

The mayor, Fausto Brancati, had seen other towns take drastic measures and had followed their lead. Becchina needed new blood, and it no longer mattered where that blood originated. At Mayor Brancati's instruction, the town seized abandoned homes and offered them for sale for a single euro, with certain strings attached. The buyer had to live in the home for at least five years and had to spend a minimum of fifty thousand euros on renovations. They were trying to lure people with a sense of adventure and romance, people who might stay beyond the five years, who might have children in Becchina and raise them here, although in his heart, Brancati had to know that most of those children would leave when they were old enough.

That's a long way off, Tommy thought. He wasn't even sure he and Kate would stay the five years needed to solidify their ownership of their new house. But he wasn't going to tell her that.

"I still have no idea how the movers' truck is going to get to the house," Kate said as the Fiat juddered through a series of potholes.

"Magic?" Tommy said. "Maybe they use a hot air balloon."

She poked him in the side.

"Hey! Don't poke the driver!"

"Hot air balloon, my butt."

Tommy snickered. "So many jokes. Brain overloading."

"I would punch you so hard, but I'm glad to see you smiling. This is supposed to be a happy day. Literally the happiest day that isn't our wedding day. It's like a dream. Look around you, Tom."

"I'm trying not to crash."

"I may punch you again if you don't look around."

He looked around.

Kate was not always right, but Tommy would admit she often showed a lot more common sense than he did. Only a year his senior, somehow she'd acquired far more wisdom than he'd managed.

Spring flowers bloomed in window boxes along the road into town. Most of the buildings were bleached by the sun, the color of sand, some so pale they looked like the ghosts of houses that must once have been full of life and laughter. A pair of elderly women walked up the steep road, arms linked, each cradling a bag of groceries with her free hand. A work crew crawled like ants over a row house with a wine shop on the first floor, new owners in the midst of having the place renovated. It made Tommy feel better to see them, a reminder that they weren't alone in starting fresh in Becchina.

The Fiat bumped through a pothole. Kate let out a little yelp as Tommy twisted to look behind them, worried as he had been every mile about the little trailer they pulled. They had bought the used Fiat partly for its price tag, but mostly for its size. The streets were narrow here, and they wanted to be able to maneuver. They had rented this trailer for the same reason. The moving truck would bring most of the things they had shipped across the ocean—a few items of furniture that meant something to him, or to Kate, and some books and artwork they could not easily replace in Sicily. The trailer behind the Fiat carried their suitcases, their laptops, and a few items of furniture they had just bought in Catania. Also in the trailer, taking up very little room, were two plastic crates of family photos and other things Tommy had rescued from the house after his mother died. They were all that was left of her now.

Everything else would be sourced locally, from merchants or artisans, or—more likely—passed down by his grandparents or their many friends and neighbors in town. Tommaso Puglisi was a ninety-six-year-old stonemason who still told stories of outrunning bombs during World War II. His wife, Raffaella—Raffi to her friends—was thirteen years younger, still spry, and knew everyone in Becchina, not to mention many of their secrets. Sicilians were notorious gossips, and his nonna was no exception. He remembered his nonno as a man who frowned in disapproval at the gossip even as he joined in, but when Tommy and Kate had visited four months earlier, Nonno had seemed less engaged, his focus drifting. He hadn't forgotten anyone's name yet, but his short-term memory had begun to deteriorate.

Age-related dementia, his googling had suggested. Entirely normal for someone who had managed to live so long. But still hard to watch.

Now, according to Nonna, the old man barely got up from his chair except to use the bathroom. His knees hurt him terribly, and he had decided it wasn't worth it to go out and socialize with their friends. Tommy knew it had to feel like a prison sentence to his grandmother, who had always been such a social woman. What had given Tommy the clearest picture of his grandfather's condition was when Nonna told him that he didn't watch much television anymore. Tommy thought that meant he had lost interest, but Nonna said it was because he had trouble understanding the stories unfolding on the screen. His mind had become so cloudy that he could not follow the plot.

Tommy was glad to be in Becchina for many reasons, but chief among them was the opportunity to spend time with his grandparents. As far as he knew, they had never visited the United States. His entire experience of them had been during the times he had spent in Sicily. When he and his parents had come here as a family, his father had been withdrawn to the point of coldness, which had always made him sad, especially because his grandparents had been so welcoming, so full of love and good humor. Nonno's eyes had twinkled with mischief, and Nonna had always behaved as if feeding her grandson was the greatest happiness she had ever known. The one time Tommy had asked his father why he was so unhappy in Sicily, all he would say was that he had left for a reason and that someday Tommy would understand.

His father had died young, dropped by a heart attack before Tommy was old enough to really connect with him as a person. After his father's death, Tommy had grown up in the shadow of a mother who gave as much love as her narcissism would allow, but whose delusional self-interest hurt everyone eventually. She had insisted that his father's heart attack had been triggered by stress from his relationship with his parents. Tommy secretly thought that if stress had killed his father, it had come from closer to home, but he never said that to his mother.

As rarely as he had seen them, his grandparents had been the best example of kindness and generosity in his life, until he met Kate.

Kate was his world.

"We're good," he said, as much to himself as to his wife. He meant the Fiat and the trailer, but he could have been referring to so many things.

She bent forward and looked out the windshield, craning her neck to look up at the tops of buildings, the street signs, and the sky.

"Next left, I think," she said.

Tommy nodded. "Then two rights."

"I see the church dome." Kate pointed, though Tommy didn't dare to look. The buildings were so close on either side that if they'd been in a car any wider than the Fiat, he would have tucked in the mirrors to avoid the risk of shattering them.

When they turned left, they were on centuries-old cobble-stones. The Fiat and the trailer rattled, and Tommy's knuckles tightened on the steering wheel. He would get used to it, he knew, but it made his teeth hurt.

They passed a market and a butcher's, a gelato stand, and a little hardware store. But his eyes were drawn to empty storefronts that had once been a dress shop, a bookstore café, and a restaurant, as well as others whose previous lives were more difficult to discern. Tommy knew what Kate would say—she would tell him those empty spaces were opportunities, and he would convince himself she was right, because he so wanted her to be. Needed her to be.

They had tried to convince many of their friends to take this leap with them, to leave behind all the absurd demands and de-bilitating stresses of late-stage capitalism and to start over in a place where they could afford to try to build a dream. Some were intrigued, but nobody had been willing to make the jump just yet. Kate was convinced that if they could make a life here, some of those friends would follow. People who didn't need to work in an office or who had entrepreneurial or artistic dreams. Tommy wanted that to be true.

He turned right. Saw the faded and patched dome of the church, and then he turned right again at the next block. The homes, row houses, were all connected here, the walls of one kissing the walls of the next. Their new place was an exception. It stood at the top of a dead-end street with an eighty-foot drop-off at the edge of the property and a breathtaking view of the valley. A waist-high split rail fence was all that separated their property from the edge of the cliff. That, and an old bench with peeling green paint. On a clear day, when Mount Etna was angry, they would be able to see the smoke of the volcano from their front stoop.

The address was 17 Via Dionisio, and the house—God, the house was even more beautiful than Tommy remembered. Bougainvillea climbed the walls, its purple flowers vivid in the sunshine, vines filling cracks and winding around the gutters. Along the side of the house that faced the cliff were lantana shrubs with their flowers growing wild, as well as bushes of prickly pear and white caper blossoms waving in the wind that blew up over the edge.

Tommy pulled the Fiat to the curb in front of the house and killed the engine.

Kate practically leaped from the car, but she paused and leaned on the roof, smiling up at their new home.

"Look at it."

Tommy climbed out of the driver's seat and glanced up. "I'm looking."

Beautiful as it was, the old stone building needed a lot of love. The entrance had heavy wooden double doors, ten feet high, so weathered and dried that it reminded him of driftwood, its paint worn away in broad swaths. The arched transom window above the door had leaded glass panes that were barely transparent. Time had taken a toll on the ornately carved stone of the lintel. In the

United States, only the oldest and most elegant buildings might have such details, but in Italy they were almost ordinary.

What Tommy liked best about the house's façade was the trio of balconies jutting from the second floor, one above the front doors, the others to either side. The balconies were just as ornate as the lintel. The wrought iron railings were rusted, and some of the glass panes in the balconies' french doors had been smashed and then boarded up instead of being replaced, but any house would begin to decay once it stood devoid of life. Without people to live there, to give it voice and a heartbeat, the house had fallen into disrepair.

Tommy and Kate would breathe new life into it.

"It's like fate," he said. "I can't believe we almost bought the other one."

Kate shut her car door and came around to join him, taking a moment to admire the house and languish in the moment of their new beginning. "The house on Via Dogali would have been fine, but this one feels like a real adventure."

They had been in the midst of arranging to buy the other place—a crumbling stone row house, sun-bleached, just another blank and ordinary residence in this forgotten town—when their real estate broker had mentioned this one. It hadn't even been listed among the homes available for the one-euro-incentive deal, but Franca had assured them that 17 Via Dionisio could be theirs for the same price, under the same terms. By the time they had completed their walk-through, both of them knew their plans had changed.

Four months later, here they were.

At their front door.

Tommy turned to Kate. He brushed a wild lock of golden curls away from her face and tucked it behind her ear. "How did I get so lucky?"

She answered that question the way she always did. "You caught me in a moment of weakness."

He kissed her softly, then brushed his lips against her forehead. They rested in each other's arms for a few moments.

"We're really doing this," Kate said.

"You're just figuring that out?"

"It's different when it's real."

Tommy studied the dreamy look on his wife's face. "Are you thinking we made a mistake?"

"Not at all." Her eyes were alight with mischief. "I feel like we're free. Like we found this secret that nobody else knows."

"Like we're getting away with something."

"Exactly. And don't forget, your family might have roots here, but I'm the one who pushed for this. I can't wait to get started."

He kissed her again, for much longer this time. The breeze gusted over the edge of the cliff, the air scented with the wildflowers of their new home.

In the midst of that kiss, the ground began to shake.

Tommy didn't notice at first. In the back of his mind, he connected the rumbling in the road beneath his feet to the passage of a massive truck, but there were no trucks on Via Dionisio just then. A pair of goldfinches took flight from the main balcony overhead. The bougainvillea on the front of the house waved and swayed.

"My God," Kate managed. And then the whole world shook.

In his head, Tommy held the word *earthquake*, but he wasn't sure it found its way to his lips. The tremor felt deep, and it traveled from down in the earth up into his bones. Somewhere nearby, dogs began barking in unison, as if a maestro had tapped his baton and the chorus had kicked off as one. Car alarms blared from the next street. Tommy and Kate clutched each other's hands, frozen. Neither of them had ever experienced an earthquake before and didn't know how to rank this one. A tremor, a full-on quake? Enough to bring Becchina down around them? Tommy remembered a news report from when he was a kid, a crumbling old hill town somewhere in Italy, sun-bleached and ancient, turned entirely to rubble by an earthquake. Part of him wanted to stay frozen, to just hold Kate, and hope.

But the house remained standing. It shook, but it stood, and he knew doorways were supposed to be safe. True or not, that was just about all he'd ever learned about quakes. For tornadoes, it was cellars or bathtubs; for floods, you kept an axe in the attic in case you had to hack your way onto the roof; and for earthquakes—

"The house!" he barked, only realizing as he grabbed Kate's hand and yanked her toward their front doors that he was shouting to be heard over the grinding roar of the earth.

Kate had the keys in the little cross-body bag strapped across her chest. She staggered and nearly went sprawling, but she managed to dig the key out. Tommy could only watch as she propped one hand against the door and scraped the key around the lock. He felt drunk, or as if she were, the way her hand wavered, but it was the ground moving, the world trying to shake off its humans like a dog shaking off fleas. He held his breath. *The end*, he thought. Just those two words. This was supposed to be the beginning, but *the end* kept echoing in his head.

The door popped open. He wasn't even sure she'd turned the key. It swung inward without a push, and Kate spilled into the dusty foyer. Just before he crossed the threshold, Tommy saw the front of his new house shrug upward. Two panes in the fanlight window over the doors cracked, and a single shard of glass came loose and fell onto the floor inside. He grabbed Kate and pulled her back so that the two of them were together beneath that ornate lintel. *Is this smart? Is this right?* Standing under hundreds of pounds of marble or granite didn't seem very clever to him.

Kate hugged him tightly. Tommy held on to her, his life preserver.

"Shit, shit, shit, shit," she chanted, squeezing him, one word over and over, but that was one word more than he could muster.

Still afraid that standing on the threshold must be a mistake, an even bigger risk, Tommy glanced into the house, scanning the arched entrances to the rooms on the left and right, the staircase, and the hall that went back to the kitchen. Dust filled the air. Plaster sifted from the ceiling and floated down like ash from an eruption. Something moved at the top of the stairs. He caught just a glimpse of it through the cloud of ash and plaster, as if through a fog. The figure flitted through the dark obscurity up there and was gone. Someone was inside their house.

"Tommy, what did we do?" Kate asked, voice muffled because her face was buried in his chest.

He looked down at her, held on.

And it was over.

3

The first thing Kate did when the world stopped shaking was step outside and make sure the rest of the town was still there. A laugh bubbled in her chest, but somehow her lips would not release it. Heart still thumping, she looked down the road, startled to see no chasms in the pavement. None of the old, bleached buildings had crumbled. The flowers were still vivid with color, and the street still looked lonely and a little sad, despite the blue sky and the birds that wheeled overhead. It was as if nothing had happened, but she couldn't convince her body of that. Her pulse raced, anxiety rattling in her skull.

Three doors down from their dead-end manse, on the other side of the road, an old woman poked her head out. She wore a floral cotton housecoat and had curlers in her dark, dyed hair, as if Sicily had never emerged from the 1950s. Curious, she looked to the left and then the right. When she spotted Kate, they locked eyes for a moment. Birdlike, the old woman cocked her head and studied the new arrival, but instead of waving or even offering a nod of acknowledgment, she withdrew into her home and shut the door loudly enough for the sound to echo along the street.

Aside from Signora Housecoat, none of the neighbors made an appearance.

"You okay?" Tommy asked. He stepped up behind her and put a hand on her shoulder.

Kate managed a dry laugh. "Hell no."

"We said we were going to share a lot of firsts when we moved to Sicily."

She turned and punched his arm. "First earthquake was not what I had in mind."

His smile remained, but she saw the gray pallor of his skin and knew it was forced. They were both still in shock. Whatever Kate had expected for a welcome, it wasn't this.

"It's so bizarre," she said. "From the way it felt, I expected worse. But I don't see any damage. And only one old lady came outside to investigate, like it's just an ordinary Tuesday for them. How often do they have earthquakes here, Tommy? Please tell me this isn't something you knew about and didn't bother to mention, because I might be willing to go to prison in Sicily if it means I get to murder you for keeping that from me."

"Wait . . . you'd murder me?"

She smirked. "In Sicily, I said. I figure the prison food must be a hell of a lot better here than in Massachusetts."

Tommy pondered that. "Okay. Fair enough. But you won't need to murder me yet. I mean, give it time—I'm sure I'll do something stupid enough to make you homicidal. Husbands usually do, if pop culture has taught me anything. But no. If earthquakes are a common occurrence, that is not a thing I knew."

Kate reminded him that she had lived her entire life in Massachusetts without experiencing a single noticeable quake, but even as she spoke, she found herself calming down. Being with Tommy always put her at ease.

Their first date had been nothing special—midafternoon coffee at a little café in Portsmouth, followed by a bit of window-shopping, then down to the harbor to watch the boats head out to sea. She had laughed so much with him, had felt so peaceful, not in spite of the way he liked to verbally spar with her but because of it. So many guys used humor as a way to create distance, to hide emotion or depth, or lack thereof. But Tommy's humor flowed from a real place within him, which meant that when a moment turned serious or somber, he remained open and honest. He didn't realize how rare that was, and she cherished him for it. The peace he always gave her—that was the reason she had fallen in love with him. The reason she had married him.

So when that openness withdrew, of course she noticed.

"What aren't you saying?" she asked.

"I'm fine. Do you want to sit for a minute, or should we unpack the trailer?" Tommy smiled, but she had seen that particular smile before.

Kate tapped his chest with one finger, hard. "What aren't you saying, Tom?"

He exhaled. Rolled his eyes a little. At himself, she knew—not at her. "It's ridiculous."

"Nothing I love more than 'ridiculous.'"

Kate had never been the kind of woman who retreated in conversation. Tommy knew that.

"Okay, look, don't freak out, but when we were standing in the doorway, I looked up the stairs and I thought I saw someone up there."

Kate cocked her head. "You saw someone, or you *thought* you saw someone? It could be the real estate broker. Franca. Or a nosy neighbor or someone squatting in the house."

"I caught a glimpse, just for a second, and then it wasn't there. So either I'm imagining things or we have a ghost."

Kate arched an eyebrow. "Okay. Let's hope it's a ghost. We can do our own reality show, like a mix of ghost hunting, European travel, and old-house restoration."

"I'm in," Tommy said. "But before we make our millions on that, maybe we should unpack. I do have to get the trailer back to Catania tomorrow."

She kissed him, and they spent a few moments lost in that kiss. The breeze came over the edge of the cliff, and the bougainvillea rustled where it wound across the face of the house. As the scent of the flowers filled her thoughts, the trepidation the quake had caused began to melt away at last.

Kate smiled when she thought of her mother, who had assumed something had gone wrong in their marriage, because they were so excited about making a new start in a foreign country. To her generation, it was the sort of thing people only did for a good job or if they were running away from something. Kate had sought kind ways to explain that her and Tommy's generation didn't want to be anything like earlier generations. Kate and Tommy wanted a better life, simpler, where they could put their happiness and the quality of their life above work. Her mom had assumed that one of them had been unfaithful or something like that, but this was the opposite of marital trouble. It was a shared striving for the future. The world seemed to be unraveling every day. American culture seemed to be rotting from the inside out, manipulated by an amoral oligarchy whose worst enemy was young people who didn't want to play their game, and Kate and Tommy were happy to be counted in that category. The irony had not been lost on them, that the nineteenth and twentieth centuries had been defined by people leaving the so-called Old World to seek their fortunes in the New World, and now she and Tommy were doing the opposite, seeking new life in the Old World. But they both believed that earlier generations had it right—a slower life, a smaller circle, a focus on home.

Now here they were.

Home.

Tommy unlocked the back of the trailer. Each of them hefted a box, and they crossed the threshold of their new home a second time, this one more slowly and contentedly. As they stepped into the foyer, Kate glanced at the top of the stairs. She didn't believe in ghosts, but they were in the Old World now, and things like that seemed so much more possible here. Fortunately, she saw only dust and gloom, and both of those could be taken care of with a little time and effort.

"All right, woman," Tommy said, "let's see those muscles in action."

Kate flexed and put on her meanest weight-lifting face. She stayed in the pose while Tommy kissed her forehead and ran his hands appreciatively along her arms. The tan and the tank top helped, but mostly it was deadlifting and boxing that gave her the definition he admired.

"You're cute," she said, "but don't think that means I won't lean on archaic stereotypes to make you carry the heaviest stuff."

With a flourish of his hand, Tommy gave a small bow. "After you, my love."

And the unloading began.

When they had made the decision to move across the ocean, Kate had worried about the cost involved in taking their belongings with them. Like most people, she had become accustomed to the habit of attributing importance to the ownership of *things*, but once they had begun debating over pieces of furniture and looking into the cost of shipping, the conversation changed. Tommy would say they needed to bring the small antique kitchen set that had been in his own kitchen when he was growing up, and Kate would ask why. Kate would say she wanted to ship the rocking chair she had acquired from her grandmother's house after the lovely old Irish woman's death, and Tommy would ask why. The answers were always sentimental rather than practical, and fairly quickly, they realized that some of those pieces could be given to other relatives or friends. Knowing they were still in the hands of someone who would appreciate them was almost as good as holding on to them. Other objects could be sold or discarded or donated.

Clothes went the same way. Both of them had closets full of things they'd held on to because they still fit, or might one day fit, but hadn't worn in a long time. They were starting a new life, and the last thing they needed was to carry the clutter of the old one along with them. That left four big duffel bags, two fat suitcases, and three carry-ons. Most of their shoes—mostly Kate's, if they were being honest—had been shipped over and would arrive with the cherry sleigh bed that had been a wedding gift from Kate's parents, along with a few other antiques and several paintings, things that their hearts could not leave behind.

That would be just the beginning of the long process of furnishing their new home's fifteen rooms. Kate still could not quite wrap her head around the size of the rambling old house. Some rooms were already furnished, but she was in no rush to get the place completely decorated. The process would be part of the pleasure of this new life. They had each taken a month's sabbatical from their jobs, with three weeks still to go, and that would be time enough to make a decent start of it.

Now, as Kate and Tommy unloaded the trailer, she smiled with each lamp and end table and old chair they brought in. Kate had opened half a dozen windows before they started bringing anything through the door, but by the time they maneuvered the antique kitchen table inside, she realized it had been a mistake not to be more thorough. A sheen of sweat covered her, a trickle traced the length of her spine. Her upper lip had grown damp, and she wiped her hand across her mouth with a shudder of revulsion. Sweaty upper lips were supposed to be the province of the elderly, at least in her mind. Sicily had a rustic, primal romantic quality. So much of the island made her feel as if they were stepping back in time to a simpler era. Even in tourist spots like Taormina, overlooking the ocean, the pace of life felt so much slower. That was what had drawn her to push Tommy into this decision. So many pressures of the modern world felt distant and unimportant here.

That was the life she wanted for herself and Tommy, and the reason she had reacted immediately when she received the junk email promoting Mayor Brancati's plan. She received a dozen such emails every day, but that one had quickened her pulse and sent her searching online real estate listings. Tommy's childhood visits to Becchina had been some of the happiest times of his life. He had often regaled her with tales of the food he'd eaten, the music in the streets, and the way his parents had laughed together in the days before their marriage fell apart. Then his father had a falling-out with his family in Sicily, and even mentioning Becchina had become a little like farting in church. When his father died, his mother had taken Tommy to Becchina once, out of obligation, and then had been constantly resentful of her son's interest in his Sicilian family, jealous of his love for his grandparents, whom she insisted were practically strangers who had alienated their only son. Tommy's father.

Mostly, Tommy had told Kate, his mother had wanted his affection for herself. After her death, grief and guilt had weighed on him. She had brainwashed him throughout his life to feel as if he were someone responsible for her emotional well-being, and though her death should have freed him from that, somehow it had done the opposite. His mother's death had left Tommy feeling as if he had somehow let her down in ways he would now never be able to cure, even though he knew he had been a good son.

Kate thought of Sicily as a new world. A new life. A kinder, slower-paced existence where she could build a future and a family with a husband who would be a good man and a reliable partner. All the things her father had not been.

She knew most of her friends would have been terrified to take such a leap of faith in a spouse or any one person. But the heat and vivid life of Sicily, the seaside spots and mountain views, all combined to give them both what they needed: freedom and a chance to have a loving, uncomplicated family for Tommy and a new start without family baggage for Kate.

It was their shared dream.

Now they were here. It was reality, instead of a dream. And it was hot as hell.

"We need to open the rest of the windows." She rested against the corner of the table.

"Can we get this into the kitchen first?" Tommy asked, using his T-shirt to wipe his forehead.

Kate slumped a bit. "I honestly don't think so."

He smiled that tired smile she loved so much. It was the smile that indulged her, the one that said, *Okay, babe, if it's important to you, then it's important to me.* The little kitchen table was a perfect example. The beautiful floral design work had been hand-painted at least eighty years ago, and it had faded so much that it almost looked like the memory of flowers instead of actual paint. It had cost a bit more than they had wanted to spend, but Kate had fallen in love with it.

"Okay. Windows it is," Tommy said.

They left the table where it was and split up, wandering through the house. While Tommy started for the kitchen, propping open doors along the way, Kate mounted the stairs. She blew a few strands of hair away from her face, wondering what summer would really be like in Sicily. If nothing else, she would have to become less self-conscious about sweating.

I'll sweat out the bad stuff, she thought. Toxins, pollution, extra pounds. There would be a lot of carbs on the menu here—just part of life in Sicily—but she knew they would be so much healthier. They would eat better and walk everywhere, and they would drink wine and make love with the ceiling fan in the bedroom twirling lazily as if they'd stepped back in time.

Jesus, she thought. *Is this what happiness feels like?*

All she'd had to do was leave the New World for the Old. And endure a little earthquake.

The floorboards creaked underfoot. Downstairs, with a few windows open, the breeze moved the air around, but up here it felt hot and stale, claustrophobic in spite of the size of the place. Franca must have sent a cleaning crew in, because the house had been dusted and swept, cobwebs removed from the corners. There were three bedrooms on this floor and a bathroom with an enormous cast-iron tub. The place had no shower, but sometime in the 1970s, a handheld showerhead had been installed, along with a curtain to keep the splashing to a minimum if someone wanted to clean up without having to fill the tub.

"File under: it seemed like a good idea at the time," Kate muttered to herself.

A gust of wind made the window in the bathroom rattle. The house groaned with age. She struggled with the lock for a moment, but once she slid the window up, the breeze washed through the bathroom and out into the corridor. Somewhere, a door slammed shut, and she jumped, a little squeak escaping her lips.

"Old houses," she whispered, and it came out like a curse.

Moving through the second floor and then up to the third, she opened one window after another. There were only two rooms on the third floor—one a slant-roofed bedroom and the other full of empty bookshelves. Once upon a time, it had been a study or a little library. Empty bookshelves saddened her, but Kate promised herself they would not stay empty for long. As she raised the last window, she leaned on the sill and let herself breathe. The smell of flowers reached her even up here, and she leaned against the door-frame and let herself begin to think of this place as home.

Out in the hall, the floor creaked with the weight of footsteps. Tommy had come up to check on her.

She stepped into the hall. "I'm here."

But Tommy wasn't.

It had just been the house groaning again.

Kate descended toward the second floor. "I told you this place was haunted!" she called down.

"This old, it has to be!" Tommy replied, his voice floating from the first floor. Clean as the house seemed, dust motes danced in the air, somehow reminding her of how large the place really was.

At the landing, she hesitated. Straight ahead, at the far end of the second-floor corridor, was a narrow door to which she had paid very little attention. Had she even noticed it when they had toured the house? Kate didn't think so. And when she had come up the stairs a few minutes ago, the afternoon sunlight reaching in from the bedrooms had obscured the shadowy parts of the corridor, where the light did not reach.

Now she wondered where the narrow door might lead. There were other rooms in the annex at the back of the house, a later addition, only accessible by passing through the kitchen. Perhaps the little door led to servants' stairs, down to the kitchen and those back rooms. Did houses—even big ones—in tiny Sicilian hill towns have servants' stairs? Had people here ever had the money to afford servants?

Kate started toward the narrow door.

Downstairs, something thumped loudly.

She flinched and turned toward the sound.

"Tommy?"

"It's the front door," he called.

Kate frowned. They'd been here for little more than an hour. Who could be pounding on their door? Her first thought was Signora Housecoat, the creepy old lady down the street who had practically shunned Kate on sight, but then she realized that anyone who so obviously disapproved of her new neighbors was not going to show up as the welcome wagon.

Little door forgotten, she trotted downstairs just as Tommy opened the front door. For a half second, Kate thought she'd been wrong, that it really was the weird old lady down the street who'd come knocking. Short and stout, curly gray hair in a bun, a frumpy blue dress that wouldn't have been out of place on a retired nun.

But then Tommy laughed in delight, opened his arms, and stepped out to embrace her.

"Nonna! You didn't even give us a chance to bring everything inside!"

The old woman stiffened as Tommy hugged her. There might have been the hint of a smile, but her consternation erased it before it could reach full bloom. In the midst of the hug, Nonna's gaze locked onto Kate, but it was difficult to interpret the emotion in the old woman's eyes. Angry, frustrated, fearful . . . whatever those eyes were trying to say, they were not happy. This was not the reception Kate had expected, or hoped for, from the woman whom Tommy loved so much.

Nonna extricated herself from Tommy's hug. She placed her left palm on his chest as if appealing to his heart. Nonna started with a torrent of Italian, only a few words of which Kate could make out. She and Tommy had both been studying the language since making their decision, but learning online was different from trying to interpret the rapid-fire admonitions of a native speaker. And they *were* admonitions, of that much Kate could be sure. Lots of questions. She heard the words for *house* and a demand to know why Tommy hadn't told his grandparents this was the house they were buying.

Tommy finally took both of the old woman's hands in his own. "Nonna, stop. English, please. Or at least speak more slowly."

Frustrated, the old woman took a deep breath. She let him grip her hands, even squeezed back. "Tommaso," she said. "This here. This is not the house for you."

"I know it's not the house we planned to buy," Tommy replied. "But the real estate agent—Franca—she showed us this one the morning before we left, and it's incredible! It's twice the size of the other one, and it stands on its own. And the view! And the flowers!"

"Flowers!" Nonna said, almost spitting the word, apparently disgusted that something so trivial could come into this conversation.

Kate decided it was time to intervene. She emerged from the house. Nonna backed away as if she feared Kate would strike her. *What the hell?* Kate felt stung by this. She had never given the old woman anything but her love, and when she and Tommy had left here months ago, after telling his grandparents they would be moving to Becchina, the old woman had wept with happiness. Her smile had been full of the kind of joy that usually only accompanied announcements of a baby on the way, and why not? Her only child—Tommy's father—had been dead for years. She had been thrilled, had treated Kate like her own blood.

Now she backed away, off the stoop, as if Kate were on fire. The look of fear—because now her expression was perfectly clear—remained on her face for several long seconds before the old woman turned away as if to conceal what she could not otherwise hide.

"Nonna," Kate said, following her.

Tommy only watched them both in confusion.

"Nonna," Kate said again, taking her arm.

The old woman took a deep breath as if to steady herself, lifted her chin, and turned to face Kate. "This is bad."

Something in her voice made Kate shiver. The elderly were often superstitious, and in her life, she had not met anyone with more superstitions than these old Sicilians. They believed in the evil eye and thought it was bad luck for a woman to give a man shoes in fear that he would walk away from her. God forbid someone give knives as a wedding gift; the marriage would end in violence and bloodshed. These were things Tommy's grandparents and their friends actually believed.

"Please, Nonna," Kate said. "Come inside and see for yourself. The house is beautiful, and there are so many rooms. Plenty of space for Tommy and me to do our jobs—"

"Plenty of room for great-grandchildren," Tommy added.

Kate smiled, knowing that was an irresistible hook for the old woman. She wasn't quite sure what their plans were for babies just yet, but she knew a winning argument when she heard one.

"Exactly!" she said, putting a hand on the old woman's arm. "Come and see. Lots of room for kids."

Nonna pulled her arm away. Her deeply lined, dark-skinned face flushed red.

"No! No babies here," she said firmly. Her rheumy hazel eyes locked onto Kate and then Tommy before she muttered a string of sentences that didn't seem like modern Italian. More like the old

Sicilian dialect she'd grown up speaking. "You come eat," she said. "Seven o'clock."

Silence fell among them. A hot breeze came up over the cliff at the end of the road and swirled the scent of the house's flowers all around. It should have been a perfect moment, but it thrummed with the anxiety and discontent Nonna had brought with her.

"Okay," Tommy said. "Seven o'clock."

Nonna did not glance at the house again or even spare another look at her grandson and his wife, who had moved across the world to start their lives over in a place where they would be near family who loved them. Now they stood and watched her march off down the road with the ticktock gait common to thickly built women of a certain age.

"Well," Kate said. "*That* was fucking weird."

4

On a little street that angled out from the church square at the center of town, the important parts of life in Becchina carried on, despite the population drain of recent decades. To find a full-size supermarket, they would have to drive more than twenty minutes, but a little grocery store called Cannistraro Alimentari had most of what they would need. The aisles were narrow, and the stock seemed arranged with no perceivable logic, but they had a little of everything, and the produce section overflowed with fresh fruits and vegetables.

Across from Cannistraro's was a small bookshop that sold newspapers and magazines in a variety of languages. On either side of the bookshop, there was a bakery. Parziale's seemed as if it had been there since the town's first stones had been laid, and according to the sign, it had been owned by the same family since 1892. The other one, Caffe Sicilia, served coffee but couldn't quite be called a café. It was mostly just a counter where you could order things to carry out, but Caffe Sicilia's sign was newer, fancier, and both the owners and the clientele looked younger. It seemed there was a kind of generational battle going on here, and although the smell of baking bread made him ravenous, Tommy didn't dare choose a side in this bakery war without first finding out if his family had an allegiance to one or the other. Nonna already disapproved of the choices he and Kate had made, and it was only the first day.

Navigating a tiny shopping cart through Cannistraro's, he

could not stop thinking about his grandmother's bizarre behavior. It seemed as if he and Kate had offended her by buying the house on Via Dionisio rather than the one they had originally settled on. He wondered if she felt embarrassed because she had told her friends about one house and now discovered she'd been giving them the wrong information.

Kate had wondered if the house had once been occupied by an enemy of the family, and Tommy felt there was a certain logic to that. Perhaps some little girl had been mean to her seventy years ago, or a man jilted her sixty years ago, or another couple slighted them forty years ago, and the offenders had lived in that house? He was proud of his heritage—proud to be named Tommaso, after his grandfather—but nobody nursed a grudge better than a Sicilian. It was their third-greatest skill, right behind gossip and cooking.

Tommy had never minded the loudness or the gossip or the constant feuding among his father's people. When he was little, his family had often gotten together with others who had come to Boston from the same region of Sicily. He loved the loudness of these people, the laughter, the food, the stories, and the language, even when he didn't understand more than a few words of it. There had been enormous outdoor barbecues at a park by the ocean up in Gloucester. His father had said it was because Sicilians all longed for the sea. As distant as his dad had usually been, those Sundays always broke through the dourness that so often enveloped him. After his father had died, those gatherings had ended, at least for Tommy. His mother refused to bring him, saying she was unwelcome, and by the time he was old enough to drive himself, the tradition had ended, the elders in the community too old to keep it going and the younger generations not interested enough.

His mother had worked seventy hours a week to pay the bills, and he had never doubted that she loved him. That effort had made up for a lot of sins on her part, but once he had met Kate, the dynamic with his mother started to change. She had been bitter and jealous and controlling, resentful of the fact that she was never going to be his top priority again. It took years before someone suggested she was a narcissist, and all it took was a bit of googling for him to have an epiphany. It didn't make his relationship with his mother any less stressful, but at least he understood. After years of feeling embarrassed and making excuses and apologies for her behavior, finally he had been able to explain.

The last thing he had expected in moving to Sicily was that he would find himself feeling that same awkward pressure to make apologies for his family the way he had with his mother, to explain their behavior. His grandparents had their quirks—mostly cultural—but after Nonna had stormed off, Tommy had found himself at a loss. He'd apologized to Kate, inwardly cringing, terrified that this move had been an awful miscalculation. If this was a sign of things to come, their dreams of a new life away from the American work-to-survive madness were doomed from the start.

They'd carried the rest of their belongings into the house, and Tommy had volunteered to make a run to the grocery store while Kate began to put things in order. They both knew he needed an hour on his own to process how weird the day had gotten, and she could use the time as well.

So here he was. Cannistraro's. A little cart full of fruits and vegetables, starches and dairy, rolling up to the register at the front of the store. There were only a dozen or so people, most of them slender olive-skinned men in work clothes or older women with just a few items each. The cashier was slim and attractive, her dark skin aglow with a sheen of sweat. She might have been thirty or forty-five, depending on how much of her life she had spent in the sun. The customer putting his purchases onto the counter was something else entirely, handsome and tall—Tommy thought probably South Asian—perhaps Indian or Pakistani. When the cashier finished adding up his purchases, she smiled at him as if they knew one another.

"No bananas today?" she said.

The man smiled. "Don't do that, Carmelina," he said in a British accent. "Speak Italian. I need the practice."

A quick exchange followed, but Tommy could only make out a few words, including one that had to be Italian for *bananas*. These two people had nothing in common apart from what he inferred were routine interactions in this very spot, and yet they shared a lighthearted warmth that felt contagious. They smiled without a trace of insincerity, full of kindness and goodwill. Despite the madness of the day and the confused shame he'd felt after his grandmother's display of disapproval, Tommy found himself smiling as well.

"The two of you seem very carefree for people who went through an earthquake a couple of hours ago," he said.

Carmelina only smiled, passing the man's items under the scanner. It beeped for a carton of orange juice and then a plastic-wrapped wheel of dried figs.

"Wasn't much of anything," the man replied. "More a tremor, really."

"It was my first," Tommy explained. "Forgive me if I can't shrug it off as easily."

"Here I am, talking like an earthquake veteran. It's only the second one for me. But I was in Los Angeles with my family when I was about eleven years old, and the world shook so hard it smashed every plate and knocked every frame off the walls. Windows shattered."

"God, that must have been terrifying."

The man laughed. "For me, yes, but the people in LA were so blasé about it."

"How the tables have turned," Tommy said. "Though I'm glad to know it's the first one you've had since you arrived here."

Curiosity lit the man's brown eyes as he turned toward the cashier. "Carmelina, do we get a lot of them? *Terremoto*? No, wait, that's singular. *Terremoti*?"

The cashier looked at Tommy when she answered. "Rohaan likes to practice Italian, but I have to use my English. We have more English moving here, so I want to learn."

Tommy felt both impressed and embarrassed at his pitiful Italian skills. "Your English is excellent."

"Sometimes we have them . . . earthquake . . . and so small you feel nothing, but you see on the news later. Like this morning? Three, four years, we get one like this. When I was twelve years old, we have a big one. Houses . . ." Carmelina looked at the man. "*Crollo?*"

"Collapsed," the man said.

The cashier nodded as she placed the man's items in a paper sack. "Collapse. My school, too. I have a cousin who died."

"Jesus," Tommy said quietly.

"But nothing that bad since then?" the man asked. "Since you were twelve."

"No. Just like today. A little shake."

She rattled off the total of the man's groceries in Italian.

"Somehow the real estate agent didn't mention earthquakes," Tommy said. "Neither did the online listings trying to get people to move to Becchina."

The man glanced up as he slid his debit card into place. "I thought you must be one of us. Another import."

"I like that. Yes, we're imports. I'm Tommy Puglisi."

"Ah," the man said as he put his wallet away and hefted his grocery bag. "An import, but with a local name."

"I'm from Boston, but I have family here."

The man held out his free hand. "Rohaan Tariq."

They shook, and Tommy felt grounded for the first time since the scene with his nonna. For their friends back home, Tommy and Kate were the canaries in the coal mine. If they thrived, others might follow. That meant aside from a cousin or two and his ancient grandparents and their ancient neighbors, they had no friends here. Yet, as Carmelina scanned Tommy's groceries, he and Rohaan struck up a conversation, and he felt like maybe they weren't going to be so alone.

The Imports were from all over, Rohaan explained. They weren't all friendly, but Rohaan and his husband, Patrick, had gotten to know several other couples fairly well, and there were occasional gatherings. By the time they were out on the street in front of Cannistraro's, they had already exchanged cell phone numbers and promised to get together with their spouses for lunch in the coming days. Tommy's thoughts ran ahead of him. He knew Kate would be relieved when he relayed the encounter to her, that she would already be thinking about hosting a gathering at the house once they had it all set up.

The thought reminded him he and Kate were due at his grandparents' for dinner at 7:00 p.m., and his stomach gave a little twist. As much as he wanted to figure out what had upset her so much, for the first time in his life, he dreaded seeing Nonna. But this was home now, and he and Kate were going to have to learn to navigate the politics of family and the town. Starting with why the hell his grandmother didn't want him to have babies in his new house.

Kate could handle letting the furniture get dusty or leaving the bathroom an extra few days before one of them cleaned it, but clutter drove her nuts. Moving house had always been a nightmare. During college, she had arrived as early as possible every semester so that she would have time to put away all her clothes, hang things on her walls, and make up her bed. Going to sleep with boxes yet to be unpacked was next to impossible for her.

She had prepared for this move, knowing it would take a couple of days to arrange furniture, unpack, and get the kitchen the way Tommy would want it—he did most of the cooking, though neither of them had much skill in that area. But as prepared as she was to allow things to remain unsettled, the idea of going to Tommy's grandparents for dinner on their first night irritated the hell out of her. Not that she blamed her husband, or even Nonna for insisting. She didn't blame anyone, which made it somehow worse. All she wanted was to deal with the move-in clutter as best she could so that maybe by tomorrow night, she could exhale. Then they could take their time acquiring other furniture and decorating the rest of the house. Months, if they wanted. A whole year. Hell, a lifetime.

But not tonight.

Tonight, they were going to dinner at Nonno and Nonna's house.

"Aaaaagh!"

Tommy was downstairs, unpacking kitchen stuff, so he didn't hear her exasperated cry. That was good. She felt better for the moment, even as she wondered how Nonna had discovered they had arrived in Becchina, not to mention that they were moving into a different house from the one they had originally chosen. They hadn't been parked in front of their house for more than an hour before she had knocked on their door, and the only person Kate was sure had seen them was Signora Housecoat.

The grapevine in this town was deadly efficient.

She and Tommy would have to remember that.

She had managed to put the bed frame together and put on clean sheets and a duvet that would doubtless prove too warm tonight. The armoire in their bedroom had been left behind by the previous owner, and Kate had begun the process of unpacking her clothes and putting them away. Fortunately, she had planned ahead, assuming they would need to eat out for the first night or two, and she had shopped in Catania for clothes that seemed to fit the local style. Now she looked into the age-obscured mirror over the bathroom sink and took stock of the result. She wore a bone-white blouse with big brown buttons, her sleeves rolled up past the wrist. She'd added a brown belt and sleek black trousers that were cuffed above the ankle to reveal two inches of skin above black boots. Her only makeup was a bit of mascara, and though she struggled with body dysmorphia, and despite the exhausting day she'd had, Kate thought she looked damn good.

But for what?

Abruptly, she felt foolish. What did Tommy's grandparents and their friends care about what she wore? They would judge her if she dressed like a slob or if her hair looked a mess, but would they appreciate this look, which would be acceptable in a trendy restaurant in Rome?

Stop. It doesn't matter. This isn't for them.

"You're killing it," she told her reflection in that dark mirror.

She smiled, blew a puff of air, and marched from the bathroom into the corridor.

"I'm all set!" she called. From the kitchen came the sound of cabinet doors clacking shut and pots rattling as they were moved around. Tommy had apparently changed his mind about how he wanted things arranged.

As she reached the stairs, she heard a sound like the swish of a dress or long coat. In the quiet of the house, the noise seemed crisp and clear. Kate glanced back quickly, one hand on the top of the banister, and felt a momentary dizziness that forced her to steady herself. She attributed it to a full day's effort and not enough food or water, but she paused and listened for the sound to come again.

Only the wind rewarded her patience. A gust that rattled the windows. Of course that was what she had heard. The wind.

But now her eyes had adjusted to the shadows at the end of the hall, and the door that awaited her there. Over the course of the day, especially once Nonna had arrived and behaved so oddly, she had nearly forgotten about that door.

Tommy could still be heard puttering around the kitchen, so he wasn't in as much of a hurry as she had thought. Kate felt a deep reluctance to open that door, a ripple of something in her chest that could only be fear, and it made her angry. This was her house now. That door and whatever lay beyond it belonged to her and Tommy. The shadowy end of the corridor had apparently triggered some childhood fright, but she was not a child now. She was a grown woman, a professional who had moved halfway around the world and bought a house in Europe, and she still had this flutter of hesitation.

"Christ," she muttered, and she laughed softly at herself as she strode down the hall and reached to open the door.

Locked, of course.

But now she was in motion. She had a set of keys from Franca in her room. Kate and Tommy each had a set. She hurried back and snatched the keys off her nightstand, then marched to the door at the end of the hall and tried to find the key that fit. There were four in all—two for the front door, one for the rear door, and a fourth one shrouded in mystery. Franca had no idea what that key opened, but it came with the others, so she had included it.

None of them unlocked the narrow door at the hallway's end.

"Katie? You ready, babe?" Tommy called from the bottom of the stairs.

"Coming!"

She frowned at the door, wishing it could feel her disapproval. Locked from the other side, she assumed, which meant they would find their way to it from another approach. But not tonight.

Kate trotted down the steps clutching her keys and tossed them onto the little antique table they'd put just inside the front door.

When Tommy saw her in the light of the foyer, his face lit up. "You look fantastic."

Kate felt warmed by the attention. She hoped he would always look at her this way. For his part, he had not planned ahead, but even in wrinkly black jeans and a faded, vintage Dire Straits concert T-shirt, he still looked good to her. A bit scruffy, in need of a haircut, so obviously American in spite of the fact that he was the one with Sicilian blood.

She rose up on her toes and kissed him. "Let's go."

Tommy patted his pockets to make sure he had his phone and wallet, tugged out his own keys, and they went out the front door for the first night in their new town. Though dusk was only now arriving, it was quiet at their dead end of the street. It occurred to Kate that this was likely always true, but Tommy still used both locks on the front door—habits from home, probably unnecessary in a place halfway to a ghost town.

As they started up the street, Kate took his hand and glanced back at the house. The dying evening light cast the whole structure in a rosy silhouette. The view combined with the scent of the flowers, and suddenly, all the tension of the day bled out of her.

"This is going to be perfect," she said. "A life we'll build without all the bullshit expectations from home."

"This is home," he reminded her.

Kate grinned and squeezed his hand a bit tighter as they walked on. But just before she turned away from the sunset-haloed view of the house, she realized something she hadn't really considered before. The rear section of the house, the part they hadn't even explored yet, had a second level. Franca had shown them photographs of the first-floor rooms back there, but now Kate realized the door at the end of the second-floor hallway didn't lead to hidden stairs but rather into a section of the sprawling house the real estate agent hadn't so much as mentioned. They had been so in love with the place when they'd first been rushed through it—a last-minute thing, before leaving for the airport—that somehow they had only paid attention to the parts of the house that Franca seemed excited about.

Tommy began to sing quietly. "O Sole Mio." During his childhood, his grandfather had taken him for walks whenever they were together. Nonno always sang that song to him during those walks, and Tommy had told her more than once how much he had cherished those times with the old man. The Italian lyrics had stuck with him.

Kate knew it meant he was happy, and so she joined in for the bits and pieces she knew.

They picked up the pace, but she spared one last glance along the street, just before they were out of view of their new home. Tomorrow, she would call Franca and inquire about a key to the annex.

She wanted a look at the parts of the house the real estate agent hadn't wanted them to see.

5

Walking through Becchina, Tommy felt reenergized—even opti-mistic. For a place whose population had dwindled over the course of generations, it felt surprisingly alive. The many vacant shops and homes were even more noticeable with night creeping in, but there were still people here. There was laughter. At a rustic tratto-ria, the floor-to-ceiling shutters at the front of the restaurant had been folded back, opening the entire place to the warm evening air. It was too early for many young Sicilians to be out for dinner, but a dozen or so patrons were seated at tables. Waitstaff in crisp white shirts and black aprons buzzed around. The scent of roast-ing garlic wafted from the kitchen all the way out to the street.

"Sebastiano's," Kate said, pointing to the sign Tommy hadn't noticed.

"I wish we were going there," he said.

"Another night," she promised. "We'll be fine. Your grandpar-ents love you."

Of course they did. He hadn't forgotten that. But he wondered if their usual warmth and joy would be tempered now that Tommy and Kate's presence was no longer novel. They lived here now, fully committed.

Bells rang in the steeple just a few blocks away. The sound echoed through the town, and he imagined it could be heard all the way down in the valley. Another sound began, almost as if it had rolled in behind the church bells, and Tommy felt his heart lighten. It was a violin, not a recording but someone playing live. Playing well enough, but not perfectly. Somehow that made it more beautiful to him, more human. He would have expected something Italian, or at least something classical—Vivaldi, maybe. Instead, the song the violinist teased out with his bow was something he knew from listening to the radio in the garage with his dad as a little kid, an old U2 song.

It felt like a good omen.

"We can do this," he said aloud, giving Kate's hand a little squeeze.

"I'm glad you think so. If we moved here and you realized we couldn't do it, I'd be very cross with you."

She said the last bit in a faux-British accent that always lightened both of their hearts. It was the sort of silliness that grew between couples, that might cause others to roll their eyes but which became part of the weave that bound them together. Tommy had no example of that with his own parents, but he'd seen it in the homes of some of his friends while growing up and always envied them. It was all he had ever wanted from his own marriage, the comfort and joy of really knowing your spouse and loving them for who they were, and having them return that honest love.

He slid his arm around her as they turned a corner and found themselves on Via Ballaro. It took a moment to orient themselves, but after a moment, they turned left. The streets were narrow everywhere in town, but here even more so. They were old and not built for cars, though cars managed to rumble down the cracked cobblestone avenue somehow. Chairs dotted the sidewalks, folding chairs and rusty metal kitchen chairs and the occasional barstool, all so the neighbors could sit out in the hot afternoons and evenings and wave hello to one another, gossip, and share news. Tommy and Kate saw several of them now, men drinking wine in their undershirts and shorts, women smoking cigarettes in housecoats.

"It's like stepping back in time," Kate whispered to him.

Tommy glanced at her. "Do you hate that?"

"Of course not. This is what we wanted. It's wonderful."

And it was. Dreaming of a future in the United States had become difficult for their generation, never mind the next one. Italy's economy had endured disastrous year after disastrous year, but his and Kate's incomes would go much further here, and health care was something with which all were provided. Their someday-children would be able to attend universities anywhere in the EU for a fraction of what it would cost at home. They had given up a lot by moving here, but they both believed they would gain even more if they could handle the change. The upheaval. If they could keep one another from growing too lonely.

"Well," he said, "get ready to go even further back in time."

Kate laughed softly, but they kept the volume down now.

They had arrived.

Tommaso and Raffi Puglisi lived in the same home where Raffi had been born, a two-story structure that was part of a block of row houses that varied wildly in height and architectural style. In some parts of town, the row of homes on a block would look identical, but here the houses were old enough not to have been built all at once. Most were painted in the beige or orange wash that the sun allowed, but Nonno and Nonna Puglisi kept their place a golden yellow that stood out from the rest. Though some of the buildings were three stories high, their place was twice the width of the next largest and had the benefit of a walled courtyard behind it that could make the place feel like a country villa when the stars shone and the humidity abated.

And they always had visitors.

Tonight was no exception.

The two folding chairs in front of the house were empty, but the front door stood open, and as Tommy and Kate strode up, they could hear a pair of men loudly debating something that involved Mayor Brancati, a schoolteacher, and a footballer Tommy interpreted as playing for Calcio Catania, a soccer club to the south. It wasn't an argument, just a typical night in Becchina. Exactly the sort of thing he and Kate had prepared for. Tommy even had his Palermo FC jersey back at their house.

"Here we go," Kate said.

They stepped over the threshold and into Nonno and Nonna's house.

The two men looked over, saw them, and raised their hands in welcome. Tommy recognized them both, one a seventysomething neighbor with white tufts of hair coming out his ears, and the other his own third or fourth cousin, Marcello Casavola. He felt a rush of gratitude upon seeing Marcello, who was only about thirty-five and spoke English better than most.

"Ah, here they are!" Marcello called with his raspy, cigarette-ruined voice.

"Welcome!" the elderly neighbor said before launching into a stream of Italian and turning to walk deeper into the house, summoning Tommy's grandmother.

Marcello embraced Tommy and then Kate, kissing them each first on the left cheek and then the right. His eyes were alight with genuine pleasure at their arrival. Nonna was Marcello's great-aunt, but he had taken to calling the Puglisis *Nonna* and *Nonno*, treating them with the love and respect he would have given his own grandparents if they were still alive.

"Cousin!" Tommy said. "It's so good to see you."

And it really was. Now that he wasn't a visitor in this town, he had needed this welcome in some profound way he had not expected.

He heard a chorus of voices, and he and Kate both looked up to see people gathered at the end of the hall—clustered in the kitchen, of course, as they always were—waving and smiling, speaking their own language. Neighbors and friends, perhaps seven or eight of them.

"Okay, okay," his grandmother said, fluttering her hands to drive them all away. In Italian, she told them to go back out into the courtyard, and then she came along the hallway toward him and Kate and Marcello.

Marcello might as well have been invisible. Nonna batted at him as if he were a pesky fly, and he laughed. She had a smile on her face, but when she had her back to him and only Tommy and Kate could see, the smile vanished and her eyes became distant and sad, almost lost, as if they were at a wake instead of a welcome dinner. The moment passed so quickly, Tommy would have thought he imagined it, if not for their encounter earlier in the day.

"Okay," Nonna said, taking Tommy by the hand. "You have pasta now."

"Nonna, you can speak Italian," he reminded her as they followed her and Marcello into the kitchen. "Kate and I are learning. We need all the practice we can get."

The smells in the kitchen made his stomach roar. A red sauce simmered on the stove, something with seafood in it. Plates of sautéed vegetables sat on the counter—zucchini, artichokes, green beans with onions. There were breaded shrimp in some kind of garlic butter. The distance in his grandmother's eyes vanished as she saw his reaction to the food.

"Eat, eat," she said.

Marcello laughed. "She wants to practice English more than she wants you to learn Italian." He picked up a couple of dishes and carried them out into the courtyard.

Kate had been quiet. Her smile was tentative, wary. "We'll have to learn how to make all of these things."

"Yes. You learn," Nonna said, nodding enthusiastically.

"Both of us," Tommy told her. "I want to cook, too."

Nonna rolled her eyes as if she thought he had made a joke. Even if the push for more domestic equity had reached Sicily, it certainly had not reached her generation. These women did the cooking and they cleaned up afterward, and the suggestion that their husbands or sons participate would be met with awkward silence or a flutter of hands to shoo such ideas away. Tommy had tried it before.

Following Marcello's lead, Kate picked up the dish of shrimp and went out into the courtyard. Nonna gestured to the pot of clam sauce and rattled off something rapid-fire that Tommy pretended to understand. He grabbed a couple of dishcloths off the counter and used them to take the handles on either side of the big pot. His grandmother seemed able to handle pots and pans right off the stove, the same way she managed to drink coffee hot enough to melt an ordinary person's flesh, but as Tommy had joked to Kate, the rest of them were just ordinary mortals.

He took the sauce out back. Nonna followed with her ladle, and soon they were circumnavigating the three big folding tables that had been set up end to end, spooning sauce onto bowls of fresh pasta.

"Tommaso," the old woman said, a bit sharply, and Tommy's grandfather looked up.

He had been staring at nothing. Now he glanced at Tommy's face. For a moment, Tommy feared his grandfather would not recognize him, but then the old man's rheumy eyes lit up, and he smiled with delight.

"Hey! There you are!" Nonno said in raspy English. "*Figlio bello!*"

Tommy thought the old man recognized him, but he didn't dare ask. He didn't want to offend his nonno, but more than that, he didn't want to know the answer. Instead, he greeted his grandfather, kissed his cheek, and told him how good he looked. He meant the part about looking good. Yes, Tommaso Puglisi had shrunken to a much smaller, stooped version of himself, whose clothes hung on his frame and whose skin seemed draped over his bones in the same way, but the man had turned ninety-six in the fall and still had a full head of white hair. His blue eyes might have lost much of their luster, and he seemed a bit unsure as he surveyed the gathering around him, but he was still aware, still talking, still able to enjoy his friends, even if he couldn't follow much of the conversation anymore.

THE HOUSE OF LAST RESORT · 45

He was a rare creature, and Tommy was grateful to have him, but sometimes when he thought of the walks they'd once taken together, and his grandfather singing to him or tossing a baseball or just sitting quietly together on a park bench, enjoying the sunshine, he felt loss like a chasm in his chest, ripping the sweetness of those memories from him like the oxygen out a broken airplane window at fifty thousand feet.

Nonna nudged him to continue, and he carried the sauce pot around the tables. The other plates and trays were spread around, along with baskets of bread and bottles of homemade wine. Soon, he and Kate were seated with the neighbors and friends and laughing despite catching only a tiny fraction of what was said. All the tension and melancholy receded, not forgotten but put away in a cabinet somewhere and the door closed.

Music played, probably a bit too loud if not for the fact that the neighbors closest enough to complain were presently seated around those tables, eating Nonna's food. Marcello sat across from Tommy and Kate, trying his best to interpret for them, but the conversation moved fast. After the twentieth confused look they received, Kate leaned over to whisper to her husband.

"We really dropped the ball on our Italian studies."

He reached under the table and took her hand. "We'll get there. You understand some of this, right?"

"I guess. But I think the old doctor at the end of the next table said he loves to cook cats. I have to assume that's a translation problem."

Tommy laughed. "Let's hope."

In spite of their deplorable Italian, by the time the plates were being cleared and pots of coffee were percolating in the kitchen, conversation out in the courtyard had turned to the arrival of Tommy and Kate, and of others who had taken the mayor's offer and moved from other countries. *The Imports*, Tommy thought. They had come from as close as Rome and as far as Australia. Marcello had met a Japanese family, several Americans, and three couples from the United

Kingdom. He thought there was a woman from Venezuela doing the restoration of a house on her own, but had never met her.

Tommy felt better knowing there were so many recent transplants. He told Marcello about Rohaan Tariq, the man he had met at the market.

"The town has so much promise," he said. His face felt flush and, as he sipped his wine, warm and red and sharp, he realized it was at least his third glass.

"So much opportunity," Kate agreed. She glanced around the table. "Tommy and I are trying to convince some friends to come here and open small businesses. If we could just increase the tourism a little, get enough traffic, that would make it so much more appealing. More people would buy these houses, invest their money in the town."

Marcello nodded. The old soccer fan who had been debating when they arrived had been seated beside Marcello, mostly ignoring them. But now he and his tall, wizened, cigarette-puffing wife were paying close attention. The soccer fan nudged Marcello and asked for an Italian translation, which Marcello quickly provided.

The man's wife—Giulia—narrowed her eyes and addressed Kate in Italian. She had to know they would understand very little of what she said. Giulia had been sitting just a few seats away throughout the meal and would have observed at least that much. Still, she did not bother asking Marcello to translate or directing her words at him.

Tommy flushed with embarrassment and wine. All they were doing was reinforcing the well-earned stereotype of Americans behaving as if the world ought to speak their language. When Giulia's pointed statement concluded, he and Kate both looked helplessly at Marcello.

"She's happy to have you here," Marcello said, but with a sly, ironic tilt of his head, half a smile on his lips.

"Sure seems like it," Kate said, giving the smoking woman her fakest smile.

Giulia replied with a fake smile of her own, polite and thin-lipped and dripping with disdain.

"She feels this is the question of the chicken and the egg," Marcello said, his accent thickened by wine. "You say more tourists will bring new people to live, to open businesses. But we need new businesses to bring the tourists here."

"There are so many things you could do," Kate said, addressing Marcello now. "Like, you guys have catacombs here. In Siragusa, they give tours of the catacombs. They sell tickets."

Tommy knew she had spoken to Marcello purposely, directing her attention to him instead of Giulia. His wife had a soft heart, a love of animals, the kind of person who always wanted to help and felt it keenly when others were in pain and she could not do anything to alleviate it. But if someone came at her with claws out, Kate gave it back in kind, and twice as savagely. Yes, they were new in town, and maybe it was naive for any newcomer to try to make suggestions for improvement to people who had lived their whole lives in this town, but they meant well, and Giulia didn't need to get snippy.

Marcello translated the suggestion for Giulia and her husband.

Giulia sniffed. It might have been a laugh. Her fake smile turned politer and even less sincere. "You make your house a tourist attraction," she suggested in thickly accented English, with a small shrug, as if it were the most obvious thing in the world.

Her husband laughed. "*La casa dell'ultima risorsa.*"

Tommy heard his grandmother's sharp intake of breath. The nearest ten people stopped talking midsentence and turned to stare. Marcello turned pale. Even Giulia seemed to realize a line had been crossed. She puffed on her cigarette and glanced away as if she could see the Mediterranean from where they sat.

"Aldo," Nonna said, glaring at Giulia's husband.

Tommy realized that must be his name.

Aldo smiled. "*Mi dispiace*, Raffi."

The man raised his wineglass and made a toast. Something about old friends and welcoming family. Other glasses were raised, and people started talking again, moving on as if the tense moment had never happened. Nonna glared at Aldo but then turned to the young boy beside her and tried to get him to go inside and help her bring desserts to the table.

Tommy looked at Kate. He saw his own irritation and uneasiness reflected back at him.

"What's that mean?" he said quietly.

Giulia and Aldo ignored him, but that was fine. He didn't expect them to answer. His focus was Marcello.

His cousin slid back in his chair and stood. "I'm going to help Nonna bring in the coffee."

"Marcello," Kate said. Her disappointment in him came through quite clearly.

Tommy leaned over the table, not enough to draw a lot of attention but enough to keep Marcello from walking away. "I got some of it. *Casa* is 'house.' *Ultima* is 'the last.' 'The house of last *what*,' exactly? What is *risorsa*?"

Marcello sighed. Whatever weirdness this was, he had not wanted to be involved with it, and now he had become its center. Tommy would have felt bad for him if he wasn't already angry at the way his grandmother's friends had behaved.

"Like 'last chance,'" Marcello said. His brows furrowed. "Not exactly. Something like that. 'Last . . .'"

"Last chance?" Kate said. "What the hell?"

Marcello snapped his fingers, remembering. "'Last resort.' Like . . . opportunity?"

Tommy stared at him. He squeezed Kate's hand under the table.

"We should go," Kate said.

"No, no," Marcello said, trying to soothe them. "Time for coffee. Tiramisu!"

He smiled again and hurried away from his seat. The conversation around the table had continued, but Tommy could not escape the feeling that everyone within hearing distance had been listening even as they carried on.

As Marcello passed Nonna's empty seat, Nonno shot his great-nephew an admonishing look and muttered something. The old man loved Marcello, but his dismay was plain.

Tommy looked at Kate. *The house of last resort?* Sicilians gossiped like crazy. Did they think that the American cousins had moved here as some kind of attempt to save a failing marriage? Or that they had failed in business in America and had come here for a last chance, a new opportunity?

The house of last resort.

Kate leaned closer to him. She whispered, "What the fuck?"

Tommy kissed her cheek. Whispered in return.

"What the fuck, indeed."

6

Their first apartment together had two bedrooms, a kitchen, a living room, and a full bath, and on the night they had moved in, they fucked in every room. Kate had assumed that when they moved into their one-euro beauty in Sicily, history would repeat itself, but after the stress and the food at Tommy's grandparents' house, neither of them had so much as shot the other a smoldering glance. Wednesday passed in a whirlwind of unpacking, cleaning, and organizing. Eggs for breakfast, local cheese on fresh-baked bread for lunch, and chicken limone with fresh asparagus for dinner.

No one came to visit. Nobody knocked at the door.

Kate passed one of the neighbors from the night before at Nonna's house, and the fiftyish woman seemed not to see her. Maybe she hadn't. The paranoia that had been slithering up her spine since Nonna's angry outburst lingered, and she felt it would be quite some time before it left her.

Thursday started with coffee at one of the nearby bakeries and a stroll through the town. They visited a fruit stand and learned there would be a farmers market on Saturday, then stopped at the butcher and picked up sausages to make that night with peppers, as well as ground beef and veal so they could begin to teach themselves how to make Nonna's meatballs. Despite the haze of tension from their move-in day, they walked hand in hand through the town. They smiled at people and began to pick up Italian words and phrases, and this new life started to feel a tiny bit like the fairy tale Kate had hoped it might become.

That night, they made love in their new home for the first time. It began sweetly, with giggles and tender kisses, and she shivered at the gentle way Tommy trailed his fingers along her back and her inner thighs, and the way he teased her with the tip of his tongue. Soon, sweetness turned to hungry abandon, and it was everything she could have wanted. Afterward, they collapsed in a sweaty heap on the bed, limbs tangled, barely able to extricate themselves one from the other. They fell asleep sweaty and naked, with the wind sighing through the house around them and the bedroom door's hinges creaking with the breeze, almost as if the house dozed with them and this was the sound of it snoring.

Sometime in the night, Kate came slowly awake. Though the creaking remained, the house felt too still. She grew aware of an unnatural quiet, and the sheen of sweat that covered her trickled along her belly toward the sheet beneath her. A frown creased her forehead.

The quiet troubled her.

They had set up an oscillating fan at the foot of the bed and a box fan in one of the windows, but the hum of the fans had ceased. Kate opened her eyes with a sigh, unsure if the profanity in her head made it to her lips. She glanced at her nightstand and saw only darkness. The face of her clock should have been shining numbers at her, announcing the time. Outside, it remained full dark, but she had no way to know how far away the sunrise might be.

Tommy lay sleeping beside her. They had separated in the night, likely driven apart by the clammy warmth of the room. She reached out and nudged him.

"Babe," she rasped, and nudged him again.

He didn't move. Like the fans. A ripple of anxiety went through her. Her mother had told her more than once what it had been like having a newborn in the house, a tiny baby in a cradle beside the bed, how impossible it was to sleep soundly while you tried to listen for the sound of the infant's breath, just to make sure it remained alive. Tommy's stillness felt alarming.

"Hey." She put her hand on his arm and shook him. "Tom."

He inhaled sharply, as if he had forgotten to breathe and she had reminded him. Blinking, he gave her a bleary look. "Hmm?"

"Jesus. I thought you were dead."

"Hmm?"

His expression made her worry fade, and she laughed softly instead. He looked so puzzled.

"The power's out," she told him.

He nodded, then sat up and swung his legs over the side of the bed. With a heavy groan, he rose and shook himself further awake before following the cord from the oscillating fan to the wall outlet. Kate did not bother to point out that if the fan had come unplugged, that would not have affected the other fan or the clock. His thoughts were still fuzzy from sleep, but he would get there.

Watching him, sleepy and naked and adorable, her thoughts returned to earlier in the night, how firmly he had held her, the way they had taken each other with such ferocity. A smile crept to her lips, and mischievous thoughts sparked in her mind.

Elsewhere in the house, a door slammed with such force Kate felt the tremor from it.

She watched Tommy's back stiffen. When he turned to look at her, even in the dark she could see he'd come fully awake. His eyes glistened.

"What the fuck was that?"

Kate didn't know. She'd stopped breathing. Now her heart restarted, along with that breath. In the dark, with the power out and only the light from the night sky to show the silhouette of her husband, it was easy to find fear. But she hadn't believed in things going bump in the night back in the United States, and she wasn't going to start just because she had moved from the New World to the Old.

"The wind blew it shut. The house is drafty."

Tommy's eyes gleamed. "I didn't feel a breeze. Not just then."

"The other side of the house. What else could it be?"

In the dark, he glanced around the floor until he found his boxer briefs and slipped them on. "I need to check the fuse box anyway. Might be just a circuit breaker. On the way I'll make sure we don't have any prowlers."

"Don't be funny."

"I'm not."

Kate refused to let herself be spooked any more than she already had, but she decided the best way to avoid that was to go with him. Being alone in the dark in their new house with strange noises and no power did not seem like her idea of a good time. She pulled her tank top off the bedpost where she'd tossed it, and she dragged it on without checking to see if it was right side out. This time of night, who cared? Who would see her?

The same rationale left her to forgo searching for her thong. Tommy had already padded out into the corridor, and she followed him, glancing behind her, despite the fact she knew they had been alone in the bedroom. Every shadow seemed ripe with unpleasant possibility, whether she believed in it or not.

On second thought, she slipped back into their room and re-trieved her phone from the nightstand. Clicking on the flashlight function, she felt a ripple of relief and yet more foolish than ever. Which seemed more ridiculous, that she'd been so unnerved by the darkness or that this small patch of yellow illumination made her feel somehow safe?

"Kate?" Tommy called softly from the hallway.

She poked her head out into the corridor again, this time pre-ceded by her cell phone's flashlight function. "I'm here. Want me to grab your phone?"

"No. This'll only take a minute."

Kate heard the amusement in his tired voice, and when she shone her light at him, his whimsical smile confirmed it. "Hey. I know what you're thinking."

"I'm thinking you're cute as hell."

"I just don't want to fall down the stairs."

"Suuuuure."

She wanted to tease him back, say something juvenile that would make him laugh. But then he had reached the steps that would take him to the third floor, and he started up.

"Where are you going?" she asked. "The fuse box is in the cellar."

"Just looking around. That door slam was weird, right?" He trotted up the steps, almost nude, as if he hadn't just implied they might have an intruder.

"You think someone's in the house?" Her voice seemed much too loud.

"Not at all. Maybe I left windows open up here. Just checking."

For a few seconds, Kate stood and listened to the creak of Tommy's footsteps on the floor above her. Her gaze drifted along the corridor, and then she remembered the phone in her hand, and its flashlight. Over her head, she heard the skidding of a stubborn window being lowered in its frame.

She began to walk toward the second-floor landing. When she reached it, she shone her phone's light down the steps, but despite the brightness, it did not offer enough illumination to see more than halfway down toward the foyer. She cocked her head, listening for strange noises from below. Now she turned, wondering about the rooms around her. Which door had slammed? Something on the first floor? The third? Or one of these, along this hallway?

A quick survey of the second floor revealed that all the doors were open except for the one at the end of the hall. She had not gotten around to phoning Franca and asking for a key, but of course it could not have been that door.

Still, she walked toward it, taking courage from the light her phone provided. The only noise in her head now was the beating of her heart. Kate shone the light around the edges of the door, confirming it remained closed. Upstairs, she heard a door creak open and then shut a moment later. Tommy's footsteps turned back the way he'd come, and she exhaled, knowing he would be down to join her in a moment.

Her light shining on the doorknob, she reached out to test it. The knob turned in her hand, and she let out a little noise that might've been profanity or just the breath fleeing her lungs. She stepped back in surprise and stared as the door swung inward, opening into even deeper darkness.

Kate stared into the dusty shadows. The door stopped three-quarters of the way open. Holding her breath, she raised her phone, not daring to step nearer the threshold but determined to see inside. Behind her, she heard Tommy rumble down from the third floor and pass behind her before starting down to the ground floor.

"One closed door up there. Probably was the wind after all," he said as he descended. "Probably what cut the power, too. I never thought about how windy it would get up here."

His voice faded as he left her there. She heard another door open downstairs—the heavy cellar door. Her gaze remained fixed on the shadows beyond the door that should have been locked. She drew a step closer to the threshold, narrowing her eyes. Kate thought she heard something from across that threshold. For a moment, she thought it might be a man's voice, words she could not distinguish, so quiet or so distant they barely registered.

In the wall to her left, the aging water pipes gave a throaty rattle that startled her. She snapped her head around and stared at the wall, then laughed quietly to herself.

"Idiot," she whispered. "*Idiota. Stupida. Topa.*"

She tried to think of other Italian words with which to chide herself, but became stuck wondering if the word for *mouse* even had a feminine form. *Topa* or *topo*? The questions a newly forged Italian had to ask herself.

Feeling foolish, she crossed the threshold and shone her light within. What she had expected to be another corridor turned out to be a small bedchamber. A single, high-backed wooden chair sat in one corner. A bureau had been pushed against one wall, and on the bureau were a pitcher and basin for the room's occupant to wash themselves. The bed had an iron frame, low to the ground, and a mattress only a few inches thick that looked as if it might once have been used to torture people with the promise of sleep it could never deliver. The walls presented only two decorations, a framed photograph perhaps eight inches square, and a black metal crucifix at least twice its size. Years of dust layered the entire scene—the cleaners Franca had hired before the move had skipped this room, or been unable to enter. Kate's phone light lingered on the photograph a moment, but she could not make out its subject without getting closer.

She lowered her light to illuminate the dust-covered floor, but found no sign of intruder footprints, whether human or animal. She was sure the place had mice—it must, an old pile like this, left empty for a time—but so far she had seen no sign of anything that did not belong here.

Kate moved farther into the room. Who had slept here, in the annex? And why here, when there were so many other rooms in the house? She flashed the light from her cell phone around the room again, this time landing on a door across from the one through which she'd entered. It stood open, yawning into a deeper darkness beyond. She tried to picture this part of the house from the outside, wondering how many rooms might comprise it, but in the small hours of the night, with the power out, was not the time to investigate.

She kept her phone light trained on that second door. Probably the sound she'd heard had been the pipes, but it had gotten under her skin, and the longer she stared into that farther darkness, the more it seemed as if the air had gone very still, a pendulum caught mid-swing, waiting for her.

When she laughed this time, quietly merry, it was forced. False. People said if you laughed without feeling, the feeling would come, but not tonight.

She told herself the annex door must have been swollen by humidity the first time she had tried to open it. Such things happened, she knew. Swollen wood might easily cause the door to refuse to budge. But her fingers still held the tactile memory of trying to twist the doorknob. It had refused to turn, which couldn't have anything to do with humidity. Could it?

"Nope," she whispered.

She retreated to the second-floor corridor. No need to call Franca now. The key to the annex would not be necessary. Tomorrow, she and Tommy would explore the rest of their home together.

When she was back on the safer side of the threshold, a breeze caressed her, eddying from some window or another. With a pop, the power came on. The stained-glass lamp on a credenza in the foyer lit up the bottom of the stairs. Down the hall, the light from their bedroom glowed.

Downstairs, she heard Tommy emerge from the cellar.

"Success!" he called through the house.

She felt herself begin to relax.

Behind her, the annex door slammed shut with such force she could feel its displaced air at her back. She cried out.

"Kate?" Tommy called, hurrying up the steps toward her.

"Christ!" she said, heart in her throat, thumping rapid-fire. She stared at the door, now closed tightly.

"What happened?" he asked, reaching the landing. Reaching for her.

Kate took his hand. She laughed, heart still thundering but filled with relief. "Door slammed. Scared the shit out of me."

"Isn't this the one you needed the key for?"

"I thought so."

Tommy said nothing. His grip did not tighten or loosen on her fingers. She glanced sidelong at him and saw the way he studied the annex door. Was he wondering how it had become unlocked or how she had believed it to be? Kate did not want to ask him tonight, because if the answer was the latter, they would have an argument, and arguments were best indulged in and dispensed with while the sun shone. Things were quieter at night. Hurtful words hurt more, and doubts cut more deeply.

Tomorrow, she thought.

"Fuse box?" she asked.

"Hmm?" He glanced at her. "Yeah. All set. No idea what overloaded it, though. Nearly everything in the house was turned off. The place passed inspection, but we should have an electrician come in and take a look, just in case."

"Some cousin or another," she teased.

"Hell no. We'll talk to some of the other recent arrivals and find out who they liked and who they didn't." He glanced once more at the annex door and then turned toward her. "Let's get back to bed. I need my beauty rest."

Kate looked at the door, stared at the knob, wondering if it would somehow be locked again. If she tried it now, would it turn? Would the door open? Glad as she was not to have to chase Franca for a key, she found herself wishing she could keep it locked now, at least until morning.

When Tommy kissed her temple, she turned with him and went back down the hall without trying the doorknob again. Better, at least for tonight, not to know. But once back in their bedroom, she moved a chair in front of the door, so its feet would scrape the floor and wake them if anyone tried to enter. Tommy smiled at the sight but did not question her. He understood what she was doing.

Back in bed, they clung to one another. It wasn't long before Tommy began to snore softly, but for Kate, sleep seemed far more elusive. When she woke in the morning, hot sun reaching deep into the room, it felt as if she hadn't slept at all but been transported from night to day with not a wink in between.

She was alone. The house quiet. As if waiting for her.

7

Even the darkest moods could be improved with sunlight and fresh air. To those ingredients, Kate added music, and the sense of satisfaction that cleaning and organizing always gave her. New acquaintances sometimes made the mistake of thinking her a naturally tidy person, but that was an illusion created by the fact that she did not typically allow anyone into her personal space unless that space had been cleaned and neatened up. She could be a slob, could let days go by with a mess accumulating, particularly because she disliked starting a project if she knew she did not have time to finish. But if visitors were expected, she liked to make a good impression. Now that they were in a place where, she'd been told, people tended to just drop in uninvited and expect coffee and at the very least some traditional local cookies, she vowed to herself that she and Tommy would keep the house in order.

It made her feel good.

Better than good.

Happy. Or, at the very least, unafraid.

"I'm going to pop down to the market to get more of that floor cleaner," Tommy said.

On hands and knees, Kate turned to look up at him. She blew a lock of hair out of her eyes and grinned. "You just trying to get out of the hard work?"

"I wouldn't dare."

"Then pick us up some fresh bread and a bottle of wine while you're out. And don't get waylaid by some cousin or other."

"Aye, aye, Captain," Tommy said, saluting her.

When he left, she turned up the music. A mix of '80s college rock that her father had put together for her during her own college days. It reminded her of those years, but also of him, and she felt comforted by such memories. Her dad had promised to come and visit them early next year, and she couldn't wait to tour Sicily with him.

Kate sat back on her haunches and surveyed the room around her. They had begun with the small annex room they had discovered during the night, what Tommy had jokingly called the *maid's quarters*. After breakfast, she had approached the room with some trepidation, frustrated by her own hesitation. Kate had never been the kind of person to buy into ghostly nonsense. During college, her friend Caroline had sometimes told stories about the haunted house she claimed to have grown up in. The stories were creepy, but the only evidence to support them were Caroline's own memories. Ghostly boy sitting on the edge of her bed in the middle of the night? Apparition of her grandmother the night the old woman died? A closet door that would not remain closed, even the night after her father had blocked it with a chair? All of it could be explained or dismissed. Kate would not believe in ghosts until one came up and screamed in her face. Her father knew one of the guys who appeared on some ghost-hunting TV series and said the guy insisted it was all real, but Kate had seen at least a dozen episodes of that show, and her bullshit alarm went off a thousand times.

Yes, she had been on the verge of terrified last night. The power outage contributed to that—things were always more uncertain in the dark—and the slamming door had felt intentional, even down to the timing of it. But in the sunlit, wide-awake world, she knew all of that could be explained away just as easily as anything Caroline had told her back in college.

Today, instead of being afraid, she was excited. With the mystery door open, they had been able to explore the rear wing of the house. Down on the first floor of the annex, that section included what appeared to have once been a study or library, and a smaller space containing several velvet screens that made her think she had found an old changing room. The velvet had deteriorated, even rotted, and the screens would be a total loss, but she thought an antique dealer might still be interested. The first floor of the annex also included a rustic shower room, its walls and floor covered in old, cracked tiles, with a drain so that the whole room could be used for washing. The showerhead needed replacing, but this room was an extra bonus, as were the two spare bedrooms. She thought of them as bedrooms anyway, though their real purpose confused her. The two chambers each contained an old stone bench, and both rooms had crosses carved into the wooden doors. It made her wonder if some previous owner had been a religious freak. She had seen a lot of the weird listings on #ZillowGoneWild and knew the stories of strange rooms found by home buyers. Sex dungeons, trapdoors, cellar graves, and worse. Like many rooms in these centuries-old homes, these were simple and spare—plastered walls and stone floors. They were also layered with dust and cobwebs and would require some love and attention to be of any real use. In time, they might be guest rooms or home-office space for expanding a business, but for now—once those rooms were cleaned— they would be little more than extra storage.

But that was all for later. The morning had mostly been spent on the second floor of the annex. Aside from the maid's quarters and an enclosed stairwell at the back of the house, the rest of the space was a single room, one chamber with six heavy wooden chairs, hand-carved with crosses and other religious symbols. On the right-hand wall was a platform that had puzzled them when they had first entered. An old iron chandelier hung overhead, and the whole long room was coated in dust, the windows caked with grime and soot, so at first they had looked around the room and wondered what it had been, why it seemed so separate from the rest of the house.

Tommy was the first to suggest it might be a prayer chapel. Kate initially scoffed at this idea, insisting that "chapel" implied the necessity of pews, or at least more than six chairs. She thought it might have been a music room, that perhaps the house had once been home to some kind of music school where students were taught Rossini or Puccini and lived in quarters that resembled jail cells more than comfortable bedrooms. She could picture such a thing in her mind. But the crosses on the walls were too numerous to ignore. A chapel it surely had been.

It was yet another strange thing for the real estate agent to fail to mention, but after the initial befuddlement and the first hour of dusting and washing the chapel, Kate had decided that she liked it. The chapel, the altar, and those carved wooden chairs gave the room character and the house a bit of history she couldn't wait to unearth. When their friends and family came to visit, the annex would be a fascination. She wanted to learn its history. They would turn the chapel into a place where they could entertain. Music would fill this room, the acoustics turning it into a symphony hall. She envisioned plants and wine racks and cushions.

"God," she'd said to Tommy, "the parties we could have."

But first, they had to finish cleaning it.

She splashed the mop into her bucket and then onto the floor. Despite the dust and dirt, and the stubborn brown spots she dared not think too hard about but which she ascribed to pets or other animals who'd slunk in during its empty years, the room had begun to smell of lemon and flowers, and the breeze that swept through dried the old floorboards almost as fast as she washed them.

Downstairs, a door banged shut, and she heard footsteps coming up the stairs at the front of the house.

"Lunchtime!" Tommy called as he passed through the maid's quarters and into the chapel. "And wine!"

Kate stood, grateful for the break. She greeted him with a quick kiss. "This room is going to be something else when we're done with it. What a place for a party."

"You don't even like people."

"Mostly true. But when you have a space like this, you either have to open an art studio or have an occasional gathering of like-minded humans. And I can't paint to save my life."

Tommy nodded sagely. "True, true."

She smacked him. "Haven't you learned by now when to agree with me and when to reassure me? It's literally the first lesson of being married."

"The important thing is that you can paint walls." He glanced back into the maid's quarters. "Any sign of our ghost?"

"Nothing. Which is mainly 'cause there's no such thing as ghosts."

He frowned. "Says you."

Kate surveyed her husband from head to toe. "The only scary thing in this place right now is that you went out in public like that."

Tommy gave her an incredulous look and spread his arms, glancing down at his attire. "What's wrong with what I'm wearing?"

"Aside from you being a wrinkled mess, the flip-flops are a dead giveaway. They scream 'American.'"

"Everyone here knows we're American."

"You have nice sandals. Italian sandals. The kind of thing they actually wear here and won't make you look like some California beach bum."

"Babe, 'California beach bum' is exactly the vibe I was going for."

Kate rolled her eyes. "Success, then." She took his hand and tugged him toward the door, her mind already racing ahead to lunch. "Let's eat. During which I will contemplate what parts of your wardrobe to accidentally burn."

Tommy hesitated, looking around the inside of the chapel. He seemed not to have heard her last line, which disappointed her.

"Hey," she said. "You okay?"

"Yeah. Of course." His smile seemed half-hearted. "I guess I'm just not as ready to forget how weird things got last night."

"The door slammed." Kate shrugged. "It happens. The wind shifts. Air pressure changes. It's an old house."

Tommy raised his eyebrows. "You've got a whole list of reasons a door can slam, but none of them apply to a door that's locked."

She tilted her head, giving him a practiced look of exasperation. He always said that look made him picture what she must have been like as a demanding six-year-old, and she couldn't argue with him. But if he didn't want her to give him her exasperated look, she had told him more than once, he shouldn't exasperate her.

"'Once you eliminate the impossible—'" she began to say.

"Don't quote Sherlock Holmes at me."

"Why not? If the Holmes fits . . ."

"You don't know that ghosts are impossible."

"But," Kate said, "I believe they are. Which means that the door wasn't locked; it was only stuck. Maybe the humidity dropped and the frame came unstuck. Maybe someone from the real estate company came by and unlocked it. I honestly don't know, and yes, those things seem improbable, but that's the rest of that quote, handsome. 'Once you eliminate the impossible, whatever remains, no matter how improbable, must be the truth.' Or something like that."

Tommy slid his arms around her back and pressed his body to hers, gazing into her eyes. "Here's the thing, Katie. You have no proof that ghosts are impossible, which means they're only improbable. So by your own reasoning—"

She groaned and slumped against him. "Okay, we're haunted. Does that make you happy?"

"You don't believe that."

Of course she didn't. But instead of repeating herself, she kissed him. "Lunch. Please."

Tommy allowed himself to be led out through the maid's quarters and back into the main house. They held hands on the way down the stairs, but she could tell his mind still lingered on the chapel and the events of the previous night. She had been deeply unnerved, even frightened, but the morning always came, no matter how frightened the dark might have made her.

"This is your mother," Kate said. "She did this to you with all of her woo-woo shit."

That woo-woo shit had comprised so many things, from tarot cards to tea leaves, astrology to magic candles, and eventually as far as séances with a friend who claimed to be a psychic medium. Tommy's mother had been a woman full of love and ambition who would do anything for her son, as long as it did not require her to admit her own flaws. Pushy and condescending, the old woman had fancied herself a masterful manipulator, and she tried to control everyone around her. Several times, it had caused massive fights between Kate and Tommy, but never split them up.

Tommy had loved his mother, even though being her son had so often caused him pain. He had fond memories of her, but he also understood who and what she had been, and that Kate had bitten her tongue a thousand times to avoid arguments over her behavior, and over his own behavior while making excuses for her.

But he defended the woo-woo shit.

"Hey," he said now. "Just because you don't believe in stuff like this—"

"Tommaso Puglisi," Kate said as they reached the bottom of the steps. "You kinda seem as if you want our house to be haunted."

He halted in the foyer, turning that one over. "I mean, 'want' might be a strong word, but I don't hate the idea."

Kate stared at him. "You are such a weirdo."

Tommy began to do a goofy little shuffling dance to punctuate her weirdness comment, but before he got too deeply committed to it, the doorbell buzzed loudly enough to make Kate jump.

"Oh, jeez!" she said, whipping around to look at the door.

"Sure. You're not spooked by our new house at all," he said as he went to the door.

It creaked as he swung it inward, and Kate was pleased to see

Franca Vitale on the other side. Tall and thin and stylish, Franca looked the perfect picture of what Kate thought young Sicilian women ought to be. Dark skin, dark eyes, dark hair, perfectly coiffed. Her sleeveless silk blouse showed off finely contoured arms, toned from routine visits to the gym. They were both happy to see her, but Kate gave a second glance at her husband to make sure Tommy wasn't *too* happy. She wasn't typically the jealous type, but Franca had something special.

"I'm so sorry I did not call you back yesterday," she said, her English accented but otherwise impeccable. "I wanted to see you when you arrived, but things got crazy, you know?"

"We know," Kate replied, taking Tommy's hand. "That's okay. We're so glad you came."

As Tommy shut the door and they walked to the kitchen with Franca, making small talk, something troubled her. Kate only half listened as Tommy and Franca discussed the house, the plans for various rooms, and the small earthquake the day before.

"Franca," Kate interrupted. "You said you were supposed to call me back. I meant to call you, but I never did."

The real estate agent brightened. "No, no. Tommy called. You wanted a key, I think, for the annex." She turned up her hands. "But I am afraid I have no other keys. We can find someone to change the locks, or just remove them, since the whole house belongs to you."

Kate wanted to ask when Tommy had called and why he hadn't mentioned it to her. Had she asked him to do that? More likely, Kate thought, that he had just known she intended to do it and suspected she would be so distracted that she would not get around to it. It was thoughtful of him, but it also stung a little. Kate tended to become a whirling dervish, unable to focus enough to cross certain small tasks off her list, and when Tommy stepped in to take care of them she was both grateful and irritated—with herself and, irrationally, also with him.

"No need," he said now. "It blew open in the night. We've been cleaning back there all morning."

Franca's forehead wrinkled. "Blew open? You said it was locked."

"I thought it was," Kate said. "Tommy thinks we have a ghost."

"A house like this could have many ghosts," Franca said as if they were talking about the weather.

Sicilian culture had many superstitions. If Franca was any example, ghosts were to be expected in an old house.

"That reminds me," Kate replied. "The annex room upstairs is huge. We've started calling it 'the chapel' because that's exactly what it seems like. There are crosses, and part of the room seems like it must have been a stage or an altar—"

"It could have been," Franca said. "I found the property in our files only a few days before I showed it to you. I asked the mayor's office, and they said yes, it could be offered as part of the one-euro program. It had been empty so long that they were happy to see someone bring it back to life."

"How long was it empty?" Tommy asked.

"Eleven years. But what I mean about the chapel is that it seems very possible because the last tenant in the house was a priest, who lived here for almost forty years."

"A priest?" Kate asked. "But if he was the tenant, then who owned the house?"

Franca smiled as if this were the dumbest question she had ever been asked.

"The church, of course. The Archdiocese of Catania."

8

Back in Boston, Tommy and Kate had lived their lives on different schedules. He would roll out of bed about eight o'clock in the morning, have breakfast, and get straight to work, waiting to shower until lunchtime. While Tommy fixed himself breakfast, Kate had been up for hours already, gone to the gym, stopped for her second coffee of the morning, and been in the shower. At night, she often turned in long before he did.

Just a few days into their new life in Sicily, all of that had changed. They went to bed early and woke before seven. By a quarter past, they were out exploring, walking for cardio and to clear their heads. It was an opportunity to get to know their new town better. They wandered the streets, ducked into empty buildings, bought fresh-baked brioche and coffee strong enough to imbue anyone with superpowers, at least for an hour or so.

Each morning after their walk, they came home and sat on the bench overlooking the lower section of town, planning their day. Thursday and Friday morning, they talked about ghosts and hauntings and the Old World versus the New. The conversation shifted from whether or not their home might be inhabited by an angry spirit to the general concept of lost souls—or souls in general—and the existence of an afterlife.

Once they vacated the bench, they retreated inside and continued the process of setting the house in order. It was cooler in the mornings, so the hard work had to be done then. Working together, music playing loud, they spent the mornings dusting and cleaning, then spent the afternoons painting walls, unpacking boxes, and arranging furniture in the main house.

The house continued to provide a symphony of eerie noises after dark, but despite the way the slamming door had unnerved him earlier in the week, Tommy found himself able to identify or explain away the sounds of his home. A scratching in the attic, which he'd first suspected of originating from rats, turned out to be a mother cat and several kittens, which he'd relocated to one of the empty row houses on the next street over.

Cats, not ghosts. The wind. The age of the place. The knocking of the hot-water pipes.

They also spoke, of course, about the previous owners of the house. Tommy found himself amused and slightly disturbed that they were living in a priest's home. More than that, a place owned for decades or longer by the Roman Catholic Church, complete with a chapel that had doubtless once been used to celebrate Mass. Yes, he'd been raised Catholic, but he considered himself in recovery from that upbringing and had no intention of ever suffering a relapse. He believed in God, but he didn't believe in organized religion. It had been used as a bludgeon or a veil of secrecy far too often for his tastes.

On the other hand, Kate was right. The chapel was going to make one hell of a place to throw a party. All they had to do was meet enough people they wanted to invite. Or persuade them to come to Sicily.

Saturday morning was hot, even for Sicily in September, so after lunch they took a nap, lulled by the whir of fans and the quiet of their half-empty town. At three o'clock, Tommy opened his laptop, and they entered a Zoom video chat with their closest friends from home. Belinda had been Kate's college roommate, best friend, and confidante. She would also be the first to admit that her mercurial nature—and her ADHD—would likely have ruined her college career if not for Kate. When Belinda had met her now husband, Gerald, Kate had been very worried that Gerald and Tommy would dislike one another immediately. Gerald raced in triathlons, but his real passion was wine, to the extent that he wrote international guidebooks based on the search for the best wines on earth, which suggested a person both healthier and more sophisticated than Tommy had any interest in becoming. Once they'd met, however, their mutual love of soccer and obscure twentieth-century punk bands turned them into fast friends.

The other couple on the Zoom were Hillary and Sara, who had always seemed the most intrigued of all their friends with the idea of moving to Becchina. Hillary did freelance graphic design while she tried to make a career for herself as a comic book artist. Sara wrote comics because she loved them, but her real job was as a journalist with Under Destruction, a news site focused on global political and economic coverage.

"Hey, Tommy," Sara said. "Did you ever find out what happened between your dad and his folks?"

Hillary rolled her eyes. "Sara, don't."

"Don't what?" Sara nudged her wife playfully. "Tommy knows I'm nosy. I ask personal questions all the time."

"That's for sure," Hillary said.

"It's fine," Tommy said, interrupting their banter. "I'll get around to it eventually. We haven't been here that long, and I'm trying to wait for a kind of natural conversational opening."

"A natural opening to say, 'Hey, why did my dad stop talking to you guys, and why did he never come back to Sicily after that one day?'" Gerald said. Even through the Zoom link, Tommy could see the amusement on his face. "You might need to bring that up on your own if you really want an answer."

"I mean, I'd like to know the story," Tommy said. "My dad would never tell me. He just said Nonno could get really ugly sometimes. I guess at one point he called my dad 'weak and immature,' and that was the last straw."

"I can't believe your grandmother didn't intervene," Sara

chimed in. "Her only child, and she went years without seeing him, all because of some fight."

"They talked," Kate said, and Tommy felt grateful. His friends were genuinely curious, but it did feel a bit like an attack. "I remember one time my mother tried to convince Nonna to come visit us without Nonno, but Nonna wouldn't even consider it. Sicilian women of her generation think their husbands will literally starve to death if they aren't home to feed them."

"It's just sad," Belinda said.

The Zoom went silent for a moment. Tommy squirmed, uncomfortable being the focus of his friends' sympathy.

"Well, she's got you there now," Hillary said. "That's gotta make her happy."

"It should!" Tommy replied triumphantly. "I am, after all, a ray of fuckin' sunshine."

They all laughed, dispelling the awkwardness of the previous questions.

"Let's show them the chapel," Kate said.

Tommy smiled. He had already given the Zoom group a little tour of the front rooms of the house, but she was right. He headed for the door that led into what he still thought of as the maid's quarters.

"I'm sorry, did you say 'chapel'?" Hillary asked.

Tommy turned the laptop screen so they could see each other. "Yeah. Wait until you see this place."

The faces on the screen all looked curious, even perplexed. In addition to Gerald and Belinda, and Hillary and Sara, the Zoom included already-high-at-8:00-a.m. Spenser up in Vermont. He had been Tommy's best friend growing up, and the bond remained, despite how different their lives had become.

"So, this place is full of surprises," Kate said as she led Tommy into the chapel. She opened her hands with a flourish, giving a tour to their friends, who were an ocean away.

She told the story of the missing key and the door blowing open, and their discovery of the chapel, and what Franca had told them of its previous owners. With every sentence, every smile from Kate, Tommy felt his heart get lighter. This move had been meant to be a new beginning and a true-life adventure. They had lost track of that for a while, but as their friends from home reacted to their story-thus-far, he found himself happier than ever that they had made this move.

"I've got to tell you guys," he said, turning the laptop so they could see his face again, "I think there's a real new life for us here. Italy's economy isn't exactly booming, but we're better off here than at home, and you can't beat the price of a house. Hillary, what did you and Sara pay for your place? Six hundred thousand for a three-bedroom in Groton?"

On the Zoom, Sara groaned. "Don't rub it in, Tom. Your place is twice the size for less than a tenth of what we paid, including your renovation cost."

Kate popped up beside Tommy. "So what are you waiting for? We could revitalize this place together, all of us. Socialized health care and university for your future kids. And, honestly, a bakery with bread so good it's worth moving across the ocean for that alone."

"It's too hot," Belinda complained.

"It's a hill town. There's always a breeze," Tommy said. "And the way the climate's changing, Boston's not much cooler in the summertime."

"Okay, okay," Sara chimed in. "You've got me and Hill convinced. At least enough to come and visit in January."

"Yes!" Tommy said. "We've got tons of room!"

"You're all welcome anytime!" Kate added. "We can't wait for you to see—"

Her words faltered. Tommy glanced at her, worried by the slack paleness of her face. Then the laptop wavered in his grip, and he heard the rumble and realized it wasn't the laptop moving; it was the floor. The house. The hill.

On the Zoom screen, their friends began to react. Their voices clashed, questions overlapping, worry and confusion and shock woven together.

The ground had already stopped shaking when Sara said, "Was that an earthquake?"

Tommy laughed in relief at the brevity of it. "Just a tremor. If you lived in LA, you'd get one of those every week."

But their focus had turned to earthquakes now, and he knew the chances any of them would consider moving to Becchina had just diminished almost beyond hope. Tommy refused to allow himself to think the chance was zero. His mind did not work that way. He and Kate would build their life here, work their jobs, invest in the local community, and get to know the others who had bought their one-euro homes—the Imports. In time, he was sure some of their friends from the States would consider joining them. He hoped they would. But by then, he planned to have passed beyond the point of missing them.

This was their home now. Tremors and all.

9

On Sunday morning, church bells reverberated through Becchina, as if insisting upon a funeral despite the absence of any recent death. Kate wondered if she might be the only one for whom that somber tone summoned such feelings. There ought to have been, she thought, more cheerful bells for less dreadful mornings. Her parents had grown up in the '70s and '80s, when Catholic churches in the American northeast were frequently host to long-haired folk singers instead of *Phantom of the Opera*–style organ music or the haunting airs of penitent choirs. Her mother had often said that church felt more welcoming in those days, and Kate had bitten her tongue to avoid sharing her own feelings about the church. Happy-hippie folk songs might put on a friendly face, but they hadn't stopped priests from committing the most horrific sins.

On the other hand, these bells were like being shushed by a stern-faced librarian. Given the choice, she'd vote for the happy hippies any day.

Fall had arrived, but summer was not yet willing to surrender its hold on Sicily. The morning had begun with sweltering heat and beads of sweat. She had showered before dressing for church in a cotton sundress patterned with tiny blue flowers. Tommy started the day by putting on a suit, but three minutes after slipping into the jacket, he hung it back in the closet. Charcoal trousers, a white shirt, and a new crimson tie would have to be enough to please his grandparents.

Nonno wouldn't notice what they were wearing, of course. He might not even remember that they had attended Mass together. It was Nonna whose expectations weighed on them. The old woman had been warm and welcoming, but this was an old-world place, full of old-world people, and with that came certain traditions and the pressure to uphold them.

Church, for instance.

"We're not doing this every week," Kate had told Tommy this morning, watching him wipe sweat from his forehead as the first strike of the church bell rolled across the sky.

"Once a month, we said," Tommy had replied. "That's a decent compromise."

Kate had nodded. She could survive going to church once a month. It wasn't that she objected to the notion of worship, even though she felt very iffy on the subject of God. She just didn't like the social pressure and the judgment that went along with it. Not only was she supposed to go to church and try to stay awake while the priest, Father Pino Ruffini, performed the Mass in Italian, but she was meant to smile and be cheerful no matter how hot it became inside the church. She wasn't supposed to ask why the church had six massive ceiling fans hanging from the rafters if the staff weren't going to turn them on. No, she was supposed to smile and be a good wife and talk to other wives when the ceremony had concluded, to pray and pretend she believed God was always with her. With them.

As Father Pino droned on, she glanced at her husband and saw him slip a finger into his shirt collar, tugging as if somehow exposing that little bit of skin to the humid air would offer some relief. Kate reached up and took his hand. Their fingers intertwined, the two of them suffering together.

She glanced over at Nonna and saw the beatific look on the old woman's face, the pride at being there with her grandson and his wife, new residents of a place where people only left and where grandsons born in America *never* came to live. It was the first time

Kate had considered how much it meant to the old woman, whose husband had been slowly sliding out of reality, to have her family in this place grow instead of diminish—and suddenly, going to church on that sweltering Sunday morning no longer seemed like such a chore.

She stood a bit straighter, clutched Tommy's hand a bit tighter, suddenly proud to be there with him and his grandparents, a part of this community. Maybe attending church once a month wouldn't be so bad, and in the winter, perhaps more frequently than that.

Father Pino gave the congregation Communion, and it was nice to be moving again. The front doors of the church were open, and a light breeze swirled around them as they made their way out of the pew and up the aisle. That relief paled in comparison, however, to what it felt like to step outside when the Mass had ended and the congregation emerged into the shadow of its blue dome.

Father Pino had exited first and waited on the marble steps to greet his flock. There were smiles and laughter, and Kate understood some small bits of conversation around her, most of which was either gossip or talk of family meals taking place later in the day. One elderly man, seemingly as old as Tommy's grandfather but with eyes bright and alert, told Father Pino he was going fishing with his great-grandson, and his smile told the rest of the story.

This is a good place, Kate found herself thinking. The thought pleased her, mostly because, although Tommy would never admit it to his grandparents, it had been Kate who had pushed for this move. After his mother had died, it had been Kate who had first brought him the article about Mayor Brancati's one-euro deal on homes in the old town. And it had been Kate who had first begun to dream aloud about helping to revive the fading community here, improving its profile, drawing new investment and new tourists.

Tommy had been intrigued, warmed by memories of his childhood visits here, but he had also been dubious about how much they might impact their new hometown. There had been some bumps in the road, but in the light and happiness of that morning, freed of the boredom of church and with the rest of the day ahead of them, her optimism began to return.

Nonna shuffled along arm in arm with Nonno, escorting him while making it appear she was the one being escorted. She was a proud woman, working to maintain her husband's dignity. Kate smiled to herself as they waited in the line of well-wishers to shake Father Pino's hand. She glanced over her shoulder for Tommy, only to discover he was not behind her.

Curious, she peered around, ignoring the unfamiliar faces in search of the one she knew best. A pair of middle-aged men had stepped to one side and lit up stinking cigarettes, laughing to each other as they smoked and showing ugly brown teeth.

When they moved, Kate spotted her husband. Tommy had drifted to the far side of the steps and now craned his neck over the edge, intent on something she could not see. She called out to him.

Ahead of her, Father Pino greeted Nonna warmly and made sure to make eye contact with Nonno, engaging the ancient Tommaso Puglisi in that moment. The priest must have known of the old man's memory loss.

Just as Nonna turned to introduce them, Tommy appeared at Kate's side, smiling and launching into passable Italian platitudes, shaking the priest's hand. Kate followed suit, and the moment the priest turned his attention back to Tommy's grandparents, she nudged him.

"What were you doing over there? Chasing a squirrel?"

Tommy smiled, but instead of answering, he saw an opening in the conversation and stepped into it.

"Excuse me, Father Ruffini, could I ask you a question?"

The corners of the priest's eyes crinkled merrily, pleased to be engaged by someone younger and from away. "*Certo.*"

Tommy pointed toward the spot where he'd been standing a moment before. "There's a small chapel over there, sort of crumbling, with a gate across the door. If I read the map right, I think that's the entrance to the old catacombs, isn't it?"

THE HOUSE OF LAST RESORT · 79

The priest frowned in a bit of confusion, trying to parse the question not in his language. Tommy turned to his grandmother, but it turned out she did not need to translate. Father Pino understood enough. The word *catacombs* had certainly gotten through.

"Catacombs," he repeated. "Yes."

Tommy leaned toward the priest as if engaged in a conspiracy.

"Tell me, Father. Is there any way you could give us a tour?"

10

By Wednesday morning, Tommy began to assume the old priest had forgotten their conversation, so it surprised him when—just about the time most of Sicily had drawn its shades to rest during the hottest hour of the day—there came a knock at the door. Tommy had given himself the afternoon to watch soccer on the massive flat-screen they had installed the day before, sipping a cocktail that seemed perfectly tailored to their new Sicilian lifestyle. The Tuscan pear on ice was even tastier than it sounded, combining pear-flavored vodka, orange juice, ginger liqueur, and Limoncello, with mint leaves and a slice of pear for garnish. It was just after lunch, and a drink like this probably ought to have been enjoyed later in the afternoon or in the evening, but they were relaxing in their new home. Tommy had fixed Kate one as well, but she was out on the little patio beside the kitchen door, shaded by the flower-threaded trellis, reading a historical romance about broken people falling in love on a tiny island with just a lighthouse and a pair of old yellow Labradors. Tommy wanted to read it next.

The score of the soccer game remained nil-nil, and he felt as if he might have been sliding toward naptime, but he set his Tuscan-pear cocktail aside and rose to answer the door. Halfway to the foyer, he heard the doorbell chime for only the second time since they'd moved in, and he smiled, for he had fixed it himself without being electrocuted.

When he opened the door, not one but two surprises awaited on the stoop.

"Father Ruffini," he said, with a respectful dip of his head. "I'm shocked to find you in the company of a scoundrel like my cousin."

The old priest stood on the threshold with Marcello, who smoked the stub of a fat cigar and was at least four days overdue for a shave, but who looked—as always—happier than anyone had a right to be.

The priest took Tommy's hand as if to shake, but instead he just squeezed and leaned in to increase their eye contact as he said, "Don Pino."

Marcello exhaled a plume of cigar smoke. "You can call him Don Pino. Or Padre Pino. Nobody calls him Padre Ruffini. There aren't enough people left to worry much for formality."

"Don Pino," Tommy repeated, stepping back. "Please come in."

The old priest's eyes narrowed. Behind the leather complexion, he might have paled a little. But then he gave the politest nod and entered the house, with Marcello behind.

Don Pino began speaking in Italian, making not even the most meager attempt at English, and Tommy understood this was the reason Marcello accompanied him. Whether the priest had enlisted Marcello or the two had arrived together thanks to some chance encounter was not clear, nor did it seem to matter once the visitors were on a roll.

"I saw Don Pino at the fountain last night," Marcello said. "He mentioned that you had asked for a tour of the catacombs and wondered why you were interested. I told him I thought you might have some ideas for tourism. That you were taking your new home very seriously and the mayor's wish to make us alive again."

Tommy smiled. "Vibrant."

"Yes. That is a good word," Marcello said. "I like it."

Don Pino had continued to talk as if confident Marcello must be translating for him, though Tommy wasn't sure if his cousin had actually shared anything the priest had said.

"Is he willing to take us?" Tommy asked.

Marcello's face lit up. "Of course! You think I didn't talk him into it?"

Tommy turned to the priest. "That's wonderful, Father . . . I mean, Don Pino. Thank you so much."

The priest turned to Marcello, who translated. "It is not a place for tourists. Or it was not built for visitors. It is a place for the dead," Marcello said. "But Don Pino appreciates history."

"Yes," Tommy said, looking at the priest's pale eyes, at his crinkled face. "People talk about the catacombs in Palermo. They're fascinated, and there is reverence for that place. Respect for the history. If people talked about our town with that reverence, they would come to visit to see it for themselves. Others may see it and want to live here. Businesses might come."

Marcello paused in his translation. "You think all of that will happen because of a few old bodies?"

Tommy grinned. "It's all in the marketing, cousin."

After Marcello translated, Don Pino gave a small shrug and spoke a bit more slowly, looking directly at Tommy. Though Marcello did repeat it in English, Tommy understood enough to get the gist. The old man thought Tommy would be disappointed, but he was willing to give the tour anyway.

Tommy thanked him, shaking his hand. "When can we do this? I'll work entirely around your schedule, Father."

Marcello chewed the end of his cigar, which had gone out. "No, no, Tommaso. Don Pino, he will take you now."

"Right now? *Now*, now?"

"*Si*. Now."

Tommy held up one finger, turned, and hurried into the kitchen to get Kate. She wasn't going to want to miss this.

The rusted iron gate looked as if it had been unopened for a generation. The chain that held it closed and the padlock that cinched the chain might have been more recent, but they were far from new. Don Pino reached into his pocket, and Tommy anticipated a ring of heavy keys, but instead the old priest's spidery fingers re-appeared clutching a length of fuzzy red yarn, at the end of which dangled a single brass key, nicked and faded.

Don Pino scraped the key around the padlock before manag-ing the trick. Tommy resisted the urge to offer to do it for him. The priest turned the key, the padlock opened, and the moment he began to uncoil the chain, its weight dragged it loose as if the gate were dropping anchor. A puff of airborne dust filled the air, causing Tommy, Kate, and Marcello to back away, but Don Pino seemed barely to notice as he inhaled it.

The priest bent to move the heavy chain.

"I've got it," Tommy said, scooping up the rusty pile and setting it aside.

Don Pino pushed open the right side of the gate, its bars shed-ding even more rust as it scraped along the stone floor beyond. Old as he was, the man's strength had not completely left him. When both sides of the gate were open, he gestured to Kate, who handed over one of the two heavy-duty flashlights they had brought along, and then the four of them entered the catacombs of Becchina.

From the outside, the sprawling church took up an entire block, its faded blue dome in desperate need of repair, and a patron will-ing to finance it. Of course, the Chiesa San Domenico was likely one of dozens, even hundreds, of churches with the same needs, perhaps even the same name, so without a wealthy patron, the town was left with two choices—finance the restoration over the course of many years with what donations the remaining residents could provide, or try to draw the attention of those who might visit and infuse tourist dollars into Becchina. It had been Kate who pointed out that this was likely the reason Don Pino agreed to show them the catacombs.

"It's definitely spooky," Kate said as they descended a few steps, leaving the sunlight and the heat of the day behind.

"It's a tomb. You think it's spooky now, give it a few minutes," Tommy said, smiling.

"The spookier the better for our purposes, I guess."

Tommy took her free hand. With the other, Kate used her flashlight to illuminate the walls, picking out iron braziers and some areas covered with tile mosaics that should not have been there. The church had been built by the Vatican, not by the ancient Greeks, who had once founded settlements here.

"It's older," he said, mostly to himself.

"What do you mean?" Marcello asked, studying the mosaics for himself.

"The catacombs. They're older than the church. Much older."

"Or at least this section is," Kate agreed.

They couldn't take much time to explore, as Don Pino had moved deeper along the corridor with surer footing than had been in evidence above the ground. He had behaved as if he intended to give them only a quick glimpse of the catacombs, but now that they were underground, he quickly warmed to the role of tour guide. His flashlight wavered a bit as he walked, but not as much as it would have if he were unfamiliar with this place. The gates upstairs might not have been opened for a quarter century or more, but Don Pino had been here longer, and he knew the way.

Behind them, Tommy heard the scritch of a match and turned as it flared to orange life. Marcello, lighting a cigarette. Don Pino heard it as well and turned around to deliver a withering glance practiced by elderly priests everywhere Rome's teachings had taken root.

Marcello dropped the cigarette, ground it beneath his heel, and then picked up the ruined butt and tucked it back into the package before returning it to his pocket.

"I am a bad boy," he said with that roguish grin. "Don Pino has been upset with me since I could talk."

"Somehow I'm not surprised," Tommy replied.

Kate had been in the presence of the dead at wakes and funerals, and she still sometimes woke from uneasy dreams about a childhood event that had never quite left her mind. Her father had been behind the wheel, driving the family to Virginia to visit old friends who had moved away. They had passed a single-car accident, a Mercedes that had struck the guardrail and flipped before hitting a lamppost, ejecting the unbelted driver through the windshield and into the breakdown lane. Eight-year-old Kate had glanced out the window just as the EMTs lifted the body to maneuver it into a body bag. Later, her father would tell her that it had been her imagination, but she had been certain that the impact with the pavement had stripped all the meat and skin off a section of the dead woman's face and that she could see bare skull before the EMTs zipped the body bag.

To Kate, that bit of bare skull was Death. Capital *D*. The sad end of all things.

Dying was a process, something people did slowly in hospitals or in their beds at home. Death itself was something different. It could be sudden, often violent, but it could also arrive in the quiet way of otherwise ordinary people who destroyed themselves with alcohol and lost consciousness in lonely bus stations while their organs failed them.

Many people might have been horrified or unnerved by the centuries-old cadavers that lay in stone pits or had been propped in niches in the wall, but Kate found them sad and slightly beautiful in the way of so many abandoned things. Old houses that had been allowed to deteriorate until they were no longer habitable had the same emotional impact on her. These were people who were not only dead but whose entire world had crumbled and been lost to history. The ever-worsening climate crisis worried her, but she always felt a certain discordant clang when people talked about the end of the world. To the people buried in this strange subterranean cemetery, the world had already ended. Everyone who had known them or been influenced by them had joined them in death. The beliefs and art and vital concerns of their world had been largely forgotten, or if not forgotten, then at least discarded.

"Hey," Tommy whispered, nudging her. "You all right?"

Kate flinched. "I'm fine. It's just spooky down here."

"I hope so. That's going to be half the attraction."

As Don Pino led them through the tunnel and Marcello translated the old priest's commentary, Kate studied her husband, happy to see how much interest this tour ignited in him.

"This is a very Sicilian story," Marcello said with a knowing smile as he glanced between Tommy and the priest. He held up a hand to pause Don Pino so that he could speak. "The story of the Capuchin catacombs in Palermo says the friars there opened a cemetery for their brothers under the altar at the Church of Santa Maria della Pace. They buried more than forty dead friars in a . . . what would you say?"

"A mass grave?" Tommy suggested.

Marcello snapped his fingers, nodding. "Yes. One chamber. But of course people continued to die, and so they broke through into an old cave system and carved out spaces in the walls. They wanted to move the original friars, but when they opened the original chamber, they found the old dead friars had become mummies."

"You don't mean *mummies*," Tommy said.

"No, no, not like Egypt," Marcello explained. "Natural mummies. Still with meat on them. Dried but still . . . I don't know how to say . . ."

"Dehydrated?" Kate suggested.

"Yes. Dehydrated. Something about the caves . . . they did not rot. They were—"

"Preserved," Tommy said.

Marcello nodded. "The Capuchin friars, they kept expanding the catacombs. They helped with the drying. They scooped out the insides and packed the bodies with hay or something, and they washed the bodies in vinegar and . . ."

He gestured to the nearest niche. The bare light bulb cast strange shadows, making the corpse look like some kind of hideous mannequin. It was leathery and looked artificial, and yet she knew it was entirely real.

"Were these prepared the same way?" Kate asked.

Marcello said something in Italian to the priest, who nodded but in a way that made it clear something troubled him.

"The same way, yes," Marcello said, "but that is their story. The one the Capuchins and the people in Palermo tell. Don Pino wants you to know it is not true—that the story of the original forty comes from here in Becchina, from the Order of Saint Birillus. The church above us now is not the first to be built there. Six or seven hundred years ago was the Church of Saint Birillus and the monastery."

Tommy stopped as if he'd struck a wall. Kate shot him a worried look, thinking he had seen something that troubled him. Instead, when he turned toward her and Marcello, he wore a smile of utter disbelief.

"Hang on, cousin. You're telling me that according to Don Pino, these catacombs and the bodies around us right now predate the ones in Palermo?" Tommy shook his head as if he couldn't make sense of the words. "You're saying there's some kind of rivalry between Palermo and Becchina over the true history of the catacombs and mummies and all of this, and that nobody knows this except the church?"

Don Pino had stopped his tour and paused to look back at them, clearly impatient, even irritated. He wore that I-don't-have-all-day look Kate had seen on her mother's face approximately ten million times.

The old priest chided them in Italian and looked to Marcello for an explanation. Marcello rattled off some reply, listened to Don Pino's response, and then nodded.

"Don Pino says yes." Marcello cupped a hand to his mouth in a sort of stage whisper. "He also calls the Capuchins in Palermo a few words that maybe a priest should not use."

The old priest understood enough English to realize what Marcello had said and that he was being teased or admonished or a bit of both. He muttered something else decidedly unpriestly and made a rude hand gesture at Marcello.

The tour continued, though a bit more quickly now. Don Pino had gotten his rhythm down there in the catacombs, and despite his age, he navigated easily and kept his balance.

Kate sidled up beside Tommy, careful not to trip and fall into one of the niches. The last thing she wanted was to end up cheek to cheek with one of the old dead men with their papery skin like the crust of a wasps' nest.

"Babe, this is incredible."

Tommy nodded, flush with excitement. "Better than we could've hoped for."

"The catacombs themselves are kind of boring once people stop being freaked out by the mummies. By the twentieth dead guy—"

"Yeah."

"But the story," Kate went on. "The publicity would be crazy. If it's pitched correctly, it would end up absolutely everywhere online. People love stuff like this—the history, the dispute, two church organizations fighting over who gets to lay claim to being first."

Marcello had been just ahead of them in the tunnel. He glanced over his shoulder. "I don't know what is the true story. You know that, right?"

"That's the best part," Tommy said. "It doesn't really matter. If Don Pino and others here in Becchina say the Capuchins wanted to claim the story for themselves, that's enough to make people curious. Enough to bring them here to have a look."

Kate found herself sharing Tommy's excitement. When they had chosen to move here, they had accepted the possibility that they would be moving to a ghost town just to watch it finish dying. Now she wondered if the fantasies she'd had about actually helping to revitalize the place might be possible.

They walked on, shining flashlights into deeper corners. Marcello kept translating, but Kate tuned them out. Most of what the old priest shared now were details about this or that particular old monk, or the wealthy seventeenth- and eighteenth-century patrons who had managed to buy their way into these catacombs, able to pay for the brothers of Saint Birillus to prepare their bodies so they would end up dried-out husks instead of just bones.

Kate had already begun to think about the catacombs in more practical terms. While it would be foolish—and certainly forbidden—for them to disturb the remains, they would need to examine every inch of the floors in those tunnels, clean them and make repairs, possibly put steps or walkways in certain places. They couldn't afford to have people injured through neglect. She had no idea what the laws about such things were in Italy, but she had a feeling Sicilians would be just as litigious as Americans.

The electricity would need to be updated and new lighting installed throughout, but what kind of precautions did they need to take for the preservation of the cadavers? They would need to consult with archaeologists, or whoever the experts were that you consulted about not damaging centuries-old corpses.

Don Pino led them to what seemed to be a dead end, but instead, he turned left and ducked his head, and in moments, they were all in a separate tunnel, where some of the funereal shelves cut into the walls and many of the niches revealed mummies whose corpses were decorated with metal crosses. Some had pottery with them, and she wondered if these were like the canopic jars of ancient Egypt, containing the retrieved organs of the dead.

Kate stepped nearer to one of the niches, and that was when she saw the crack in the wall.

Inhaling sharply, she took a step back and looked up. The crack ran along the ceiling overhead. On the opposite side of the tunnel, it led directly into a darkened alcove, and when she shone her flashlight there, an alarm began to sound inside her skull. Freshly revealed rock gleamed in the tunnel ceiling. A cavity had opened there, and on the floor below it, her flashlight illuminated a small pile of stone that had fallen from above.

"Tommy."

Marcello had been midsentence, but the tone of her voice made all three men stop and turn. Don Pino had gone farther and had to backtrack a bit to see the crack, the cavity in the ceiling, and that pile of broken stone.

"*Il terremoto*," Marcello said. "The earthquake."

Tommy gave a thoughtful nod. "I guess we should be surprised there isn't more damage."

Kate glanced back the way they'd come. "There probably is. We just didn't notice it until now."

"Fair enough, but if the tremors and little quakes are as routine here as we've been led to believe, and this place hasn't caved in yet, I don't think there's anything to worry about." He turned to look at her. "Do you?"

Kate knew the answer he wanted from her. The crack triggered her anxiety and a little bit of claustrophobia, but there was logic to Tommy's point. If the earthquakes were a serious issue for the catacombs, they would have collapsed centuries earlier. Still, she shone her flashlight around and tried to picture the kind of support columns that might help prevent the worst-case scenario. In addition to an archaeologist, they would need a geologist and a structural engineer. Suddenly, this project was starting to become expensive, even just in her head.

Fortunately, it would be up to the mayor to foot the bill.

"Do you want to go back?" Tommy asked.

"No," she said, "but watch your head."

11

Tommy grew impatient. As grateful as he was that Don Pino and Marcello had taken the time to give this tour, now that they had a publicity angle and a sense of the condition of the catacombs, he wanted to get out from underground and start planning. First order of business would be to have a conversation with Kate about what they envisioned and how deeply involved they wanted to get in a project like this. Then they could set up a meeting with the mayor to see if the town shared their enthusiasm.

The thought of what a talented publicist could do with the story of this place excited him. He and Kate both had real jobs that would start occupying most of their time once their sabbaticals had ended. Even so, he couldn't help feeling it would be worth the extra effort to put a spotlight on Becchina.

"Marcello, we should wrap this up," Tommy said. "I'm grateful to Don Pino, but I think we've seen what we need to see."

His cousin nodded. "Good. If I don't have a cigarette in the next few minutes, I think I will murder someone."

Tommy laughed. Marcello caught up to Don Pino, smiling as he spoke quietly in Italian. Don Pino glanced back at Tommy with something like disappointment on his face. Apparently, now that he had fallen into familiar old patterns, Don Pino did not want to leave without completing the tour.

"Hey, Tom?" Kate said, off to his right. "Look at this."

Her flashlight had found a narrower tunnel that branched away from the main passage. Kate shone the light into a darkness so deep it seemed to swallow the illumination. No bare bulbs hung from the ceiling in that tunnel, and a quick pass of the beam revealed no wiring. Wherever this tunnel led, it had never been intended for regular visitors, and yet there were niches in the walls here just as there were in the main tunnel.

"I wonder how deep this goes," Kate said.

"I wonder how many there are," Tommy replied. "There could be dozens of little tunnels and shafts, like in a mine. We need to explore every inch if we're going to try to convince them to allow tourists down here. We can't have anyone getting trapped or falling into some hole."

"Or lost," Kate said. "Can you imagine being lost down here?"

Tommy shuddered. "Shit, yeah. I can. Thanks for the nightmares I'll have tonight."

Kate tipped an invisible cap. "Happy to help."

Marcello and Don Pino were engaged in a quiet conversation, the tour suspended. Tommy waved to his cousin and pointed to indicate that he and Kate were entering the side tunnel, and off they went. The moment they stepped into that narrow passage, he felt the silence envelop them. The stone overhead seemed lower, heavier, almost ominous, and the air went still. The tunnel walls had a stale, moldy smell, though the cadavers in the niches along the walls were just as dehydrated as the others had been.

"It's weird down here," Kate said, and he knew she meant this tunnel, not the catacombs in general. "I feel like we just walked into a library." She lowered her voice. "Like we should be whispering."

"Somber," Tommy replied. "That's the word that comes to mind."

"It's all somber. It's a cemetery. Dead guys all over the place."

"The rest of it feels like a museum. As if the cadavers are meant to be on display. But down here . . ."

He couldn't find the words to finish the thought, but Kate must have understood what he meant, because all she said was, "Exactly."

This place felt private. The absence of electrical lighting emphasized the intimacy of that cramped space, but he wondered if the lack of illumination was responsible for the frisson of uneasiness that rippled from the base of his neck down his spine, or if the foreboding intimacy of this part of the catacombs was the reason no light fixtures had ever been installed. The monks had not put lights here because they knew nobody would want to explore.

"Look at this," Kate said, her flashlight trained on symbols engraved in the stone to her left, between two of the niches. "What do you make of these?"

Tommy studied the engravings. One of them looked like the cross-keys symbol often used in Catholicism. Kate let her flashlight beam illuminate farther portions of the wall as they continued along the tunnel and examined other symbols.

"Alpha and omega," she said.

"And that looks like a sheep," Tommy added.

"Or a lamb. Lamb of God, that kind of thing."

The engravings were crude, which seemed strange to him, given the delicate and ornate nature of the art and sculpture found in many churches, no matter their age. He assumed local artisans had carved these, less for the sake of art and more for their religious purpose, marking the graves.

They were so engrossed in examining the walls that they were nearly at the tunnel's dead end before either of them noticed it. Kate kept her flashlight trained on the side of the tunnel, and Tommy noticed a gleam in his peripheral vision that caused him to turn just a moment before he would have walked straight into the wall at the end.

He made a little noise, not quite a word, just enough to draw Kate's attention. As she turned to face the dead end, her shoes caught on something and she tripped, fumbling forward. Her flashlight flew from her hand and struck the wall, blinking out. In the darkness, Tommy only had the memory of her position, but he managed to reach out and catch her before she collided with the wall face-first. Momentum caused him to bump his back against it, and he stood for a few seconds, blinking in the darkness, surprised to be holding her.

"Wow. Good reflexes, babe," Kate said.

"I'm secretly Spider-Man."

The joke fell flat. Both of them had tried for levity, but the air felt suffocating back here. Tommy saw the gleam of light from the main tunnel, and the urge to rush back to it was primal and visceral. It felt childish and cowardly, but also ridiculous. They could still hear Marcello and Don Pino talking, voices muffled, and although they had watched their share of ghost-hunting adventure shows pretending at reality, he had no fear that the dead around them would begin to whisper or to reach for them.

Even so, he had to settle his nerves a moment before he kissed Kate's temple and separated himself from her.

"You all right?" he asked as he crouched and ran his hand along the floor in search of her flashlight.

"Ready for fresh air," she replied.

Tommy concurred, but when his fingers brushed the flashlight, he knew they could not rush out of there without inspecting the dead end. He clicked the flashlight off and on again. The bulb might have broken, but it was equally likely that the contacts that kept the batteries circulating energy inside the simple mechanism had been jarred loose. He unscrewed the top of the flashlight, slid the batteries partway out into his palm, then put them back in and screwed the top on again. It always amazed him how so many problems could be overcome simply by turning something off and then on again.

When he clicked the rubber button, the flashlight winked to blazing life.

The dead-end wall had a crack in it from floor to ceiling, but that was not the first thing they noticed.

"Holy shit," Kate whispered.

The wall was the height and width of the narrow tunnel, barely

more than seven feet high and four feet wide. Crosses and crucifixes had been set into the wall, each of them different from the
others in size and design. Some appeared to be bronze, others iron.
The largest of them, in the approximate center of the wall, was at
least nine inches high and made of gold that glinted in the light
despite the tarnish and the dust that had accumulated over time.
The crosses were the first thing that struck him, but immediately
thereafter, Tommy saw the crack in the wall and took note of the
fact that this was not a natural formation.

"This is weird," he said.

"In so many ways," Kate replied. "Why is this here?"

"That's the first question, for sure."

Someone had built this wall out of rocks and blocks of stone,
likely rubble that had been broken away while excavating niches
for dead monks. The mortar between the stones was of varying
age, with some sections having clearly been patched in more recent years. The crack in the wall was also of more recent vintage—
possibly from the quake that had caused the other crack they had
seen.

Tommy shone the flashlight overhead and found another crack
there, along with a divot where stone had broken away and fallen
to the floor, explaining the origin of the rubble Kate had tripped
over.

"Thirteen," Kate said.

"Huh?"

"Crosses. There are thirteen of them."

Tommy ran the flashlight beam over them again, not to confirm
her count but out of simple curiosity. There were symbols carved
into these stones just as there had been in the walls down at this
end of the tunnel.

"There's something written here," Kate said, down on her left
knee, cocking her head to trace words that had been engraved into
one of the largest of the stones in the wall.

"What does it say?"

"Latin, I think. *Extremum fato.*"

"Extremely fat?"

Kate shot him an admonishing glance. "Somehow I don't think that's the translation."

"Yeah, it doesn't seem very likely."

Tommy heard shuffling steps back along the way they'd come and glanced back to see Marcello and Don Pino starting into the narrow tunnel.

"What are you two doing?" Marcello called. "Don Pino says it can be dangerous down there. There are cracks in the ceiling."

Tommy shone his flashlight upward again. There were other, less recent cracks, but none of them seemed to present any imminent danger.

A low scritching noise caught his attention, and he swung the flashlight beam down to the right, where the natural tunnel and the man-made wall formed a dark and jagged corner. Tiny, putrid-yellow eyes glittered in the shadows.

"Jesus Christ!" Tommy hissed, jerking backward in revulsion as the flashlight beam illuminated the foot-long rat crouched in that corner.

Silent, twitching, the rat stared brazenly up at him, unafraid. It watched him with apparent disdain, as if to let Tommy know that he was the intruder here, not the rat.

Kate scowled and took a step backward, staring back at the rodent. "Brave little bastard, isn't he?"

As if responding, the rat inched toward her. Kate braced herself, and Tommy knew that pose. She wasn't going to run from a rat. If it came any nearer to her, Kate would do her best to stomp it to death. Rodents bothered him a lot more than they did her.

"Ha!" Tommy shouted, and stamped his foot down about two feet from the rat.

It retreated, scurrying toward the corner. His flashlight beam pierced the deeper shadow there, and for the first time, he saw there was a hole in the mortar, down at the bottom of the man-made section of wall. The rat paused there. And turned toward him again.

This time there were others. A pair of skinny rats slid over one another like baby weasels and crept up behind the first. They waited, panting, while a fourth emerged. In the darkness of that hole in the mortar, something else moved. Tommy could have crouched and shone the light there, but he would have had to get nearer to the four rats to do so, and that was simply not in the cards.

"We should go," Kate said.

Tommy agreed. He nodded toward Marcello and Don Pino, who were still approaching through the narrow tunnel, and Kate didn't wait for any further signal. As she retreated, Tommy kept the flashlight on the rats. Scratching came from inside the mortar hole, and he told himself it was another rat, possibly more than one. But if it was a rat in there, why did it not come out and join the others? Little bits of broken mortar came spitting out of the hole.

The first rat crept forward, staring up at him.

Tommy backed up farther.

As he began to turn, he nearly collided with Don Pino. Reflexively, Tommy turned his flashlight away from the rats and shone it into the old priest's face instead. Don Pino squinted in the glare and pushed past Tommy with greater strength than a man his age ought to have been able to muster. He held up a hand and made the sign of the cross in midair, facing the cracked, dead-end wall and those thirteen crosses, and facing the rats.

Don Pino prayed aloud in Italian, something about Saint Michael the archangel. As he prayed, he took a step closer to the wall.

The rats beat an urgent retreat, scurrying back into their hole, every rat for itself.

Don Pino stayed at the dead end until he finished the prayer, and then he made the sign of the cross again and turned to leave.

Tommy blocked his way a moment, flashlight still illuminating that hole in the mortar in that jagged corner. Nothing stirred there now. The one golden cross glinted as he turned away and strode back along the tunnel toward the main section of the catacombs.

When he reached Kate and Marcello, he took his wife by the hand, and they started for the exit, and more importantly toward fresh air and daylight.

"This place gives me the creeps," he confessed.

Kate squeezed his hand. "Me, too. It's fantastic."

Tommy shot her a sidelong glance. "What?"

"Oh, babe," she replied. "Tourists are going to eat this story up."

12

Tommy lay in bed wondering what had woken him. He could see Kate snoring lightly beside him. The room was dark except for the dull-orange glow of the salt lamp they'd picked up the day before—something to do with better sleep, ironically. The darkness told him sunrise was still hours away. He closed his eyes, waiting for dreams to claim him again, but a memory echoed in his mind. A voice crying out. Tommy frowned, wondering if that had been a dream or if it had been what woke him.

The wind gusted, rattling the window in its frame. He listened to see if the cry would come again but heard nothing beyond the sighs and creaks of the old house. Sometimes it made sounds that reminded him of his late mother's knees when she walked up the stairs at home, popping and crunching the way elderly joints tended to do.

He sighed.

Awake.

Shit.

He listened to Kate's soft snores and the house creaking in the wind, and he shifted his head in search of the perfect position on his pillow.

Something was amiss.

He opened his eyes—the bedroom door stood halfway open, and light reached in from the hallway. He glanced at Kate, assuming she had gotten up at some point, maybe gone downstairs to the kitchen for a snack or a drink, and left the light on. Tommy looked at her again, her face smooth and peaceful. But now that the hallway light had caught his attention, he decided he might as well get up, use the toilet, and shut off the light.

He slid from beneath the covers so Kate wouldn't feel a draft, then went into the hallway. The switch plate was at the landing, where the stairs led up and down from the second floor. Head still muzzy from sleep, Tommy padded over to it, reached out, and froze.

In the short bit of hall that led to the annex, a massive rat sat on its haunches and glared up at him. Its thick black tail weaved on the floor behind it, a serpent with a mind of its own. Its eyes were sunken and dark, with a little glint that felt to Tommy like intelligence.

"What the fuck?" he whispered, not aware he was speaking until he heard himself.

It can't be the same rat.

The thought sprang into his mind, and for a moment, it confused him. Why would he think it was the same disgusting rodent from the catacombs? As he studied it—and it, him—he understood. It wasn't the look of the thing; his memory of that moment in the catacombs didn't have the clarity to compare. Instead, it was something in his gut, his own reaction to its presence, that made him feel it must be the same creature.

Tommy touched the wall, scraped the pads of his fingers against the surface to feel the texture of it. He glanced down at his hands. His mother had been into all kinds of new age stuff and had once told him that you couldn't see your hands in a dream, but he could certainly see his own. Everything seemed real and tangible and ordinary except for the rat.

"Okay. Let's play," he said, but he hesitated to approach it. He'd worn blue socks to bed, but socks weren't shoes, and he wasn't thrilled about putting his toes anywhere near the gray rat.

Almost as if it recognized his hesitation, the rat turned and scurried away. *Scurried* might have been the wrong word, Tommy realized, because it made that awful scritching noise on the floor, and its tail dragged behind it.

He followed.

For the first time, he noticed that the door into the annex stood open—again. When he had gone to bed, that door had been closed, but now it hung completely open. The rat crossed the threshold and continued on, passing through what he still thought of as the maid's quarters and then into the chapel.

The glow from the open door behind him was enough to see by, but the whole space was filled with blue-black shadows. The chairs were lined against the left-hand wall, just where he had placed them. To the right, the iron chandelier still hung over the low platform he had reluctantly allowed himself to think of as the altar.

The rat stopped in the center of the room, sat up on its haunches, and turned to face the altar. Its tail went still, laid out straight behind it, and the rat lowered its head as if bowing.

Tommy's mouth hung open. He stared for several long seconds, waiting for some other explanation for what he'd just seen. It was impossible, of course. Human brain interpreting animal activity through the lens of its own rationality and experience. It wasn't what it looked like. It couldn't be.

A shudder of revulsion went through him, and he tasted bile in the back of his throat.

"Hell no," he muttered, and he strode toward the rat, prepared to stomp it to death.

Then he remembered the absence of shoes.

Tommy diverted toward the chairs, picked up the nearest one. It was heavy, ornately carved wood, but not so heavy he could not hoist it. Striding quickly, he raised it over his head and swung it downward.

The rat darted away, toward the altar platform. The chair struck the floor, and one leg snapped off with a crack like a gunshot. Heart pounding, Tommy let the broken chair fall from his grasp, thinking how stupid he'd been. These half dozen chairs were all antique, gorgeously handcrafted, and probably worth real money, and he'd broken one because a rat had freaked him out.

Stupid, he thought.

That scritching came again, and he watched as the rat peeked from beneath the platform and then crept out, staring at him.

"You've got to be fucking kidding me."

Tommy picked up the broken chair leg. As fluidly as he could manage, not wanting it to dart back beneath the platform before he could kill it, he took a step forward.

Two more rats came out from under the altar. Then another, and another, and he backpedaled quickly, broken chair leg now held up in breathless defense instead of murderous offense. There were seven of them now, counting the original, and he saw a row of yellow eyes glaring from the darkness beneath the altar, making it impossible to know how many there really were.

"Filthy little bastards," he muttered, thinking about exterminators, but also—in that place where your childhood self lives beneath the adult you've become—thinking he wanted to run from the room. From the chapel. Because this wasn't normal, was it? This was the stuff of dreams, nightmares, except that Tommy could see his hands, and that meant he couldn't be dreaming, and he could feel an ache beneath his shoulder blade from picking up the heavy chair and smashing it against the floor.

He couldn't be dreaming.

"Fuckers," he breathed, and he took a step forward, raising the broken chair leg, not caring which of the rats he killed as long as he got one of them and drove them back into hiding, and then it could all wait until morning and the exterminator.

The rats opened their mouths as one, and they screamed.

Tommy stumbled backward and tripped over the chair he'd broken. The horrid, shrill chorus followed him as he fell. He twisted to avoid hitting his skull, and instead, his shoulder struck the floor and sent a jolt of pain down his arm and up to his neck, but he barely noticed. The scream continued, the worst sound he had ever heard. His stomach roiled, and his skin prickled in disgust. He dragged himself away from the broken chair, glad for the pain in his shoulder now because it still worked. Nothing was broken.

He scrambled backward until he bumped into the other chairs, knowing he had to get up because they were coming for him. The rats, the shrieking vermin, they were going to come and get him now.

Tommy shoved himself up off the floor, bumped against the chairs, lost his balance, and fell into one of them. Sitting, he stared into the nearly dark chapel, and he listened. Only then did he realize the shrieking had ceased.

No screaming.

No rats at all. They were gone, as if they had never been there at all.

He stared at the two-inch gap between the floor and the base of the altar platform, waiting for those filthy yellow eyes to reappear, but only the darkness gazed back.

"Jesus," he whispered, rising quickly, wanting nothing more than to get out of there and back up to his bed. To close his bedroom door and stare at the windows until the sun came up and he could call the exterminator.

But that was when he heard the other sound in the room.

Either it hadn't been there before or his focus had been so much on the rats that he had not noticed.

Quiet weeping, so soft he could barely make it out.

Trembling, he rubbed his eyes, trying to get a better look at the shadowy corner in the back of the chapel. He realized he was blocking what little light came in from the doorway behind him. When he stepped aside, he could finally make out the pale silhouette in the corner. She looked, in that moment, as if she were made of the blue-white static of a television screen with no input. Only the effects of the gloom, of course, his eyes trying to fill out her image in the dark.

She wore only a thong and a little T-shirt, and she had her back to him, but of course he knew his own wife.

"Kate?" he said quietly.

As he started toward her, reaching for her shoulder, he remembered that this was not possible. He had left Kate snoring in their bed upstairs. But when he touched her, she was real.

"Katie," he said, a bit louder now.

Tommy took her by the shoulders and gently turned her around. Her body cooperated, but when he could make out her face in the gloom, he saw that she seemed in a kind of trance, like a sleepwalker, her eyes barely open. Tears streamed down her face, and she looked sadder than he had ever seen her. Sadder, he thought, than he had ever seen anyone.

He glanced once more at the altar platform, but there was nothing there. Only the chair he had broken gave any evidence that any of it had happened.

"Come on. Back to bed," he said, and when he put his hand on the small of her back, she fell into step beside him.

"You're okay," he whispered, because he desperately needed her to be okay. He needed her to be with him in the morning, when the sun came up, to help him make sense of this night.

They shuffled out of the chapel and through the maid's quarters. He maneuvered her through the door ahead of him and then followed, closing the door tightly behind him, wishing he had the key in hand, although locking this door didn't seem to be enough to keep it from opening again.

"Tommy," Kate said.

He stiffened and turned, half-afraid she would be calling him from the top of the stairs, disturbed in her sleep and coming to check on him. But no, when he turned around, she was right there where he'd left her in her T-shirt and thong. Now, though, Kate hugged herself and shivered with the chill of the old house. Her eyes were narrowed in confusion, and she glanced around the landing and then looked at him again.

"Where is the priest?" she asked.

"Don Pino?"

Kate shook her head in confusion. "How did I get down here?" she asked.

Tommy didn't have an answer.

13

Tommy opened his eyes shortly after 8:00 a.m. and kept them open just long enough to check the time on his phone screen. His head seemed full of cobwebs, and his body felt too heavy in the bed. If Kate had already been awake, he would have gotten up, but he closed his eyes again and slid gratefully back into sleep.

When he woke the second time, he shivered and burrowed more deeply under the covers. Gray daylight shone weakly between the drapes, and he recognized the sound that had been there all along—the patter of rain against the windows. The curtains billowed in the breeze. The windows weren't open more than a few inches, but the wind blew hard enough that the sills would be wet with rain. He worried about water damage, but not enough to drag himself out of bed.

Tired, uneasy from the night before, he rolled over and reached for Kate. She nodded as he slid his arms around her, already awake but just as reluctant to get out of bed.

"Good morning," he rasped.

"Morning." She slid herself backward on the mattress, contouring her body to fit perfectly against him. Days like this, when they didn't have to get up, and her body felt so good cleaved to his, he often found himself with a morning erection made more urgent by her warmth. His hands would start to roam, and Kate would respond.

But not today.

"You okay?" he asked.

Kate rolled onto her back and looked up at him. She reached up to caress his stubbly cheek.

"Not really, babe," she said. Her gaze held a tired sadness. "I'm happy it's raining, though. I always feel like days like this are meant for staying in bed, having breakfast for lunch, and watching old movies. I need something funny and sweet."

"I'm funny and sweet," he said, mostly because he knew she'd expect it.

"You are. But I was thinking more about something with Hugh Grant in it."

Tommy propped himself up on his elbow. "You want to watch *Notting Hill* again, don't you?"

"I mean, since you suggested it, sure." She gave him an adorably mischievous smile. The one that had made him fall in love with her in the first place.

He kissed her forehead, then her nose, then her mouth. "But right now, we just listen to the rain, right?"

Kate pushed him backward so that his head landed on his pillow, and she slid beside him so that he could hold her. She put one leg across him and closed her eyes again, and for half an hour, they did precisely as Tommy had said—they listened to the rain. She might have drifted off again during that time, but Tommy found he could not sleep. Eventually, he grew uncomfortable, and he nudged her slightly.

"Getting restless?" she asked. "On a rainy day when we don't have to work?"

"I need coffee."

"I could let you up, on the condition that you bring me some."

"I think I can manage that."

Kate disentangled herself from him and lay on her own pillow. Tommy slid out of the bed and dug into the closet for a sweatshirt.

"I take it you don't want to talk about last night."

Kate looked up at him from their rumpled bed. "I'm okay talking about it. I just don't know what to say."

"You still don't know how you ended up—"

"Sleepwalking?"

Tommy frowned. *Is that what it was?* he wanted to say. But he didn't want to challenge her, especially because he didn't have any rational alternatives. He also had no explanation for the bizarre behavior of the rats he had seen come out from beneath the altar platform.

"Last night, I asked if you had a history of sleepwalking," he said. "You didn't know, which is strange, right? Isn't that the sort of thing your parents would have mentioned? Teased you about or told me about to embarrass you, the way parents always do?"

"Probably? But just because I don't remember doing it before, what does that mean? Obviously, I went sleepwalking last night, or you wouldn't have found me in the chapel in my underwear. I assume it's just my subconscious being weird while we're adjusting to so much change in our lives."

Tommy wanted to say more. The way his grandmother had behaved about this house—not to mention the glimpse of someone moving inside on the day they'd arrived—it had started to get to him. And then the behavior of the rats last night, as if they had been trained for some kind of rodent circus, had really freaked him out. Thinking about the rats now, he had difficulty summoning up images of exactly how they had moved. He wasn't any kind of expert, but he supposed it was possible that rats exhibited some kind of uniform movement, like certain herding animals or the murmurations of starlings.

That made a hell of a lot more sense than anything sinister.

"My mother walked in her sleep," Kate announced.

Tommy smiled. "She did?"

"Yep. She fell asleep in front of the television a lot. When I was eight or nine, I remember waking up in the middle of the night so many times and hearing her making noise in the kitchen. I'd go in there to see what was happening—at two or three in the morning—

and she would be eating or smoking a cigarette, but her eyes would look right through me. I'd talk to her, and she'd mumble nonsense, like she thought she was talking but she wasn't really saying words. I'd tell her she needed to go to bed and kind of take her hand, and she'd get up and shuffle to her room. Then, in the morning, she wouldn't remember any of it."

"Was she sleepwalking or drunk?"

Kate frowned. "That's not nice. No, she wasn't drunk."

"That was so dangerous. Lighting cigarettes while she was asleep. She could've burned the house down."

"I know."

"You think maybe you inherited something from her? Whatever made her walk in her sleep?"

"I don't know how it works," Kate replied. "But I definitely don't remember getting out of bed last night, so I'm going to guess that, yeah, like mother, like daughter."

Tommy worried about this new wrinkle. It frightened him to think Kate might go walk about in the middle of the night, fall down the stairs, and break her neck. The idea of life without her scared him more than anything else he could imagine.

"I might need to put a bell around your neck," he said. "Or tie you to the bed."

She arched one eyebrow. "Oh, really?"

He nudged her. "Not what I had in mind."

Kate pouted. "That's a shame. You did say moving to Sicily was going to be an adventure."

Tommy slid toward her as if summoned, slipped his arms around her, and gave her a lingering kiss that promised many things. He knew how predictable he was—how predictable most men were. Any kind of salacious talk elicited a response, no different from pulling the string on the back of a talking doll. He might as well have said, *You're my favorite deputy.*

Or, *There's a snake in my boot.*

He laughed to himself, mouth still pressed to Kate's.

"What's so funny?" she demanded. "Are you imagining me bound and gagged, and laughing about it?"

"Wait, so you're gagged now, too?"

She shrugged, mock innocently. "In case of the screams."

Tommy felt a delicious shiver go through him, but he only kissed her forehead and stepped back, still holding her hands. "This has been a fascinating morning so far. I have no idea how the conversation veered into such extremely interesting territory, but there's something else I need to talk to you about."

"Turn the page?"

"For now," he replied.

Turning the page was their version of changing the subject. And if ever he hated to turn the page, this was the moment. But even if they followed the threads that Kate had just begun to pull, he knew the things troubling him—haunting him—would remain in the back of his mind, and she deserved his full attention, especially when she had decided to embark on a new adventure.

"Coffee first?" Kate asked.

"Wouldn't dream of anything else. I know the rules."

Really, there was only one rule, and Kate had just stated it. *Coffee first.*

They went downstairs. On the landing, the door to the annex remained closed. He noticed that Kate took pains not to even glance at it as she passed, but he didn't draw attention to that. They would be back in the annex soon enough.

In the kitchen, Tommy ground the beans while Kate prepped the coffee maker and took out mugs. The conversation had been suspended, a time-out, and for several minutes, they poked around, cleaning up dishes from the night before, sweeping the floor, and just holding each other in the middle of the kitchen, swaying together like two kids at a middle school dance.

When the coffee was ready, cups were poured, creamed, sugared—that last part only for Kate—and they sat at the table in the gray light of the rainy day. Even down here, they could hear the rain pelting the roof. Despite the tension and awkwardness they had experienced, it felt like home.

"It's been weird," Tommy said, cupping his hands around his coffee mug. The rain had made the house damp and cold.

They were married. Kate didn't have to ask him to elaborate. "I can't disagree."

"We knew it would be weird. The adjustment was always going to be a steep climb."

Kate sipped her coffee. He envied her ability to drink it that hot. He needed to wait a little for his to cool off.

"But we didn't expect ghosts," she said, like she was asking for more sugar.

Tommy sat back, watching her through the veil of steam rising from his mug. "On a scale of one to ten, how serious was that comment?"

"Probably a four."

A four. He could live with that. "I don't believe this house is haunted by anything but its age and the memories of the people in this town. The chapel excited me when we first went in there. So much possibility there, not to mention the rooms on the first floor of the annex."

"Maybe we could rent the rooms out to priests. Or start our own church."

She smirked. Being a wiseass. Which let him breathe a little easier. They were both so anxious that there were layers of tension to strip away.

"After last night—between the rats and you sleepwalking—the chapel weirds me out even more."

She sipped her coffee again. "You seem like you have an idea what you'd like to do about that."

Tommy tried his coffee. Still very hot, but tolerable. "This house is ours. We need to claim it. Put our stamp on it."

"I'm with you."

"We've talked about getting involved with this community."

Kate studied his face, openly intrigued. "I've been pushing from the start. If the point of the town selling these homes for practically nothing is to reinvigorate the area, it's on us to contribute to that. I know you want to lure some of our friends from home, but everybody has their own story. We should be assuming none of that's going to happen. Instead of dragging our old life to Sicily, we have to build the new one here."

"You won't get an argument from me about that. Not anymore."

"I'm glad. It's our life, Tommy. Our home. It's up to us to build it." Kate took another sip. "I'm assuming it's our tour of the catacombs that prompted this epiphany?"

"It's that, but more than that. Based on the way this town treats those catacombs as a curiosity—sort of an afterthought—I realized that the only way we're going to be able to help Becchina capitalize on its history is if we do it ourselves."

She cocked her head. "You want to, what, take charge of the town's tourist trade?"

He leaned back in his chair. "I do."

"Tommy, you have a job—"

"We both have jobs. But together, we can do this, too. Not alone—I'm not completely nuts—but we can create the momentum Becchina needs."

"You want to elaborate on that?" Kate asked.

So he did.

Two hours later, with Kate out grocery shopping, Tommy opened the door to find Don Pino standing on the front stoop beneath a black umbrella, rain sluicing off into a kind of waterfall all around the old priest.

"Don't stand there, Tommaso!" Marcello called from the steps, just behind the priest.

"I'm sorry, Father," Tommy said, ushering the old man inside. "*Mi dispiace*, Don Pino."

The priest moved to allow Marcello to pass him, then set

his dripping umbrella—still open—upside down on the tiles as Tommy closed the door. A gust of wind whistled through the gap just as he turned the lock, keeping the storm outside.

"Marcello, thank you so much for coming out on such a terrible day. *Grazie*, Don Pino."

The old priest replied in Italian. His brows knitted as he glanced around the foyer, and he shivered. Tommy told himself it was the weather, the priest just happy to be out of the storm.

"You said it was important," Marcello said, translating for Don Pino. "But to be honest, cousin, you sounded a little strange on the phone. Maybe happy, maybe drunk. I thought I should come see you."

Tommy smiled, warmed by Marcello's concern. "I appreciate that. I haven't been drinking, but I sort of feel like I have. Kate and I had a conversation today that gave us a new perspective on what we want our lives to be, here in Becchina. I'm sorry to drag you out in the rain, but we're both starting back to work in a couple of weeks, and our new plans mean we're going to have to do some renovations in the house. I really want to get them done as quickly as possible."

Marcello gave him a dubious look and then translated for the priest. Don Pino listened, and slowly, his wrinkled features contorted into the same sort of expression Marcello wore.

Don Pino said something in Italian.

Tommy understood it before Marcello even translated.

"You don't need a priest," his cousin said. "You need a painter, maybe a carpenter."

Tommy grinned. He knew how stupid it was going to sound, but he said it anyway. "We're going to renovate the chapel. Kate and I both get a weird vibe in there—"

"What does this mean? A 'vibe'?"

"It's creepy, that's all." Tommy laughed at himself, but inside, it didn't seem amusing. The laugh came from discomfort. "There are rats in there. And there are stains that I don't want to think about. We're going to do the whole thing over, but before we do any of that, we hoped Don Pino would do a prayer in there. A blessing on our new home and our endeavors."

Marcello cocked his head. "You want him to send the ghosts away."

His sarcasm came through loud and clear.

"Real ones, imaginary ones, bad feelings lingering in the place. But basically? Yes."

Marcello translated quickly, wearing a grin that matched Tommy's.

Don Pino didn't grin. His only reply was a solemn nod, and then he walked toward the stairs, headed for the chapel.

He knew the way.

14

Five days later, so much had changed that Kate could not quite wrap her head around it all. At random intervals, she would find herself grinning for no reason, so happy that the muscles in her face ached from smiling. Moving here had been a leap of faith, an investment in the quality of their lives and the future they hoped to have together, but from the moment their plane had landed in Sicily, she had been plagued by doubts she never dared confess to Tommy. They'd vowed to make their life together an adventure, unbound by the constraints of prior generations.

And now here it was. Their adventure.

For five days, they had spent nearly every waking moment fast-tracking the process of settling into their new home, focused mainly on the kitchen and the main rooms at the front of the house, and on the second floor of the annex. She and Tommy had debated what to do with the chapel. It might have been a shared office, except that seemed a waste of such a grand room, and they both admitted they would find the presence of the other distracting. It might have been a home theater, but Kate had reminded Tommy that they didn't know enough people who would want to attend regular gatherings where they would be subjected to his favorite goofy action movies.

Now it was all coming together. Kate hoped to install an elegant Italian skylight dome, the sort of thing found in museums and fancy restaurants, something that would add stunning architectural beauty while also flooding the space with natural light. It would be very expensive, but the more she thought about it, the more determined she became. When Tommy had tried to argue with her, she reminded him that he had set this in motion . . . and after all, it was going to be beautiful. It would transform this space.

Until then, they had to reimagine the chapel as best they could. With the clock ticking toward the resumption of their actual day jobs, they had hounded Franca until she got them an electrician who could come immediately. They paid extra for faster service, and now the chapel had been rewired and new electrical outlets had been installed, along with gorgeous antique-looking wall sconces and some recessed lighting.

With help from Marcello, they had ripped out the altar platform. Tommy had expected to find dead rats beneath it. Fortunately, there were no bodies, but there were holes in the wall. Exterminators showed up that afternoon to put poison through those holes and lay traps, and then the contractor—a friend of Marcello's named Onofria—went to work. Adorably tiny but formidably no-nonsense, Onofria tore up the existing baseboard but found herself so dismayed by the state of the floor that she persuaded them to rip it all out. In the U.S., Kate would have gone with hardwood for the chapel, but this was Sicily, and only tile would do. Of course, the cost of such an undertaking should have been shockingly high, but Onofria had a kind of magic all her own. She knew everyone in town and managed to cajole the tile merchant and drag an elderly tile setter out of retirement to help guide her through the process. When the tiny contractor had finished, the chapel looked like a room in some modern palazzo.

Kate and Tommy had painted the walls before the tile went down and cleaned the windows inside and out. Onofria had given them the name of a woman who made custom drapes, but they did not want to wait and instead bought some gossamer white curtains embroidered with fleurs-de-lis that had been ordered by another customer who had never picked them up. It felt like kismet because if they had been forced to go through a thousand fabric samples and pages of designs, Kate knew she and Tommy might have murdered each other. But these were perfect, not the ominously heavy curtains the Sicilian women of Nonna's generation favored but something far simpler and more attractive, and the young Puglisis agreed on them without debate.

That Friday, about 8:00 p.m., Kate stood on the chapel's threshold. It barely looked like the same room.

Voices drifted in behind her. Smiling, she turned to see Tommy coming through the maid's quarters with Franca in tow. The real estate agent lit up, delighted at the change in the place, and she hadn't even entered the chapel yet.

"We're calling this the *vestibule*," Tommy told Franca as he guided her through that anteroom, which now contained only a few chairs and a small table, a small space for quiet conversation.

They crossed the threshold. Franca glanced around in open amazement. "You did this so quickly."

Kate greeted her with a small hug. Franca quickly kissed her on both cheeks, her focus still on the room around them.

"*Vestibule* seemed a good word, considering it's the entrance to the chapel," Kate said.

Franca looked at the wall sconces and then down at the new patterned-tile floor. "I am surprised you are still calling it a *chapel*."

"Tommy wanted to call it *the great room*, but as big and beautiful as it is, that seemed a little pretentious to me," Kate explained.

Franca beamed at her. "It all looks so beautiful."

Kate felt a warmth blossoming in her chest. Despite her early misgivings about the house, and her growing worry that she might have been wrong all her life to say that ghosts did not exist, they really were building a home here. Their life in Becchina could be something truly special if they wanted to make it that way.

And she really did.

Their beautiful adventure. With just a hint of haunting. She had decided that if ghosts really did exist, as long as they kept their mischief to slamming the occasional door, she could survive that.

A voice called up to them from the front-entrance foyer, reaching all the way to the annex. Tommy excused himself and raced off to escort the next guests up to the chapel.

The first meeting of the Becchina Tourism Board was about to begin.

Laughter erupted in the chapel. There had been a lot of that tonight, mostly due to Rohaan and Franca trading stories about pampered Americans who had come to investigate the possibility of starting new lives in Becchina.

Tommy laughed as much as the rest of them, but he set his wine-glass down and raised both hands in surrender. "Hang on. They can't possibly *all* have been so ridiculous."

Rohaan Tariq sipped his wine. He gave a small shrug and looked innocently at his husband, Patrick. "To be fair, the British are nearly as bad."

"Let's not pretend you're not British, love," Patrick chided him.

Rohaan arched an eyebrow. "Never British enough for most Britons."

"Fair," Patrick said.

They had all turned to Franca as if to make her the referee. Three glasses of wine into the evening, her English had deteriorated, but she still had no trouble understanding them. When she glanced at Tommy and Kate, she wore an apologetic grin.

"I show houses to thirty, forty American buyers since last year. Only two came to live."

Kate snickered. "You mean 'two' as in Tommy and me? Or us and another buyer?"

Franca pointed at her. "You and the other buyer. In September, a man from Chicago. But he is already gone. Too boring, he said."

Rohaan slapped the table. "You see? Americans!"

The conversation went on, but Tommy let himself soak it in.

He looked around the table, happier than he had been since arriving in Sicily. Earlier in the week, Rohaan and Patrick had organized a kind of introductory coffee date at their place to introduce Tommy and Kate to the rest of the group who'd come to refer to themselves as "the Imports." Aside from Rohaan and Patrick, the other Brits were an older couple from Northern England called Graham and Sue, who'd done a lot of traveling in their lives and found the offer of a nearly free Sicilian retirement home irresistible. The others at that coffee date had been a young Senegalese couple whom Rohaan had described as a West African Romeo and Juliet, children of wealthy families who were business rivals. Their names were Serigne and Roukia, and of the members of the Imports who had shown up for that coffee, they had seemed the most excited about the ideas Tommy and Kate had presented.

There were others, of course, but it was those six who had gathered for coffee with Tommy and Kate. All of them were gathered around the long table in the chapel, with Marcello and Franca making a total of ten. They had all admired the table itself, forged of lava from the volcanic eruption of Mount Etna, and then hand-painted in a classic Sicilian pattern of blue and white, with bouquets of yellow flowers done in exquisite detail. Tommy had already known the story about the American from Chicago who had given up and left Sicily out of boredom, because this table and a number of other items had come from the man's house. Tommy had bought them for probably half what the quitter had paid, but the table had been the biggest score. There were ten of them now, but the table would have fit another six with elbow room left over.

"Tommy," Kate said, raising her glass to get his attention. "This is your baby. Lay it out for them."

He raised his glass to his wife in return, then took a sip of wine as he settled his thoughts. The aroma of fresh paint filled the room, and he liked that—felt it was auspicious—the smell of new beginnings.

"I explained some of this at coffee earlier in the week," he said, looking around the table. "Marcello and Franca weren't there, but they know some of the basics. After our tour of the catacombs, Kate and I came away very excited about the potential there—"

"One of us more excited than the other." Kate sipped her wine, a mischievous glint in her eyes.

"Don't let her fool you," Tommy said. "This is just as much her idea as it is mine. Honestly, we wouldn't even be living here if Kate hadn't been so enthusiastic about the opportunity the mayor's re-population plan offered to people like us . . . and most of you."

There were nods around the table.

Marcello shot him a quizzical look. "But it's your family that lives here."

"And I'm glad to be here with you, cousin," Tommy said. "But I had to be persuaded. It's a big move, a leap of faith, and it took a lot of courage to put our country and our old lives behind us and start over. Part of our courage came from knowing that Becchina was a town looking for a fresh start, just as Kate and I were. We tried to talk some of our friends into buying into the same plan, moving to Becchina, but none of them had the guts. Some were definitely intrigued, though. We've been keeping them up to date, but the truth is, in my heart, I doubted any of them would end up following us here."

"So did I," Kate admitted. "For most people, it's just too hard. They have too many ties they'd have to break, or they're afraid of the unknown."

Tommy studied her, surprised to hear that she also had lacked faith in their ability to persuade any of their friends to move to Sicily. In all their Zooms, their Instagram posts, even texting with friends, she had never let on that she harbored such doubts.

Kate looked at Rohaan. "As intrigued as Tommy was by the catacombs, I confess I went along with him mostly out of basic curiosity, not because I thought there would be anything interesting enough to build a tourist trade out of virtually nothing."

Rohaan nodded, but Patrick leaned forward. "The catacombs are really that special?"

"Haunting," Tommy said, thinking about their walk through the subterranean hive of cadavers. "If we hadn't already visited the ones in Palermo, I would have found them shocking, but also fascinating in their history and the preservation of the bodies."

"But Palermo—" Rohaan began.

"That's just it. That's the draw for tourists," Kate said.

Patrick smiled, glancing around at the rest of the Imports. "Tommy explained that part to us. The people of Becchina claim the church in Palermo stole the origin story for their own catacombs, that ours are older—the original. I'm sure that'll draw a lot of curiosity, but my husband doesn't have enough faith in people's love of drama and their morbid curiosity."

The conversation picked up. Tommy laid out the particulars again, focusing especially on Marcello and Franca. As the two locals on the new tourism board, he would need their support in dealing with Becchina's merchants and politicians. The meeting with the mayor had been just the beginning.

"We can't do this alone," Kate said as if she had been reading his mind. "Yes, with the right publicity and a face-lift, the catacombs could be an excellent draw not just for foreign tourists but for Sicilians and those from the Italian Peninsula interested in searching for the true history of this place. The point of creating the Becchina Tourism Board is to focus on what those visitors will find when they get here. Not just the catacombs but the steps and the church dome. Tommy and I have talked about a unifying logo for the town, about the kinds of souvenirs that might be available."

"You're talking about branding," said Roukia, the young Senegalese woman. She had perked up considerably. Her husband, Serigne, encouraged her with a wave of his hand, and she went on. "But there is more to branding a destination than putting a logo all over the town and selling T-shirts."

Tommy felt stung. "We're aware it isn't that simple—"

"Of course," Roukia interrupted him. "I did not mean to imply otherwise. It is why we are creating this group, yes?"

"Yes," Kate agreed.

Roukia smiled, glancing up and down the long table. She had declined wine, taking coffee instead, and now she placed her hands around her mug as if a chill had settled in.

"We need to create an identity that is real and tangible," Roukia said. "This place needs to have a reputation as more than the ghost town where the mayor is selling off homes for pennies to keep the place from being utterly abandoned."

Franca bristled. "Becchina is more than that. It is generations of families, centuries of history—"

Marcello shrugged. "All right, Franca, but where are the younger generations? Gone, except for a handful. It's really mostly history now. Our reputation, if we have one, is just as Roukia says."

"We have famous local dishes," Franca said.

"We do?" Tommy asked.

Marcello nodded. He reached into his pocket for his cigarettes, then paused and grimaced in frustration as he remembered he had been forbidden from smoking in this house. "Pasta Becchina," he said.

The rest of them exchanged baffled glances, and Marcello laughed. "You have not eaten in many restaurants since you have been here."

"We have, actually," Patrick said. "Now I remember. It's that dish with the aubergine—"

"That's half the pasta dishes in Sicily," Rohaan replied.

"This one has sausage and peppers and would almost seem like a stew except for how much bucatini is in the bowl. I had it months ago at the little place with the cats on the patio."

"That's it," Marcello agreed. "But there are others. My mother always told me granita al caffe was invented here."

Roukia tapped her finger on the table and looked at Kate. "That is precisely the sort of thing I am talking about. Coffee-infused Italian ice? Other parts of Sicily will certainly argue, but if the Becchina Tourism Board creates a web presence and begins to spread news stories and travel-magazine pieces showcasing 'the forgotten hill town where Sicilian history and culture were born,' then that becomes an identity."

Silence around the table as they all pondered the audacity of the plan.

"We would have to involve a lot of merchants and restaurant owners," Rohaan said. "We couldn't do it without them."

"And some of them will have to invest in updating their places of business," Serigne added.

"We'll help them," Kate said. "The mayor, the town . . . We'll have to persuade the people here to invest in their own future."

"We need a tour." Tommy looked at Marcello and Franca. "A vineyard, a glassblowing studio, a place we can watch arancini being made from scratch. Historical interest, too, and not just the catacombs. Obviously the church would be included, but we have to do some research and find buildings designed by famous architects or where historical figures once lived. Anything of interest."

At the far end of the table, Graham snorted with derisive laughter. Tommy flinched. The old man, son of a coal miner, had been so quiet that Tommy had forgotten he and his wife, Sue, were even in the room. Now Graham leaned low over the table, his bulbous nose and cheeks ruddy with too much wine, his eyes dancing with a merriment that verged on mockery.

"Come on, lad," Graham said. "You're livin' in a place called the House of Last Resort, and you're really not going to put it on this tour you're dreaming up?"

Tommy went still. His stomach clenched. He'd heard that phrase before, and it took only a moment to remember where. Marcello had translated the words for him at Nonna's house. Tommy turned to stare at his cousin.

"Where'd you hear that?" Kate asked.

Graham leaned back in his chair, half in shadow. The light from the wall sconces didn't reach him. "Rohaan and Patrick heard it from the fella who sold them their place."

Tommy stiffened. Everyone around the table turned to look at Rohaan and Patrick.

Rohaan lifted one shoulder in half a shrug. "When I'd heard someone was moving into this place, I asked him why he hadn't shown it to us when we were searching for a home here. He told us the history, and we were . . . well . . ."

"You were what?" Kate asked.

Patrick took a deep breath. "We were happy we hadn't been the ones to buy it."

Serigne and Roukia shifted awkwardly in their chairs.

Serigne looked as if he might be sick, but he also looked confused. "This is the first time we have heard this name, the House of Last Resort. Someone please explain?"

Tommy tossed the question to Rohaan. "Go ahead. You seem to have the answers. My cousin obviously does, too, but I asked him once already, and he wasn't very forthcoming."

Marcello took out his cigarettes. "I would have told you. Nonna made it clear I wasn't to do that."

Kate reached across the table and snatched his cigarettes away. "There's no smoking in here."

Marcello rolled his eyes. The tension in the room grew thicker.

They all looked to Rohaan again. He nodded.

"According to our real estate agent, this house once belonged to the Vatican," Rohaan said.

"For centuries," Patrick added.

"For centuries," Rohaan repeated. "The Catholic Church used to do a lot of exorcisms. Maybe they still do. But for a very long time, this house was apparently the place the Vatican sent people who were possessed by demons that couldn't be exorcised."

Tommy felt the blood drain from his face. "What?"

"You've got to be fucking kidding," Kate said, biting off each word with a bitterness he had never heard in her voice before.

Marcello shook his head. "You're making too much of it. The things people believe, the superstitions, we are not bound by these things."

Tommy barely heard him. He felt numb, thinking about the chapel, running through his memory of each room, wondering about the bizarre religious rituals that had taken place in them. How insane must someone have been for the Vatican to decide they were full of demons and nothing could ever cure them?

"Why here?" Kate asked.

Rohaan began to reply, but Marcello cut him off. "It's far from Rome. Far enough that they could pretend they had driven the devils out of every person who was possessed. But it was called the House of Last Resort because of the priests here. The most experienced exorcists . . . some of them went a little crazy. Of course they did. If these things were real, anyone would go a little crazy, right? And if the demons were not real, then these exorcists were already crazy. They were sent here, and they would keep trying to drive the demons out of the possessed."

Kate looked as if she might be sick. "The House of Last Resort. Okay. But what happened if they couldn't cure these people? Where did they put them then?"

Marcello shook his head. "Nowhere, Kate. The priests here did not ever give up. They would try again and again until they succeeded or the people died."

Kate got up, swayed a bit, and then walked from the room. "Jesus Christ," she muttered on her way out.

Tommy watched her go, then looked around at the others. Serigne and Roukia whispered apologies as they rose and departed without another glance. They could not stay another moment in such an evil place, Roukia said. Tommy winced at the words. If the priests were doing good and important work here—if you believed in any of that shit—then how could this be an evil place?

But the answer floated in the back of his mind.

The ones who died without being exorcised—what happened to the demons who had possessed them? Where did that evil go?

"This is bullshit," he said. "Demons? Exorcism."

"To be honest," Patrick said, "I agree with Graham. If you're going to all the effort of creating a brand identity for Becchina with the story of the catacombs at the center of that brand, then the story of this house could be just as much of a draw."

"You want me and Kate to make our house a tourist attraction revolving around exorcism and demonic possession?"

Patrick heard the edge in his tone and said nothing. Instead, he opened his hands in surrender and stood up, the legs of his chair scraping the tile as he slid backward. Rohaan blinked, realizing his husband had decided it was time to go, and then he stood as well. Graham downed the rest of the wine remaining in his glass. Sue tugged his arm, and then the two Northern Englanders stood.

"Thank you for the wine, and the conversation," Sue said politely.

Graham inclined his head in something that looked like half-thanks and half-apology, but not really either one. Sue muttered some recrimination at him as they hurried out. Rohaan and Patrick said something else, trying to take some of the shock out of the news they had given Tommy tonight. After a few seconds, they left. Rohaan patted Tommy on the shoulder before they departed. He wondered if Kate would let them out downstairs or if she had retreated to one of the rooms in the house and left them all to find their own way.

After a moment, Marcello got up. He walked around the table and retrieved the cigarette pack that Kate had snatched from him.

Tommy's eyes narrowed. He looked up not at Marcello but at Franca.

"You've been awfully quiet," he told her.

Franca gave him a half-hearted smile. Her chin trembled as if she might cry. "I think you and Kate have wonderful ideas for

Becchina." She rose from her chair, obviously intending to follow Marcello out. "I'm sorry the evening did not go as perfectly as—"

"Are you kidding me?"

She flinched. Looked stung, even a bit frightened.

"Tommy," Marcello cautioned.

But Tommy couldn't take his eyes off Franca. His real estate agent. Who, in this small town, was one of those working with the mayor on his program to sell old homes to foreigners for insanely cheap prices. There couldn't have been many local real estate agents, and fewer still who were entrusted with this task by the mayor. Whoever had helped Rohaan and Patrick buy their house here, Franca had to know him. Which meant it was very likely she had known the true history of the House of Last Resort and chosen not to mention it.

Tommy stood up, took a hard look at Franca. "Get the fuck out of my house."

He turned and left the chapel, out through the annex vestibule into the main house, and up the stairs to his bedroom. Marcello and Franca could let themselves out.

This changed everything.

Kate sat on the edge of their bed, body locked in place. She wanted to haul back the covers and burrow underneath, just cocoon herself away until morning. The anxiety buzzing inside her made her want to get up and pace, just walk back and forth until she wore a path in the floor or she collapsed from exhaustion. With her body driven both directions, cocooning or pacing, she found herself unable to do either one. It paralyzed her, as she perched there on the bed with her eyes closed. The best she could manage was to rock back and forth, just a little.

"Shit," she whispered. "Shit, shit, shit."

It would have been so easy to free-fall into superstition, but did she really believe any of this? Facts were facts, of course, but what were the facts? If she took this story at face value—and nothing they had learned up till now conflicted with these new details—it wasn't the local archdiocese that had owned this property but the Vatican itself. That made sense, and might even be a matter of semantics. No matter what might be written on a property deed, the Vatican controlled every archdiocese and could make decisions related to their properties at any time. The fact that priests had lived in this house for generations was something they had already known. If she pondered on it, she would have assumed that the place had earned the nickname "the House of Last Resort" because old priests came to retire here. Something like that would have made sense.

But this story about exorcism, about the ones the Vatican didn't want to admit they couldn't save . . . That also worked very well with the house's nickname.

Gossip, she told herself. Rumor and folk tales among a people still profoundly influenced by tradition and superstition.

"But let's assume it's true," she whispered to herself, face buried in her hands.

The chapel would have been where the rituals took place, where people the Vatican believed were possessed by demons had been strapped to the altar, or a bed or table. There had been stains on the floor, now covered by new tile, that she had believed to be blood. Old stains, the color of rust, soaked in and left to history. She and Tommy had barely talked about those stains, and she thought she knew why—because they both believed people had bled there, and neither had wanted to make it a reality by discussing it.

The rooms on the first floor of the annex would have been perfect as cells to hold people who could not be allowed to roam free. Possessed, or simply mentally unstable, they might have been violent and certainly could not have been given the run of the house. And the vestibule—what she and Tommy had originally called the maid's quarters—Kate could see it now, in her mind's eye, a single priest stationed in that room at all times, a guard or sentinel outside the chapel. Or perhaps it had just been a place for the exorcist on duty to lay his head when exhaustion overtook him.

She could see it all, inside her head. Could even believe it, though she didn't want to.

"That doesn't make it real," she told herself.

The thought made her open her eyes. She stared into the corner of her bedroom, listening to the house breathe and creak, and realized that was true. That the Roman Catholic Church had stood by its belief in demonic possession well into the twenty-first century; that they had exorcists among their ranks, priests whose supposed role was to use ancient rituals and the fortitude of their righteousness to drive demons out of human beings . . . All of that was irrefutable fact. Kate had been aware of that for as long as she could remember and thought it vaguely amusing.

No, more than amusing. She had thought the church's position on demons and exorcism to be ridiculous and pandering to their most gullible faithful to keep them frightened of evil, and thus obedient to the church.

That could all still be true.

The House of Last Resort might have been used for precisely the things Rohaan had said, but that didn't make any of it real. Broken-down old exorcists, retired from fieldwork, had lived in this house. Rome had sent the worst cases of supposed possession here for those exorcists to keep working on until they regained control of their souls—or their sanity, more like—or died. It was ugly and it was sad, but that didn't mean it was real. The church had been taking advantage of the fear they nurtured in the faithful, and the fragility of people who were obviously mentally ill.

"Jesus," she whispered to herself.

And smiled at the irony.

No. She did not need to believe in demons to accept the history of her house, although she wasn't just going to take Rohaan's word for it. They needed to do some digging. If the story was true, then she and Tommy would have to discuss what to do about that. Could they still live in this house, knowing the tragic things that had happened here? How did it all figure into their plans for Becchina?

If they were going to draw tourists with macabre curiosity about the catacombs, did this house now figure into that scheme?

Sitting there, she could hear the usual creak and moan of the house. She thought about doors slamming and what sounded like footsteps in the middle of the night, and how easy it would be to let herself believe there were ghosts in the house. Even if she did not believe in demons or exorcism, the nature of the things done in her house meant a lot of pain and sorrow had filled these rooms, and doubtless, people had died in the annex. And what about her sleep-walking and the question she had asked when she came awake— *Where is the priest?*

Somehow it was much easier to believe in ghosts than in demons, but even so, she could not bring herself to really embrace the idea.

"It wasn't supposed to be this complicated," she said, dropping her head and closing her eyes again.

The bedroom door creaked. The floor groaned with Tommy's footsteps.

"Please tell me they're all gone," she said.

No answer.

Kate opened her eyes to find herself alone in the room. A chill traveled up her spine, and it made her laugh at the absurdity of it all. Finally, she could move, and she rose from the bed and went to the open bedroom door. Of course it had been a breeze, and the sounds had been a result of the house shifting in the wind or settling after the recent earth tremor.

Or maybe it had been a ghost. She chuckled to herself. Really, would that be so bad? Given the alleged history of their home, it could be so much worse than open doors and creaking timbers.

She poked her head in the hall just as Tommy came up the stairs to join her.

"They gone?" she asked.

Tommy nodded. "Marcello and Franca are finding their own way out. I'll go down and lock the door in a bit."

Kate opened her arms to receive him. Tommy embraced her, and they stood in the hall outside their bedroom for a minute or so, just resting against one another.

"This is nuts," Tommy said, his breath warm on her ear.

"This is Sicily," she replied.

His laugh was quiet, soft, but she heard it. As long as they could both laugh, they could get through anything.

Tommy stepped away from her. He gave a thoughtful shake of his head. "This is why Nonna freaked out about us moving into this house. The whole thing about not wanting us to have babies here—that had to be because of all this exorcism bullshit."

"To be fair," Kate said, "if she really believes any of that, I don't blame her for not wanting us to have babies here."

Tommy studied her. "But you don't believe it?"

"That exorcists lived here? If they did, they did. But if you're asking if I believe people actually possessed by demons lived and maybe died here? Of course not. Do *you*?"

In the yellow hallway light, Tommy seemed pale.

"Of course not," he echoed. "It's just a house."

"Not 'just a house,' Thomas Puglisi. It's *our* house."

"Soon to be our museum of horrifying exorcisms gone wrong?"

Kate stared at him, a sick feeling in her gut. "Ah, fuck. Probably, yes. That's probably exactly what it's going to be. The House of Last Resort."

15

Late the following morning, Kate sat at Nonna's kitchen table with a cup of coffee and a plate of the S-shaped cookies she seemed to bake every few days. They had very little flavor but were hard and crumbly and perfect for dunking in coffee. Kate broke one in half and stared at the two halves before setting them onto the table in front of them. Tommy had made her an omelet for breakfast, and she hadn't been able to eat more than a few bites. She wasn't any hungrier now than she had been three hours earlier.

She sipped from her cup and looked across the table at Tommy's grandfather. Nonno took a drink of coffee, but his attention remained locked onto the small TV on the counter. Nonna said he couldn't really sustain interest in a movie or television series anymore, but if there was some kind of performance, a game show, or a comedian, he could follow along. Tommy had confided in Kate his feeling that this might be wishful thinking. He doubted his grandfather could follow anything for more than a few minutes.

The door to the laundry room creaked open. The smell of detergent wafted into the kitchen, stronger than the aroma of freshly brewed coffee. Nonna came into the kitchen, stuffing two handfuls of clothespins into the pockets of her apron. She glanced over her shoulder as Tommy emerged behind her.

"Don't drop," she said, then added something in Italian.

Nonno didn't look up from the TV.

Tommy carried a basket of sodden laundry straight from the

washing machine. Nonna had a clothes dryer but hardly ever used it. The electricity drain placed enough of a burden on the house's wiring that it often led to a blown fuse, but more than that, Nonna preferred to hang her laundry out in the back courtyard. She liked the fresh scent of air-dried laundry and the routine of hanging things out to dry. This morning, the moment they had arrived, Nonna had pressed Tommy into service as her assistant.

Kate sipped her coffee. She tapped half her broken cookie on the table, waiting for Tommy to say something.

Tired of waiting.

"Nonna, can I ask you something?" she said.

The little old woman stopped and turned to her. "You like more coffee?"

Tired, Kate did her best to summon a smile, knowing it would be the least sincere effort she'd ever made. Tommy shifted the laundry basket and gave a single, curt shake of his head. *Not now*, that look said.

"No more coffee, thanks. I just have to ask. You knew the history of our house—you know the church owned it, that they used to do exorcisms there."

She felt so stupid just saying it.

Nonna looked almost angry.

Scratch that, there was nothing *almost* about her expression.

"What you mean?"

"*La casa dell'ultima risorsa*," Kate said, mangling the Italian. "One of your friends referred to our house by that name on our first night in Becchina. You were not happy about him giving us that information, which means you know that people around here have called our house by that name for a long time. *La casa dell'ultima risorsa*. The House of Last Resort. Last night, we learned where that name comes from."

Nonna's spine had gone rigid. Expressionless, she stared at Kate, waiting for the rest. The old woman had gone to her hairdresser that morning. In a clean apron and with her hair freshly dyed, sitting like a cap on her head, she looked like the sweet old Sicilian grandmother she had always been. But Kate saw a different part of her now. At first, it seemed like strength or bravado, but was there a bit of fear in there, too? A tremor in the ferocity she wanted them to see?

"This house no good," Nonna said. "But now is yours. Maybe you do something good with it. Make better."

"That's exactly what we plan to do," Kate replied. "We just wish you had told us about this yourself so we didn't have to find out from strangers."

Nonna gave her a disapproving look and left the room without another word.

Tommy stared after her. "Nonna?" he called as he hurried to follow her out to the courtyard with her wet laundry.

Kate heard the back door squeal open and slam shut, then again as Tommy went outside. Their voices were muffled as Tommy tried speaking to her further, but Kate wasn't sure what he hoped to get out of the conversation.

Fuck it, she thought, sipping her coffee.

Her stomach rumbled, suddenly aware of its emptiness. She regretted not eating this morning's omelet.

Kate slid back her chair and carried her cup over to the counter, where she discovered that the coffeepot remained half-full. She poured a hot refresher into her cup and looked over at Tommy's grandfather. The old man had barely moved. He spent most of his time these days napping in a reclining chair in what Tommy called the TV room, but this morning, he seemed to have nodded off in the much less comfortable chair at the kitchen table. Despite her agitation and the trill of anxiety that rang in her head, she felt a pang of sympathy for the old man. Far better, she thought, to leave the stage when the curtain came down and not linger on long after the lights were out and the audience had gone home.

Laughter erupted on the small kitchen television. The slumped old man blinked and sat a tiny bit straighter.

"Nonno, there's still coffee in the pot. Do you want another cup?"

He seemed not to have heard her. Kate walked the coffeepot over to him. Even if his hearing had started to fail, he would notice if she was standing right next to him, and she wasn't above a bit of theater to get through the language barrier. She put her own cup down on the table, then reached out to tap a finger on the rim of his cup.

"Nonno? Do you want more coffee?"

She prepared to shake the pot a bit to illustrate, but why was that necessary? He might not speak more than a couple of hundred words in English, but surely *coffee* would be one of them. Pointing at his cup and holding up the pot ought to get the idea across even if he'd forgotten every English word he'd ever learned—even if he'd forgotten every word in every language. She was speaking the international language of caffeine, and that was impossible to misinterpret.

If he would just look at her.

Kate glanced at the doorway through which Nonna and Tommy had taken the laundry. Something was off here. Something more than just the gradual slide into the abyss of dementia. The old man's eyes were open, and he seemed to be looking at the television, but as she watched him, a little bubble of drool appeared on his lips and then slid over the edge to become a dangling string of it.

Her chest tightened.

"Nonno? You okay?" She didn't feel close enough to Tommy's family yet to touch him, but trepidation overrode any hesitation.

Kate laid her free hand on his shoulder. "Nonno?"

Nothing. She stepped back and studied him, but she could see his shoulders rising and falling slightly as he inhaled and exhaled, so she knew he hadn't died there in the chair. The little string of drool broke off and landed on the second button of his shirt, then slid farther down the fabric.

"Shit," she whispered. "Oh shit."

Gripping his shoulder more firmly, she gave him a shake. "Nonno. Can you hear me?"

Another ripple of laughter came from the tinny television speaker. A wave of sadness crashed over Kate. What would happen now? The old man seemed to have had some kind of stroke. Tommy would be frantic and would feel obligated to take responsibility for both of his grandparents. She did not blame him for that, but she wished she could take that burden from him.

She had to go out into the courtyard now. Right now. He was ninety-six years old and had dementia, but she knew with a stroke that speed was essential.

Kate shook him one more time, not wanting it to be true. "Nonno?"

The old man's head swiveled toward her. His ice-blue eyes were bright and clear, and he smiled wide enough to show all his teeth.

"Why can't you leave me alone, you stupid *cunt*?" he sneered in perfect English. "Can't you see this is not about you?"

The coffeepot fell from her hand and hit the floor hard enough to crack the tile. Kate backed away, staring at the open revulsion in his eyes. At the alertness in his gaze and the knowledge there. She felt stripped bare and bruised.

"What the hell did you just say?" she managed.

Nonno grinned merrily. Playfully. "I have waited a very long time for what is about to happen, but if you insist on making this about you . . . we can do that."

He stood up in one fluid motion, spine straight, taller than he'd been before. His chair fell backward and clacked on the tiles. More laughter came from the television. But really the sound did not come from the TV at all. Nonno opened his mouth, and the sound emanated from the dark place behind his teeth. From the depths of his gullet.

He bent to pick up the coffeepot she had dropped. She had backed away from him without realizing it. Now he picked it up and stepped right into the puddle of coffee that had dribbled out of it, and he tested its weight in his grip, nodding happily. Even before he looked up at her with grotesque intent and took another step toward her, Kate knew he intended to bludgeon her with that pot. This ninety-six-year-old man who could barely walk, never mind speak English.

"You should have let me be," he whispered, his voice a deep rasp.

Kate backed into the counter. No more room for retreat.

She screamed, and Nonno rushed at her. Kate put her hands up to defend herself, but he batted them out of the way and grabbed her by the throat with his left hand. With his right, he swung the coffeepot. She caught his wrist to stop him, and the pot flung from his hand and clattered across the kitchen counter and into the sink.

His fingers squeezed her throat. She wheezed for air but managed to get both hands on his chest. With the counter behind her for leverage, she shoved him backward. The old man could barely lift a coffee cup without his hand shaking, but for a few moments, he had seemed impossibly strong. Now he flailed as he stumbled backward and crashed into the table.

Down the corridor, the patio door squealed open and banged shut.

"Kate!" Tommy called as he came running.

Nonno collapsed to the tile floor, wheezing and clutching at his chest. He went rigid a moment, gaze riveted to her, eyes inhumanly black, and then his head lolled to one side, and it seemed as if all the lights had gone out inside him.

Tommy came into the room, saw his grandfather on the floor, and rushed to him. Kate knew she ought to explain, or at least stand by her husband and calm him down, but she could not bring herself to move a step closer to the old man.

Nonna came into the kitchen, a pair of clothespins still in her hand. She'd abandoned the hanging of her laundry when she'd heard Kate scream, and now she seemed to have forgotten those clothespins.

They fell from her fingers and clattered on the tile.

"Tommaso," she whispered.

Tommy turned to her. "Nonna, call for an ambulance."

The old woman's rheumy eyes narrowed as if she might argue with her grandson. For a second, she looked like she was weighing the wisdom of calling for help. Then she turned and ambled to the small side table, grabbed her telephone, and started to dial.

On the floor, something rattled wetly every time Nonno drew a breath. Something down inside him, caught in his chest. Something that didn't belong.

16

There were places bustling with people where it was possible to feel a part of something greater. A triumphant concert. A darkened theater. An Irish pub when the music began to play. A wedding, in the moment of the first kiss. But Tommy had always thought a busy hospital must be the loneliest populated place on the planet. You could feel alone almost anywhere, but rarely with so many people surrounding you.

Nurses rushed along corridors; people sat worrying in waiting areas; visitors crowded into patient rooms, wearing uncertain smiles. And it was so much worse when you were in a hospital where everyone around you spoke a different language. It felt like landing on an alien world during its last days. Nobody had time to explain anything.

Tommy felt numb as he walked past the nurses' station, not sure if it was the right direction. The signs were simple, but they were in Italian. How had he and Kate thought they were going to start a new life here with the language barrier they faced? A new adventure, they'd told each other, with the lightness of heart that only youth allowed. They'd had no kids, no mortgage until they'd bought this house, no obligations to keep them in the United States, and they'd had ambitions and dreams of a simpler life in a kinder world.

They hadn't counted on what would happen in a crisis.

Part of the reason they had moved to Becchina had been the

serendipity of it being one of the towns offering houses for next to nothing. It had felt a bit like magic—a gorgeous, rambling home in a beautiful hill town where his grandparents lived just a few streets away. They were old, no doubt, but he'd had this fantasy about finally getting to really know them, maybe to know his late father a little more by spending time with them. Maybe he wouldn't feel so much like an orphan if he embraced his father's family, in a way he had never really felt free to do while his mother had been alive to push his buttons and pull his strings.

Intellectually, he had known his nonno could not live many more years. At ninety-six and in declining physical and mental health, even elderly Mediterranean people in so-called blue areas, where people enjoyed extraordinary longevity . . . even they could not live forever. But it had only been days. Barely more than two weeks.

A nurse came bumping through a swinging door ahead of him. While it remained open, he spotted the glass partition and the door that led out to the waiting area. He should have felt grateful to be leaving the patient rooms behind. The constant noise—the buzzing of alarms on medical machinery, the dinging of signals only the staff understood, the ringing of phones—that was bad enough. But the smell was worse, the layer of antiseptic cleaner and air freshener on top of the stink of human waste, rot, and slow decay. The smell of sickness and dying.

When Tommy passed through the swinging door and then the automatic glass door slid out of his way to allow him into the waiting area, he should have been thrilled to leave all of that behind. But the moment he saw his wife, he wanted to turn around again.

Kate didn't look up. She sat slumped forward in a chair, face buried in her hands, not as if she were mourning but as if she had fallen asleep that way.

Tommy approached and stood in front of her, thinking she might notice the scuff of his shoes or see his feet standing there, but she did not.

"Kate."

She jerked in the chair as if he'd poked her with something sharp. Her head snapped back, and she looked at him with such naked worry that Tommy didn't know what to say next. Kate had told him she wanted to go home, and the way she'd said it—in that moment—he had been sure she meant Boston, not Becchina. But she had been the only one in the room with Nonno when the old man had collapsed, and Tommy had insisted she come to the hospital in case the doctors had questions for her.

"How is he?" she asked hopefully.

If he hadn't known any better, he would have thought the hope in her voice was that Nonno had already died. He told himself that was crazy, and he sat down in the chair beside her.

"He's stable," Tommy said, "but the news isn't good."

Still bent forward, Kate worked her fingers together, kneading first the left and then the right as if she'd been out in the cold and needed to get her blood flowing again. She didn't ask him to elaborate, and though her silence hurt, he went on.

"He's had a stroke. I'm not sure I understand it all. Marcello is still in there with Nonna, and he tried to translate for me. From what I could gather, in addition to the stroke, he has congestive heart failure. There's fluid building up in his body, including in his lungs and around his heart. With someone his age, and after this stroke, there's so much damage that there's no coming back from this."

Kate nodded without looking up. She took a shuddering breath and reached over to take his hand and squeeze it, still without meeting his eyes.

"I'm sorry, babe," she said, her voice sounding hollow.

Grief washed over him, not for his grandfather, whom he had never really gotten to know well, but for the things he had hoped for when coming here.

"Nonna says he would want to die at home. That he would hate being in the hospital on machines or something. Being in this place, I can understand that. So they're going to bring him home."

Finally, Kate looked up, her face pink and her brow furrowed. "Is that a good idea?"

"It's what he'd want. I'm sure he'd prefer to have died in his sleep without any of this, but—"

"I don't think it's safe," Kate said.

Tommy cocked his head. "I don't know if 'safe' means much anymore. He's dying. They'll have a nurse visit every day, and the rest of us will be in and out. They have plenty of friends and family around."

For the first time since Tommy had come into the waiting area, Kate sat up straight. She glanced at the people around them, the young woman with her toddler, the old man sitting alone with tears in his eyes, and the others who were lost in their thoughts, awaiting news that would change their lives. Tommy wanted to tell her that these people weren't eavesdropping on them, that they had their own troubles, but he did not want to interfere with the thoughts in her head. He could see that she was tormented.

"When you say, 'the rest of us,' I assume you're including me. That you expect me to help take care of him."

Tommy slid forward on his chair, reaching out to turn his face toward her. Her eyes were red from crying. Her hand felt cold in his. She seemed skittish and ready to bolt.

"Whatever happened when the stroke hit—"

Her eyes went hard. "Tommy, I told you exactly what happened."

"You told me Nonno tried to attack you. That he said awful things to you, in English."

"Perfect English. Yes."

"I don't have to tell you why it's hard to imagine all of that."

Kate closed her eyes and took a breath, steadying herself. Tommy squeezed her hand a bit more firmly, hoping she understood.

"Your grandfather hardly speaks any English at all," Kate began.

"Exactly."

"As far as you know," she went on. Her eyes opened. She stared at him. "But I'm telling you what happened. I'm not stupid, I'm not on drugs, and I'm not someone with a history of hallucinations or psychotic breaks. I'm willing to admit that I don't understand what happens to the human brain when someone has a stroke. If you want to say the stroke caused it and that his trying to hurt me—"

"Kate, come on. Why would he—"

"Tommy, are you seriously going to do that to me? To your wife? Fuck it, to any woman? Stop interrupting me."

He nodded.

"If you want to say all of that was his brain short-circuiting because of the stroke, okay. I'll go along with that. But you have to respect that I am completely freaked out right now, and I've got to work through some of that, and I will not be alone in a room with your grandfather while I do. If you'd seen the look in his eyes . . ."

She let her words trail off. Tommy's skin prickled with heat. It wasn't embarrassment but some other emotion he could not name. It felt as if the world had become very unsteady beneath his feet, not because their new home had occasional tremors but because nothing felt reliable to him. Not even his wife. He couldn't blame Kate for that. Something had happened that scared her and left her profoundly unsettled, and he had to respect that. But the reality of Nonno's stroke and the demands that it would place on Nonna were real.

He took both her hands. "I love you. I wasn't there, and I can't explain what happened. But I need to help my grandmother—"

"Of course you do."

Tommy stood up, giving Kate a gentle tug that brought her to her feet. "He's stable right now. I told Marcello I was going to take you home and then I'd come back in the morning when he's going to be discharged. But before we go, I want you to take a look at him. Just see him, the way he looks now. I don't want the picture of him in your mind to be of someone who tried to hurt you."

Kate hesitated. He could see she didn't want to go with him, but she gave a small nod and they walked together back into the ward, through the swinging door and past the nurses' station. He guided her along the corridor until they reached Nonno's room.

Tommy looked into the room. Nonna sat in a chair that had been drawn up beside the bed. A machine beeped, tracking the old man's heartbeat and other vital signs. Marcello sat perched on the windowsill. He gave Tommy a small wave, but both men kept quiet so as not to disturb their elders.

Kate stood on the threshold. Tommy gestured for her to step inside. He saw her swallow, and she licked her lips to moisten them, more anxious than he'd ever seen her. Kate entered the room and stopped, staring at Nonno where he lay in his hospital bed. Needles had been jammed into his hand and arm, feeding him liquids and drugs. Oxygen tubes were taped to his face. Something rattled in his throat as his chest rose and fell.

He's dying, Tommy thought. Standing right on the precipice of death. *He can't hurt you.*

And he wouldn't if he could.

Kate watched him intently, as if she thought he might spring up from the bed.

"Okay?" Tommy asked quietly.

Kate looked a moment longer and then turned her back on the hospital room.

"I need to go home," she said.

This time, Tommy was pretty sure she meant their new house and not Boston, but something had happened. The momentum they'd both been feeling had broken, the hope and excitement extinguished, and he wasn't sure how long it would take before they could get it back. But they would get it back eventually.

They had to.

For better or worse, this was home now. They had both known it wasn't going to be easy. New life or old one, life was never easy. As Nonno's pale, withered, unconscious body back on that hospital bed reminded him, death was always waiting just around the corner.

BOOK TWO

OCTOBER BELOW

1

October began with the kind of weather that made it feel glorious just to be alive. Early that morning, the breeze rustling the curtains had felt chilly, and by noon, the temperature had only risen to seventy-four degrees. Kate sat in her home office, sipping her third cup of coffee, contemplating the project she'd been working on since starting back to work two weeks before.

Before they had moved, she had worried that the time difference between Sicily and Boston would cause endless anxiety and frustration, keeping her out of the loop when it came to urgent matters and irritating her employers. Instead, she had never felt so relaxed about her job. Most mornings, she sat down at her desk around 8:30, took a ninety-minute lunch hour, and wrapped up at 5:00 p.m., when the team back in Boston had only been at work for two hours. There were frequent Zoom meetings at the end of her workday, so everyone could be sure they were on the same page, but otherwise, she was left to her own devices. In an emergency, they could always call her, but so far, that had only happened once.

It was bliss.

Her phone buzzed, drawing her attention away from her computer screen.

Belinda calling.

Kate leaned back in her chair as she answered the phone. "Is it that time already?"

"What do you mean 'already'? It's oh-my-god-o'clock back here, but I've dragged my ass out of bed for you."

"I think we'll both be glad you did," Kate replied.

"Fine. I just want you to know I'm pouting."

"Oh, I can hear your pout halfway round the world."

They had gotten into this new routine together. At home—though Kate kept chiding herself to stop thinking of Boston as "home"—Belinda would drag her butt out of bed at 6:00 a.m., drink coffee, use the toilet, and force herself into workout clothes. By six thirty—half past noon in Sicily—she would call Kate, and the two of them would go for a walk together.

"How's the weather there?" Kate asked as she popped her Air-Pods into her ears.

"Oh, go fuck yourself," Belinda replied.

Laughing, Kate slipped her phone into the pocket of her shorts, patted the other pockets to make sure she had her house key, and then trotted downstairs and out the front door.

"Come on," she said. "I love October in New England."

"Yeah, October is beautiful. All the autumn foliage, sweater weather, pumpkin spice everything. But it's gray and wet and cold this morning, and I'm too grumpy to go out for a walk this early. It's lunchtime for you—"

"It's also seventy-five degrees with a nice, dry breeze and not a cloud in the sky," Kate interrupted.

"Now you're just being mean." Belinda's breathing grew a bit labored from effort. She had started her own walk.

"Hey, you could move here anytime you like. There are empty houses just waiting for you."

"Don't start."

The two of them had gotten into this rhythm when Belinda began to complain about weight she had gained and that she didn't have the discipline to lose it without help. She had been enthusiastic about Kate's suggestion that they start to walk "together," or as together as two people could be who were separated by a sea, an ocean, and thousands of miles. Thanks to a free international calling app, they had spent an hour together nearly every day since.

"Is the housecoat lady out today?" Belinda asked.

Kate happened to be passing the old woman's house. "You mean the lady who sweeps the street for fun when she isn't glaring at me? Sadly, there is no sign of her today."

"Are you going to the church?"

"You don't like to say 'the catacombs,' do you?"

"You know it creeps me out."

"Wait till you come visit next month and I give you the tour," Kate said.

"Did they get the braces up yesterday?" Belinda asked.

"The first section, I think," Kate said. "But it's going to take a while."

That had been part of the new routine as well. Work had begun on shoring up the ceilings inside the catacombs. An archaeologist had come from Rome to evaluate the project and issue guidelines to the town engineer. The newly formed tourism board had Kate and Tommy as its engine, driving things forward, but they had made Marcello the director of the group so that the people in the mayor's office would feel comfortable, knowing one of their own would be in charge. But with Marcello and Tommy both trying to help the old folks as much as possible since Nonno's stroke, Kate had been the one keeping tabs on the project and making sure it kept moving forward.

"I love Europe, and Sicily in particular," she told Belinda, "but you can never accuse anyone here of being in a hurry."

"I envy Europeans that lack of urgency. It's an American disease," Belinda replied.

"All the more reason for you to move here," Kate said. "But you know what? Never mind. I'm going to stop badgering you."

"Thank you."

"Only because we both know you want to. You and Gerald both. And once you come and visit—"

"We'll see there are other Black people in Sicily?"

"I promise, you will not be the only Black people."

This was not a lie, but it was purposely avoiding the point. Of course there were Black people in Sicily—particularly in its capital, Palermo—but if Belinda and Gerald did move to Becchina, they would be part of a very small minority, including the couple from Senegal who had briefly been a part of the new Becchina Tourism Board, before the history of the House of Last Resort freaked them out.

She still hoped Belinda and Gerald would come to visit and make their own judgments. Certainly, Sicily would have its own prejudices—and plenty of ignorant, hateful people—but in a place as quiet as this, she found it hard to imagine it wouldn't be an improvement over the way they were treated at home. Maybe she was being naive, but she hoped not.

"Any more earthquakes?" Belinda asked.

"Not even a tremor, I'm pleased to report. I'm sure the workers down in the catacombs have been pretty happy about it, too."

Kate picked up her pace. Sometimes the cobblestones could be treacherous, so she spent most of the walk looking at the road instead of around at the town, but when she turned down her favorite side street, she made a point of looking up. She had discovered the street purely by accident one day, and now she would never consider going for a stroll in town without including its serene beauty. Flowers of every color grew in window boxes, on trellises, and in small gardens in front of the homes. It felt like slipping into some kind of fantasy world for two long blocks and made Kate want to cultivate the flowers on their own property more vigorously.

"How are you doing, Kate?" Belinda asked. "Truly?"

"I can't complain, Bee. I'm the one who pushed us into this, remember?"

"That's why I'm asking. You can't complain to Tommy, but you can complain to me. It won't make me and Gerald any less excited to come and visit."

Kate inhaled the smells of the flowers along that quiet, secret street. "I promise I'm fine. Better than fine. I'd be lying if I said there weren't moments every day when I still have mini panic attacks about how huge a decision this was, and Tommy is so sad about his grandfather, but even with that, it feels like our lives belong to us here. Nobody's in a rush to define us by where we work or how much we earn. We're always going to be outsiders, but mostly, it's about what to make for dinner, how fresh the ingredients can be, and whose family has a wedding coming up."

"A simpler life," Belinda said, breathing hard.

Kate could hear the smile in her words. "It really is."

"What about Tommy? How *is* his grandfather doing?"

"Still with us," Kate said. "Though not for long."

"That's so sad."

"It is, but he's nearly a century old, and he was in good health until just a few years ago. Nobody can ask for more than that."

"Tommy's having a hard time, huh?"

"It's a lot. He and Marcello visit them almost every day. Fortunately, we're really close to their place. It only takes fifteen minutes to walk from our house. The doctors didn't think Nonno would last this long, honestly. A few days, they said, but it's been nearly a month. I suppose it helps Tommy's grandmother to get used to the idea of a life without her husband after almost seventy years—"

"Seventy years. I can't even imagine it."

The conversation continued that way as Kate turned uphill toward the center of town and La Chiesa San Domenico. She could see its dome in the distance, rising above the other buildings. Its blue seemed almost to blend into the sky.

Belinda shared some gossip about their mutual friends back in Boston as Kate crossed the road toward the church, then diverted to the left of the front steps, toward the entrance to the catacombs. Two dusty pickup trucks were parked nearby. One worker leaned against a dented vehicle, smoking a cigarette and leaning his head back to catch the sun on his face. Two others carried heavy metal piping down the stairs into the catacombs. Work was underway. She had a quick flash in her mind, an image of what it might look like here when it was all done—a little ticket booth in front, a sign, a brand-new black wrought iron gate across the entrance. It occurred to her that she would have to come up with a pamphlet, some kind of guidebook, and she mentally added that to her to-do list. But it felt good to have such things on her mind.

"—ghosts?" Belinda was saying.

Kate blinked. She'd let her focus drift. "I'm sorry. I just got to the catacombs entrance, and I got distracted. What was that?"

"Just asking about your haunted house. Any more ghost sightings?"

A chill trickled along her spine. "Ugh, I don't even want to think about it."

"Oooh, what happened?"

"Nothing," Kate said. "It's just an old house with a really bizarre history. We're trying to stay focused on what's next, so for now, it's just our house. It's clean and freshly painted and enormous and has plenty of room for guests, and I'm insisting to myself there are no ghosts."

"I'm excited that we'll be your first guests, but honestly, I might be a little disappointed if I don't see at least one little ghost."

Kate felt a warm flush of happiness. "I can't wait for you to see the place. I'm so excited I might be willing to hire a ghost just to entertain you. You're really going to love Sicily, Bee. There's so much to see, so much beauty here."

"Can't wait. But I don't want to keep you," Belinda said. "Before I let you go, I have to thank you again for doing this with me. It's so much easier to commit myself to this exercise when I know I'm going to have your company while I'm walking. I still miss you, but I miss you less, and I get to shed some pounds at the same time."

"You know it isn't just for you," Kate said. "We have started to make friends, but it's still pretty quiet. Kind of isolated up here on the hill. And things with Tommy have been a little strained since his grandfather's stroke. I feel better knowing you're on the other end of the phone."

"Always," Belinda said.

Kate waved to the smoking worker as she descended the steps into the catacombs.

"I'm heading down, so I'm going to lose you. Talk to you to-morrow," she said.

"At the crack of dawn," Belinda groaned. "But we will talk then."

Happy and looking forward to the rest of her day, Kate went down into the darkness, where the dead and the rats were always waiting.

2

Tommy had spent most of the day at his grandparents' house. Over the past couple of weeks, he had taken to visiting in the late morning for coffee. He always tried to leave before lunch to avoid Nonna feeling as if she had to prepare something for him, but she usually insisted he stay—that she was going to make herself something anyway—and he never had the heart to disappoint her.

Today, he had brought his laptop with him and stayed through lunch, and afterward. When he had left home this morning, he had told Kate he wanted to have dinner at his grandparents' house and that she should come there when she had finished work for the day. He wanted to help Nonna go through some of their personal papers, he'd told Kate, and that was true enough, as far as it went.

But there was another truth, layered beneath that one.

Nonno was fading. He might have lingered for years if not for his stroke, but now his time in this world had begun rapidly winding down. His breath rattled in his chest, and he slept nearly all the time. Several days earlier, Nonna had held his hand while he slept and told Tommy that her husband of nearly seven decades was just resting as he waited for God to claim him.

Tommy was no doctor, but it seemed like God might show up with that claim ticket anytime now. He couldn't be with his grandparents every minute, night and day, but he thought if he worked out of Nonna's kitchen for a few days, there was nothing wrong with that. Unless she grew tired of his company and told him to go home, he would stick around this week and hope that when the moment arrived, he would be there for her.

He sat with a cup of decaf, staring at his laptop screen. His back hurt from sitting in the hard wooden chair at Nonna's kitchen table, but the stiffness would pass. His inbox dinged, and he opened the email to find a company-wide missive about cost-cutting measures being implemented. A quick skim confirmed that the email did not mean he would be losing his job, so he deleted it, not even attempting to fool himself into thinking he would read it later.

Nonna buzzed into the kitchen. That was how Tommy had come to think of her—as someone who buzzed here and there. Despite her age and the stoop of her body, she seemed constantly on the move.

"Did he eat anything?" Tommy asked.

Nonna scowled. "No!" Then she switched to Italian. *A few bites of pasta*, she told him.

He would not say it to her, but it surprised Tommy that his grandfather had eaten even that much. It was a testimony to his love for his wife that he attempted it. Thinking about Nonno as a man capable of such love, Tommy could not prevent himself from thinking about his dad. Ever since he and Kate had first come to visit Sicily, he had been consciously avoiding the temptation to dwell on the rift between his father and grandfather. Whatever had happened would obviously have been painful, and the last thing he had wanted to do was reopen old wounds. His father had been gone for years, and he told himself stirring up old drama would not be good for anyone.

But now, with Nonno drawing toward the end of his life, he kept coming back to it.

"Tommaso," Nonna said. "What?"

He smiled at her but knew the smile would be unconvincing. Her husband was dying. It wasn't fair to hit her with this right now. But somehow he knew the moment had come.

"I haven't wanted to ask," he began, "but I never knew what

happened between my dad and Nonno. Why we stopped visiting you guys when I was young. All those years, we could have seen each other. I feel like we missed out on a lot, and I don't know why."

Nonna stared at him. Her eyes had grown damp with tears, but she was not a woman prone to crying, and she took a deep breath. The tears did not fall. If Tommy had any doubt that she had understood him perfectly, those damp eyes were enough to convince him otherwise.

"*Tuo padre* . . . Nonno want you safe," she said, a sickly expression on her face. Nonna averted her gaze, as if embarrassed or ashamed.

"He wanted us safe?" Tommy said. "That's what they fought about?"

"No, no. *Per questo.*"

"That's 'why' they fought? I don't understand what you're saying. Nonno and my dad fought because Nonno wanted to keep us . . ." A spark of clarity flared in his mind. "Wait, Nonno fought with my dad on purpose, to keep us safe?"

Nonna nodded, still unwilling to meet his gaze.

"To keep us away," Tommy said as pieces of the puzzle clicked into place. He knew that Nonno had said things that his dad had found unforgivable, and part of that revolved around Nonno telling him that he was weak. But the idea that Nonno had purposely created a rift between them, and that Nonna knew about it and did nothing to heal that rift . . . it was too much for him to accept.

"Why?" Tommy asked. "Why would he do that? Why would you go along with it, unless it really wasn't safe for my dad to be here?"

Nonna glanced in the direction of her husband's room, as if the old man could have overheard the conversation from his deathbed. Maybe she feared repercussions from him or just did not want to betray him by sharing family secrets. Either way, she seemed to shake herself awake and poured the last of the coffee into a cup, ignoring the question as if Tommy had never asked it.

"Come on, Nonna," Tommy said. "Don't you think—"

From the front of the house, there came a knock at the door. Tommy and his nonna exchanged a glance as they heard the door open, and then a voice called out.

"Marcello," Nonna said, hurrying from the kitchen with a look of relief at having been rescued from Tommy's questions.

Moments later, she returned with Marcello in tow. She told him to sit and busied herself putting on a fresh pot of coffee—no decaf for him or for Nonna.

"You worked here today?" Marcello asked, spotting the laptop.

He took out his cigarettes, then glanced at Tommy and set them on the table. It was a quiet courtesy, unspoken, and Tommy felt strangely emotional. He had no siblings, but suddenly, he wanted to hug this unexpected big brother.

"I thought I'd keep Nonna company. She's got a lot on her hands," he said. It felt as if, with Marcello's arrival, the moment of truth had been disrupted. Tommy wondered if the answers really mattered now, when the people it had affected the most were already dead or soon would be.

"Thank you. It's nice." Marcello studied him as if seeing Tommy for the first time not as someone foreign but as true family. The imminence of death brought them nearer to one another. "It surprised me when Nonna said you were coming to live here," Marcello went on.

Tommy sipped his coffee, closing his laptop. "Me, too."

"When your father died, my mother said we would never see you again."

At the kitchen counter, Nonna clucked her tongue in disapproval. Tommy wasn't surprised—this was too near the territory they had just been discussing, and which had made her so uncomfortable.

"For Nonno," she said, raising the cup of coffee she had poured, and she hurried from the room.

Tommy stared after her a moment before returning to Marcello's point. "It was a pretty reasonable assumption," he said. "The idea that I'd never get back here. My mom never made it a secret that she didn't love Sicily. She didn't like competing with anyone else for Dad's affection. Or mine. But she wasn't the reason we stopped coming to Sicily. Not originally."

Marcello perked up. "No? What was the reason?"

"My dad," Tommy said. "I thought you knew that. He had some kind of fight with Nonno and Nonna and said he'd never go home again. Whatever it was, he had such resentment about it. I remember thinking they must have been awful to him, even though I only remember them being sweet to me when I was little. My dad wouldn't talk about it to me, but he kept after my mother. Even when he was dying, he told her he didn't want me having anything to do with the Puglisi side of the family."

Marcello had grown pale. He said something in Italian, too quiet and too fast for Tommy to understand, and then shook his head. "These things happen in all families, I know. But I never heard this. It is sad to think of the times you could have been here, with family—and poor Zio Giovanni, that he did not have that time with his parents and cousins. And for why? Something small, probably. Nonno said something, or they argued and nobody would apologize, and for that . . ."

"I know. When Kate talked me into visiting at the beginning of this year, I didn't know what to expect here, and now look where it's brought us."

Marcello smiled. "I am very glad you are here, cousin."

He raised his coffee mug to toast. Tommy did the same, and they clinked the ceramic together.

"Me, too."

They spent a moment in companionable silence before it was disrupted by Nonna's return. She bustled into the kitchen with a scowl on her face. She carried the coffee cup that she had brought in for Nonno and dumped its entire contents into the sink.

He didn't want it? Marcello asked in Italian.

Nonna rinsed the cup, back to them. *He said it tasted . . .*

"I didn't catch that last word," Tommy said. "It tasted what?"

"Bitter," Marcello said.

Tommy had no reply for that. The coffee tasted fine to him. It surprised him to think that Nonno even had the strength to take a sip and had been conscious enough to do so. He figured it was more that Nonno had zero interest in consuming anything now, as his clock wound down, but he could not express that to Nonna, and she would not have listened even if he did.

He watched Nonna's back as she busied herself at the sink; then he glanced at Marcello, who sipped his coffee. It occurred to Tommy that everything they did now, every conversation and activity that did not revolve around Nonno dying, was a kind of performance. It felt as if they were putting on a show, delivering lines, improvising for some unseen audience even though the three of them knew it was all pretense. Somehow, in some soul-crushing metaphysical way, breaking character would hasten the arrival of the Grim Reaper.

Nonsense, of course, but Tommy realized people did this sort of thing all the time, when death or heartbreak drew near.

A soft knocking came from the front of the house. Tommy looked up at the antique clock on the wall and saw that 5:00 p.m. had come and gone while he sat there. He slid his chair back.

"Probably Kate," he said as Nonna went to her refrigerator and took out something wrapped in butcher's paper.

Even at her age, with her husband dying two rooms away, she intended to cook for her grandson and great-nephew. He would have tried to stop her but knew that would be interrupting the performance of normalcy in which they were all participants. He couldn't do that to her.

With a nod to Marcello, Tommy went out through the living

room and down the corridor. Before he reached the door, it crept open, and Kate slipped her head through. When she spotted him, she visibly relaxed.

"Hey," she said, slipping inside and closing the door behind her. "I tried to be quiet. I wasn't sure how things were going and I didn't want to intrude, all happy and stuff."

"It's okay," Tommy said. "No real change today. He's still . . ."

"Dwindling?" she offered.

The brutal accuracy of the word made him falter. "Yeah. It's just a matter of time."

Kate slid her arms around him and held him for a minute or two, stroking the back of his head until their breathing had fallen into sync. Inhale, exhale, inhale, exhale, in unison. It was a calming thing they had begun doing for one another several years earlier, and it felt warm and quiet and beautiful.

"I love you," he said.

Kate whispered it back.

"What made you happy this afternoon?" he asked.

"Belinda and Gerald are definitely coming to visit. I hoped for next month, but it's going to be January, I think. To be honest, I thought the earthquake while we were on Zoom with them had short-circuited any possibility of anyone still considering a move here, but I guess it's a good thing it was just a tremor and not a full-on quake."

Aftershock, Tommy thought.

"That's wonderful," he said quietly. "I'd love for you to have people here."

Kate wrinkled her nose. "Dumbass. You're my people."

"You know what I mean. I have family here."

"And I have you," she said. "You're my family."

They heard footsteps. Tommy turned to see that Marcello had come out into the hall, right about the spot where they had reconnected on the night Tommy and Kate had moved into their house.

"I checked on him," Marcello said. His expression seemed perpetually lighthearted, the sort of wise, amused-with-the-world countenance Tommy associated with old men who played chess in public parks or surprised everyone at a party by sitting down at a piano and playing something beautiful.

But not this afternoon.

"He's awake," Marcello went on, gray and pale, as if the truth of the moment had only just broken through. "His breathing is not good, but he knows who we are. He knows what is happening."

None of them needed him to elaborate further.

"Thanks, Marcello," Tommy said. "We'll be right in."

Marcello nodded and retreated toward the kitchen. Tommy appreciated that he did not go back into Nonno's room, giving Tommy and Kate the opportunity to visit with his grandfather alone.

Tommy hesitated, taking a deep breath.

Kate took his hand. "You okay?"

"I think so. It's just weird." He lowered his voice. "I know he's ancient and everything, but I thought we'd have more time. All the years my dad kept that wall up, keeping us apart from his family here, feels like such wasted time. But you can never get that back. Even if he lived another few years, his mind's not all there anyway. The time when things might have been different is already gone."

Kate hugged him again. "I'm sorry. But you had this little time at least. And you'll be here for Nonna, and I'm sure she's grateful for that." With a kiss, she pushed back from him. "You should go in while he's still awake."

Tommy nodded, taking her hand and starting back down the hall.

Kate resisted.

When Tommy looked back, her grim expression shocked him enough that he released her hand. "You're not coming?"

"This is something you should do on your own."

The words were kind and thoughtful, but her face revealed more. Her eyes had become small, her mouth a thin line. They had been married long enough for him to know when she had put on the mask meant to disguise her emotions. Her mouth gave away everything by giving away nothing, and those small eyes held the emotion she tried to hide—fear.

"Kate, come on," he whispered, trying to understand. "You can't be afraid of him. He's on his deathbed, for Chrissake. I know you were with him—"

"You weren't there, Tom."

"I know that. And I know it had to be really unsettling, watching him have a stroke, having him get delusional and babble at you—"

"And try to strangle me."

Tommy sighed. "Jesus. Kate, you know that's . . . We've talked about this. Was he trying to hurt you or reaching out for help? You know what the doctor said."

Kate seemed to muster up her strength. She took both of his hands, met his gaze. "I love you, and I'm here to support you. Yes, I know what the doctor said, but he wasn't in the room, and neither were you. Maybe all of it can be attributed to the stroke, and maybe I just saw a part of him that he couldn't hide in that moment—"

"Jesus Christ. Are you kidding me with this?"

Kate let go of his hands. "Of course not. I want to comfort you, not make this worse for you."

"Then do that."

"I will. I am," she said. "But I'm not going into that room. I don't need to see him. I'll wait here as long as it takes, or I'll go home and wait there if that makes it easier for you, but I'm not going—"

Tommy felt numb. Lost. He blinked several times, just staring at her with his mouth partway open. "How can you be so selfish?"

A little noise came from Kate's throat. She flinched, and the mask crumbled. Tears welled in her eyes, and she backed away from him. "That's not . . . Ah, shit, this isn't what I meant to . . ."

Kate retreated to the door, bumped into it, turned, and opened it.

"Hang on," Tommy said. His thoughts whirled, grief and hurt and confusion all tangled together.

Kate did not hang on. She went out the door and started to pull it closed behind her. Tommy caught the door before it could shut, then followed her into the street. The angle of the sun this late in the day cast the narrow road in shade. With the sky still blue overhead and the tops of the houses still limned with golden afternoon sunlight, the shaded street felt like a quiet, secret place, until the thunderous roar of a distant motorcycle broke that illusion.

"I didn't mean it like that," Tommy said.

Kate had not gone far. Just across the street, in front of a house painted something like yellow that seemed more peach or orange this time of day. The neighbors might have been inside, listening in, but Tommy didn't know how to wave this moment away so that his grandparents wouldn't be embarrassed by him. Fighting with Kate was the last thing he would have imagined happening today.

In the midst of the momentary silence, a hard wind blew along the street, strong enough to rock them where they stood. A loud cry overhead made them both look up to see a quartet of gleaming black crows take flight from the roof of Nonna's house. Their cawing continued as they flew out of sight, ragged-voiced and urgent.

The moment passed, the birds gone, the wind subsiding.

"Go inside," she said.

"Kate, please."

Her arms were crossed. She stood a dozen feet from him, head bent, shoulders protectively inward. Tommy walked toward her, thinking to take her in his arms. He felt angry with her, and himself, and his grandparents, and somehow his mother, too, as if she'd had anything to do with this. This should not have been happening, not today.

"No," she said, holding up one hand to keep him from coming any closer. Kate wiped her eyes and looked up, trying to rebuild her mask. "I'm fine. I'm not being selfish, Tommy. If I were being selfish, I would have stayed away from this house since the second you brought him home from the hospital."

"Kate—"

"Stop. Listen."

He did. Still angry, still confused, but loving his wife.

"You weren't there when it happened. I understand that," she said. "What's important right now is that you be here for him and for your nonna. I'm going to go home. You call me when you can, but if not, I'll see you tonight."

Tommy heard her. He still didn't understand. There were opinions about her behavior that he would not share, because they would only cause more hurt. Kate was right when she said the priority was for him to be there for his grandparents—and for himself. He needed to do what he felt was the right thing so later he could find comfort in that.

"Okay," he said.

This time when he approached her, Kate hugged him. She kissed him quickly on the lips, and he tried not to be hurt by how perfunctory the kiss felt, like a reflex. He wasn't usually that sensitive, that prickly, and he knew he would shake it off.

"I love you," she said.

"I know," he whispered in her ear.

In reply, she kissed him again, then gave him a gentle shove toward Nonna's front door. Tommy watched her start back up the street toward their home, and then he hurried inside.

He found Marcello waiting for him in the living room, sitting on the arm of the sofa, smoking thoughtfully. His eyes glistened.

"Nonna's in there with him now," Marcello said, puffing at his cigarette. He exhaled a plume of smoke. "He's gone, Tommaso. I think he was waiting—it seemed like he was waiting to see you— but he couldn't wait anymore."

The words held no blame, no attack. Marcello shared them only as cold fact.

"Nonno's dead?" Tommy rasped.

Marcello nodded, still smoking, and glanced away, wiping his eyes.

Tommy thought again about time and the way it only ever ran in one direction. The way it swept them all along, and the only way to escape its current was to be left behind forever.

"My God," he whispered. He hung his head, and, though most days he didn't think anyone was listening, he offered a little prayer that Nonno would find peace and rest.

Elsewhere in the house, Nonna screamed.

Tommy and Marcello exchanged a panicked look as they raced from the living room. They rushed into the side hall, to the room where Nonno had been sleeping. Nonna ambled out into the hall, staring back into the room. Though her eyes were red and her face streaked with tears, she looked disgusted and angry.

Get it out of there! she shouted in Italian. *Get it out!*

Tommy pushed past Marcello and entered his grandfather's death room just in time to see a fat gray rat dart under the bed. Aware of his grandfather on the mattress, the husk of the man, he pulled out his phone and shone its flashlight into the dark underneath. He saw the hole, just behind the leg of the bed, and spotted the long, twitching tail as it slipped into the wall and was gone.

3

At a quarter past nine the following morning, Kate carried two cups of coffee out to the bench on the cliff overlooking the valley. Tommy had been there for nearly an hour, lost in his thoughts. Kate sat beside him and handed over his coffee without saying a word. With clear blue sky above, they could see almost to the curve of the world.

They were quiet for a time. Kate shifted her coffee to her left hand so that she could lace her fingers with his, side by side.

"Tommy, I—"

"No, Kate. Don't say you're sorry."

"I am sorry. Not that I wouldn't go in to see him. I wouldn't do that even now, and I hope you can understand that. I'm not the kind of person to say something like that without a real reason. I'm not hysterical, and I don't imagine things."

Except maybe strange sounds in the night, she thought.

"I know that."

Kate squeezed his hand. "You're the best person I know, and I love you. I'm sorry I wasn't with you when you found out. I wish I'd been there for you."

Tommy nodded. "I'm okay." He glanced at her. "I just feel guilty that I wasn't with him. That I didn't really say goodbye."

She laid her head on his shoulder, coffee mug clutched but ignored in her left hand. The benefit of snuggling up to him was that she didn't have to look into his eyes.

"I'm going to be blunt with you right now, okay?" she said.

"You always are," he said.

"He was your grandfather, but you barely knew him—"

"True. I just hoped I'd have more time."

"At his age, and in his mental state," she said, "I'm not sure more time would have meant you getting to know him better. And as for you not being in the room with him, the state he was in, he probably wouldn't have really known you were there. The truth is that you basically sat a vigil with Nonna, looking after her, helping her through this, and that was and is more important. I have to assume he loved her, and if he did love her, then certainly your grandfather would have thought you taking care of his wife when he couldn't was more important than being in the room when he passed."

Tommy took a deep breath. "I know you're right, but it's going to take a little time for me to accept it." He shifted on the bench to look at her. "I'm just going to wallow in my guilt for a while, okay?"

Kate smiled. "Of course it's okay. I'll do a bit of wallowing, too."

He picked up her hand, kissing the back of her knuckles. "Fair enough."

"You're not still upset with me?" she asked.

Tommy glanced at her, a wary look on his face. "I don't want to fight. I don't have it in me right now."

"But—"

"But fuck, yes, I'm still upset. I still think you were selfish. I won't say you were overreacting, because you're right—I wasn't there when he had his stroke. And I know you're not some delicate flower. If he swore at you and grabbed your throat . . . I can't explain that, except that he was in the middle of having a stroke. But by the time he got around to dying in his bed, he posed no threat to you." Tommy looked at her, not trying to hide the hurt in his eyes. "You should've gone in there with me, Kate. I needed you."

Kate swallowed the sour taste in her mouth. Her heart beat a little harder as she stared at her husband, studying his face. "Maybe

I should've. Maybe. But he scared me, got under my skin in a way nothing ever has. It freaked me the hell out, and so yes, okay, be pissed off as long as you like, but it comes down to this—I couldn't go into that room with you. I couldn't be near him. Whether I should have been there for you doesn't really matter, because I could literally not do it. I guess you're going to resent that, but eventually, you'll either have to accept it or not. Either way, I'm sorry."

Tommy nodded slowly. Maybe he did not know how to respond, or maybe he simply did not want to. The tension had waxed and waned between them, but for the moment, it had found a certain balance.

They both sat back and looked out over the valley, drinking coffee, feeling the breeze. Kate knew she had to remind him of the time, but she waited a few extra minutes just to be in his company. Finally, she knew she couldn't wait any longer.

"You know it's just about nine thirty, right?"

"Shit, really?"

"Really." She took the coffee cup from his hand as he jumped up from the bench. "Go. I'll see you when you're back. I love you."

Tommy said he loved her and cursed under his breath as he quick-marched down their street, heading for the church. Too self-conscious to run.

The church bell tolled once to signify the arrival of the half hour.

It rang out across the valley, as if that one somber note might carry forever.

4

The strange thing about churches, Tommy thought, was that they never felt empty. He pulled open the door of the Chiesa San Domenico and hesitated at the wall of quiet that awaited him inside. There were no people in view, and he walked up the aisle toward the altar almost on tiptoe. The fans overhead remained unmoving; there were no worshippers, no one there to sweep or to distribute missals. Yet he could feel eyes on him, could feel the weight of someone's attention. The small hairs at the back of his neck bristled in the nexus of that silent, weighty focus, though he knew he was alone.

He knew what people of strong faith would have said about that feeling. They would have told him that he felt the presence of God. He would have argued that what he really felt was the lifeless gaze of the many statues and icons, and the saints immortalized in stained glass windows. But if he let himself think about it, it wasn't merely the feeling of being watched but the atmosphere of the church itself, which felt to him like the moment when a conductor raised his baton, the instant before the symphony began to play.

In his life, Tommy had lost many people he loved. His father, his mother, his dear friend Luke in a high school drunk-driving accident, the teacher who had made him care about learning when he was in the seventh grade, and now his nonno. As he walked up to the altar, glancing around for Don Pino, he thought it would be nice to find, deep within himself, an unexpected and uncomplicated faith. He would trade a great deal to know without doubt that God existed, that heaven waited for kind souls.

Yes, churches felt occupied, as if a presence filled them. But even in that moment, when it would have soothed him greatly to believe, he trusted the evidence of his eyes. No matter how it felt, nobody was home.

"Don Pino?" he called, thinking he might have to go back into the sacristy, the room where priests prepared for Mass, where they hung their robes and vestments. His office would be back there as well.

"Tommy, *grazie dio.*"

He turned to see not Don Pino but Marcello. Pale and anxious, his cousin hurried toward him, and Tommy met him halfway, right in the center of the church, with Christ gazing down at them from on high.

"What's wrong?" Tommy asked, confused. The stricken look on his cousin's face puzzled him, and then Tommy thought the worst thing. "Oh, shit, please tell me Nonna's all right."

"*Si, si,*" Marcello said, waving his concern away. "She is fine. But, Tommy, this is crazy."

"What is?"

Marcello huffed. "You don't know yet? Nonna didn't tell you?"

"I haven't seen her this morning. Tell me what, Marcello? Settle down."

"Ha. See if you settle down when I tell you they're going to put Nonno in the catacombs. They're going to prepare his body the way they did with the others down there."

Tommy stared at him. "That's crazy—"

"*Si.* I told you!"

"Why would they do that? Nobody's been buried that way for decades."

Even as he asked the question, he saw Don Pino come out from the back of the church—the same direction from which Marcello had come. Tommy realized the meeting had started without him, and his cousin's upset was the result.

"Father," Tommy said. "Don Pino, is this what my grandmother wants?"

Don Pino raised both hands in that condescending, placating way of priests going back two thousand years. "Come, come. I explain you," he said in the best English he had.

Tommy patted Marcello on the back, and the cousins followed the priest along a side corridor and into the sacristy.

"It is not right," Marcello said.

Tommy glanced around the sacristy. It felt as though they were backstage at a theater, and in many ways, he knew that was not far off. The priest would have said God was the star of the show, but he was the one in the spotlight when he went out onto the altar, and this was his dressing room.

Don Pino sat at a small conference table in the middle of the large room. Marcello huffed again as he went to a chair that had been pushed out, and Tommy envisioned the two of them sitting at this table minutes ago, waiting for him, and Marcello learning of the burial plans for Nonno.

Tommy took a seat. "Let's just focus on why, okay?"

Don Pino looked a bit confused. Marcello translated into Italian. When the priest began to reply, Tommy thought he understood about half of what was said, but the words amounted to something he could not believe, and so he waited for Marcello to turn them into English.

Instead, Marcello stared at the priest. *"Questa è solo una storia."*

"No. Mi dispiace," said the priest.

Don Pino gave a small, apologetic shrug that Tommy understood without translation. It was an abdication of responsibility. The sort of gesture that meant, *Sorry, but I don't make the rules.*

Marcello looked as if he'd swallowed something rotten.

"You want to tell me what's going on?" Tommy asked. "That

was a lot of Italian from him, and I'm pretty sure you said, 'That's just a story.' What's 'just a story,' Marcello?"

His cousin stared at the priest and then shook his head as if he refused to believe what he'd been told. Marcello slid down in his chair like a petulant middle schooler.

"I need a cigarette," he said.

Tommy sat forward. "Just tell me. This is ridiculous."

Marcello nodded. "Yes. It is ridiculous." He shot a disdainful look at the priest. "You didn't know much about your house when you bought it, did you, Tommaso?"

"You know I didn't. We'd already moved in before I found out the church used to own it."

"And you know what they used it for. That night at your house, with your friends . . . The Englishman . . . he told you that the priests were exorcists."

"You were there," Tommy said. "But the first hint came the night we moved in, with that guy Aldo and his wife at Nonna's house, when he called it 'the House of Last Resort.' I should have pushed that night for more explanation. Everyone in Becchina seems to have known the history of my house except for me."

Don Pino began to speak, but Marcello cut him off. If he felt any regret at being rude to the elderly priest, he didn't show it.

Marcello put his elbows on the table and leaned in, searching Tommy's eyes. "You understand, Tommaso . . . the Vatican sent the ones who were . . ." He paused, searching for the word, and then found it. "Hopeless. They sent the ones who were hopeless."

Tommy wanted to scowl at this bullshit. Once upon a time, the church had taken people who were severely mentally ill and decided they were possessed by demons. The ones who could be forced to behave in a manner others considered "normal" were said to have had their demons driven out of them by priests performing the rite of exorcism. The ones who couldn't be forced to behave were secretly transported from Rome to Becchina, at great effort and presumably great expense, where several priests lived in the house at 17 Via Dionisio, and where the attempts at exorcism would have become more desperate and more damaging to the poor souls kept captive in that house.

It sickened Tommy to think of it.

"Hopeless," he echoed, but his version of "hopeless" and the Vatican's would have been quite different.

"Most of them died," Marcello said.

Tommy tapped his fingers on the table. "I know this. They died and were buried in the catacombs. Probably in a section separate from where the monks and wealthy people were mummified and buried down there. What does this have to do with Nonno?"

Even as he asked the question, Tommy knew the answer. The old priest had told Marcello that Nonno had been one of the possessed. The hopeless cases.

He smirked. "Oh, come on. That's ridiculous."

Marcello sat back. "I do not think Don Pino would invent such a story. Also, I very much doubt Nonna would agree to this if it is 'ridiculous.'"

Tommy wanted to lash out at Don Pino with as much creative profanity as his mind could muster, but the old priest's eyes were downcast in sadness or shame. It unsettled Tommy to realize that Don Pino, at least, believed this Vatican mythology.

And yet something about this didn't make sense.

"Don Pino, I'm very confused," he said. "If my grandfather survived, then he was . . ." It embarrassed him even to talk about this aloud. "He was *cleansed*. The exorcism worked. Why should he be buried with the ones who were never cured?"

Marcello began to translate, but the priest waved him to silence. He understood the question, perhaps had even anticipated it.

"They send him home," the old priest said, the crow's-feet at the corners of his eyes crinkling.

Tommy didn't understand. "He survived, and they sent him home. Where else would they have sent him?"

Don Pino looked at Marcello, growing more animated, perhaps

frustrated at still not being understood. He spoke rapidly, and Marcello nodded sadly along. When the priest finally ran out of rapid-fire Italian, Marcello turned to Tommy.

"Don Pino was not here when this happened," he said. "All of this, he learn from the priests who were at San Domenico before him. They tell him, watch over Tommaso Puglisi. Always keep an eye on him. On his family. In case something happens."

"In case what happens?"

"They never took Nonno to Rome. He was a boy, twelve or thirteen, when his parents bring him to *la casa dell'ultima risorsa*. They knock on the door and beg for help. Their boy has a demon in him, they say. And after watching Nonno for two days, the priests agree. They try to make the demon leave him. For weeks he is there, a prisoner, and they pray and bless him and try to make the demon go. They fail again and again. Then, one morning, this boy—Nonno—he seems okay. Happy. *Come si dice . . . normale?*"

Tommy's mouth had gone dry. "Normal," he said.

"*Si*, normal. Two more days they wait, but he is only a boy again, and they send him home to his mother."

"Like the demon just decided to leave him in the middle of the night," Tommy said. "It had him, and then he woke up one morning and it was gone."

Jesus, listen to me. Talking like it's real.

"The priests, they thought this is very strange. So they watch him."

"For more than eighty years," Tommy said, thinking of the events Kate had described to him on the night of Nonno's stroke.

The cousins both looked at the old priest then. Don Pino nodded slowly.

"Now," Don Pino said, and he put his hands together and made a fluttering gesture, mimicking a bird in flight. Or a soul departing. "*È finita.*"

It's over, Tommy thought. But they wanted to bury him in the catacombs, where they had put the bodies of those who had supposedly died while still possessed. Near the bodies of the exorcists who had tried to drive their demons out, sanctified bodies of men of God, as if to guard the remains of those who had been tainted by the devil.

All superstition, of course. The idea of evil as something real and breathing, malignant, instead of just one end of the spectrum of human nature, had always seemed both childish and convenient to him. To be able to pass off insidious behavior as the influence of some malevolent force, some poison in the soul, seemed designed for human beings to avoid blame. Demonic possession was mental illness and "the devil made me do it" just something psychopaths said in court when trying to avoid the death penalty.

But Nonna agreed with the priest. Tommy didn't know if she had learned of her husband's story before or after they married, but Don Pino claimed she had agreed to see Nonno buried in the catacombs, his body dried, prepared, mummified—likely the first person in Becchina to undergo that process in a generation or two.

Tommy nodded. "Fine."

Marcello stared at him. "Fine?"

"If Nonna is okay with it, why should we stand in the way? I've been to my father's grave, and my mother was cremated, but I rarely went to the cemetery before I moved to Sicily. Now they live in my memories, and that's where Nonno will live, too. I'd only ask that they put him somewhere out of sight down there, where tourists won't walk by."

And where I won't have to see his cadaver when I go down there, he thought.

"There is more," Marcello said. "Don Pino says that in the back of your house, there are stairs that go down into the tomb where the . . ." He searched for the word, and then it came to him. "The place where the 'possessed' were buried when they die. Like the catacombs. They close this up years and years ago. Don Pino says we have to open it again, to bury Nonno."

Tommy stared at him. "This is under my house?"

Don Pino nodded. *"Certo."* As if it was the most natural thing in the world.

Tommy supposed there was a certain logic to it—if you were trying to save the souls of people possessed by demons, but they frequently died in your care, it only made sense to want somewhere nearby to entomb the bodies. Maybe the church had wanted to hide their failures, or maybe the families of people crazy enough to be thought of as infested with literal evil had not wanted the bodies of their loved ones to be returned to them.

"Oh, right, of course," Tommy said, wondering if the panic-edged sarcasm would be lost in translation.

Marcello glared at Don Pino. Tommy wasn't sure if what bothered his cousin was where Nonno would be buried, or why. When it came to death and religion, it was all guesswork. All superstitious nonsense.

That was what he told himself.

Yet beneath that certainty, there ran a trickle of doubt, which had begun the day of Nonno's stroke, with the things Kate had told him about the episode leading up to it. The way Nonno had spoken to her, the things he had said. The cruelty and malice she described.

If you'd seen the look in his eyes, Kate had said.

Tommy shook himself, drove out the memory of those words.

But minutes later, when he and Marcello had left the church and walked out into the morning light, he did not feel warmed by the sun.

He only felt haunted.

5

Kate stood in the room they were now calling the vestibule. Now that they knew that the chapel had been used for rites of exorcism, she suspected this room had been a place where a priest might sleep while taking a break in the midst of an exorcism that had lasted days or weeks. Could such a thing have taken months? She had difficulty imagining it—but then, she had difficulty imagining so many things regarding their house now that more of the truth had come out. If not for gossip the other Imports had picked up around the town, they might never have known. Their neighbors certainly were aware of what this house had been, and Tommy's family had known.

"Honestly, Belinda, I don't have a fucking clue what to do next."

The phone remained silent in her hand. She had it on speaker—didn't like to keep it pressed to her ear—and when she looked down, she saw that the timer on the call continued to tick away the seconds.

"Are you there?" she asked.

"I'm here," Belinda replied. "I'm just trying to absorb it all."

"I know. It's crazy."

"Maybe it feels more outrageous to me because I'm still in the U.S. I think in Europe, everything is so old that you sort of expect a certain level of superstition and stuff."

Kate leaned against the doorframe separating the vestibule from the chapel. They had turned the former "maid's quarters" into a sort of sitting room, just two comfortable chairs and a little table with a lamp by which to read. A breeze billowed the sheer curtains.

"I know what you're saying about Europe. The age of so many places here makes things we associate with fairy tales and story-books seem more believable, but they are still fairy tales."

"Of course they are," Belinda said.

"But this is real, Belinda."

"Kate, come on—"

"I don't mean demons," she said quickly, as if afraid of being overheard endorsing the reality of evil. "The church has always believed in exorcism, and it isn't just Catholics. There's a long history of people thinking they were being influenced by demonic forces and some ritual or other being needed to drive them out. In Catholicism, it starts with Jesus doing it in the Gospels, but as recently as 2017, Pope Francis told priests not to hesitate to call on Rome to provide experts in the rite of exorcism if they were needed."

"You're shitting me."

"No, Bee. I swear. Twenty fucking seventeen."

"That's nuts. But it's still just mythmaking, Kate. The more people believe in evil, the better for them. There's never been a better marketing campaign for God than the invention of the Devil, and demons are just little lowercase versions."

Kate looked into the transformed chapel, with its elegantly tiled floor.

"I swear, Bee, if you were standing where I'm standing, you'd have your doubts."

Belinda laughed, but kindly. "Oh, honey, it can't be that bad."

"It's not bad at all. That's the weirdest part," Kate said. "The house is beautiful. I love it here. After dark, it can be a bit creaky, and spooky, and . . ."

She nearly told Belinda about her experience with Tommy's grandfather, but she didn't want to talk about it anymore. Didn't even want to think about it. Her interpretation of those moments had already caused such strain in her marriage, the last thing she wanted was for Belinda to join him in second-guessing what she had witnessed. Or, possibly worse, to support her and cause her to bring it up with Tommy again.

But staring into the chapel now, she shivered.

"Spooky and what?" Belinda asked.

"Huh?"

"Earth to Kate. You're drifting. You said the house got creaky and spooky at night, but there was something more. You kind of blanked out."

Kate walked into the chapel. "I guess it's just that in this frickin' ghost town, everything seems spookier. Throw in finding out that my new house used to be the go-to spot for the church's most difficult exorcisms, and you can imagine it's gonna take a while to get used to living here."

"You do realize it's a gold mine, right?" Belinda said. "You want tourist attractions. Tons of people would want to visit a place with that kind of history."

"That's what the other Imports were saying."

"Sorry, the 'Imports'?"

"It's what we call the foreigners who've moved here to get one of these bargain homes. We had a bunch of people over, and they were all saying the same thing. Haunted houses, places with weird history—if we play it up, we could make money giving tours of the house."

"More than that," Belinda said. "You could buy a second house under the same deal the mayor's offering and turn this one into a demon-infested bed-and-breakfast."

Kate halted in the middle of the chapel. "Belinda, that's a brilliant idea."

"Really?"

"Yes! I don't know if the rules for this thing would allow us to buy a second property at the same price, but if we explain what we want to do, as part of our tourism efforts here, Mayor Brancati might go for it. We're moving pretty fast, and we've already asked him to put a lot of trust in us—"

"Which he has, probably because Tommy's family goes back a thousand years there," Belinda said.

"Yeah," Kate agreed.

"You're quiet now."

"Thinking."

"Elaborate?"

Kate smirked. "If we can get them to do something like this, I'm going to need help. Definitely going to need you to come visit for at least a couple of weeks."

"I'm sure we can work something out."

The chapel loomed around her—*breathed* around her—but suddenly, instead of being unsettling or oppressive, the room's gloomy nature inspired her. Even if there were ancient spirits here, or the echoes of the pain and sorrow that had filled the room, that would be exactly what ghost-loving tourists were looking for.

"Maybe," she said, mostly to herself. "Maybe."

Somehow the light coming through the windows in this room did not reach very far. Quiet, vacant, almost expectant, it waited to be occupied. It was easy to imagine the right tour guide spooking the hell out of tourists who came looking for something that would unsettle them. Alone, even with Belinda on the phone, she found it all too easy to imagine the screams that had resounded off these walls. The profanity and obscenity, the bodily fluids, the pain and humiliation. She had only seen the movie *The Exorcist* once, but once had been enough to engrave indelible images in her mind. Surely a real exorcism did not involve levitation or vomiting, but how was she to know?

In her mind's eye, she saw a young woman strapped to a bed in the center of the floor—or on the altar platform that had been there before she and Tommy had ripped it up. She tried to imagine how terrified the people brought here must have been. Mentally ill, surely. Even haunted—she could allow such a possibility. Driven insane by ghosts? Somehow it was easier to believe in demons rooted so deeply in a human soul that no amount of prayer could drive them out.

"Of course," Kate mused, "if we did that, we'd end up having to undo most of the work we just did to spruce the place up."

Something moved in the far corner of the chapel.

Kate stopped breathing. It had been at the edge of her peripheral vision, in the shadowed corner, near where the floorboard had been rotted, and she thought the rats had come through.

"Shit," she muttered.

"What's wrong?"

"We might have another rat."

"Are you kidding?" Belinda said. "Didn't you put tons of poison down there and seal up the wall?"

Kate thumbed on her cell phone's flashlight and walked toward that corner. Outside, the late-morning sun was bright, but the nearer she went to that corner, the more it felt as if evening approached.

"We did," she said. "But rats and mice and things . . . I guess you never know what it takes to get rid of them."

"I guess," Belinda replied, voice heavy with doubt. "You'll make sure the place is rat-free before I visit you, right?"

Kate wished she could have summoned up a polite laugh, but she couldn't manage it. The flashlight revealed nothing in that corner, just the standing lamp they had bought a few days earlier in a shop down the hill. Its cord had not been gnawed, and the baseboard seemed undisturbed. She scanned the floor for rat droppings or any other sign that they had gotten up to the second floor again.

"I think it was a false alarm," she said. "Just me imagining things."

"I hope so. Rats are nasty."

"Nasty they are." Kate shut off the flashlight. "I think I'm going to go down and pour myself a fresh coffee, then check the first floor of the annex and make sure there's no sign of them down there."

"What about the basement?"

Kate gave a hollow laugh, no trouble mustering this one. "Not a chance in hell. Creepy cellar in the exorcism house? There aren't many things that will make me succumb to antiquated gender roles, but that is one job that I will leave to my husband, thanks."

"Agreed," Belinda said. "Okay, babe. Keep me posted on how it's going."

Kate promised she would and ended the call. She glanced at that corner again, then smiled to herself about how jumpy she had become. She checked the time, wondering when Tommy would come back from his meeting with Don Pino, and saw that he'd been gone more than an hour.

She slipped her phone into her pocket and turned to leave the chapel.

The scratching noises began behind her. In that same corner.

Kate would have laughed if it hadn't creeped her out so much. Instead, she inhaled sharply and turned, staring at that corner. Studying the shadows, she shuffled backward toward the vestibule. As she turned, she saw the first of the rats scuttle out into the light.

"What the hell?" she whispered, even as fear trickled down her spine.

Another appeared, and a third. They could not be there, she told herself. She had just checked the wall, and the baseboard and the paint had not been marred. No new hole had been dug or gnawed to let them squirm their fat gray bodies through the wall. But the scritching of their tiny claws on the new tile was the only sound in the room aside from the quickening of her heartbeat in her own ears.

They skittered toward her, and she kept retreating until she bumped against the doorframe.

Kate spun, relieved, and crossed into the vestibule.

Someone stood just in front of her, on the threshold between the annex and the main house. The sunshine in this room bright-ened and she narrowed her eyes, trying to shield them, inhaling sharply in surprise. She saw the priest's collar and knew it must be Don Pino, come back to the house with Tommy.

Only it wasn't Don Pino at all. The priest stood taller, straighter, younger, steel-gray eyes intense, even though the rest of him was barely there at all. He crossed the threshold, and Kate screamed and threw up her hands, twisting as he rushed past her. She felt him go, though she could barely see him because he was barely there. A shimmer in the sunlight, the suggestion of a man.

She turned to watch him storm into the chapel, this barely glimpsed shade, hardly more than the afterimage of a bright light when she blinked. The rats scurried back toward that shadowed corner. She could hear their claws on the tile still, and then sud-denly, not at all. The corner became quiet shadow once again, and the chapel stood empty, only the breeze passing through that room.

"What the hell's wrong with you?" she asked herself.

Barely able to breathe. *A ghost.* Either that or she was losing her mind, because this wasn't a slamming door or creaking timbers. *Holy fuck.*

She shook her head. Losing her mind? It was a hallucination, of course. Too much talk of demons and dead men.

But when she blinked, it reappeared, a shimmer of a man, an afterimage on the inside of her eyelids. She cried out and stumbled toward the main house, because when she blinked again, it had gotten closer, hurrying toward her, and now all she could think to do was to run. Get out of the annex . . . and out of the house.

"Fuck, fuck, no," she whispered to herself as she hustled down the stairs to the foyer. "This is not real."

Real or not, she could not pretend she hadn't seen it or that it hadn't terrified her. Real or not, she opened the front door and dashed outside, pulling it closed behind her without bothering to lock up. If anyone wanted to sneak into her house while she was outside, they were welcome to do it.

"Christ," she said, heart pounding. She bent over, not to vomit, although for a moment, that seemed possible. Kate took deep breaths and realized this must be panic. Her fingers tingled and her skull thrummed, and she didn't know what to do or say, wondered if she would ever manage to summon up words again.

From the corner of her eye, she saw someone move.

"Kate?"

"Oh, Jesus!" she shouted, spinning round to find it was only Rohaan Tariq, the charming British man who had drawn her and Tommy into the society of the Imports.

Rohaan had just parked a pale-blue Vespa and came toward her, his forehead creased by concern, hands up and nearly tiptoeing, the way one might approach a wounded tiger.

"Are you all right?" Rohaan asked.

She could only imagine what might be going through his mind.

"Definitely not," she replied, surprised at her own honesty. A laugh burst from her throat, and she thought shock might have turned her a little bit crazy, at least for the moment. "I think our house is actually haunted."

Embarrassed, she put a hand over her mouth, but the words were already out.

Rohaan frowned, perhaps wondering if she was playing some sort of joke on him. When his suspicion faded, he looked amused and fascinated, but certainly not frightened, and Kate found his lack of fear began to alleviate her own.

She looked up at her house, watching the windows, expecting to see dead priests in every window. Instead, the house was only a house, old and gorgeous and surrounded by flowers, windows open to let in the light.

"Do you want me to go in there with you?" Rohaan asked.

Kate laughed again, though not quite so insanely this time. "No, my friend. I want you to put me on the back of your Vespa and take me somewhere to get hot coffee and something indulgently chocolate. We can come back when Tommy's home, and you can be there when I tell him we're buying another house."

Rohaan smiled and escorted her back to his Vespa. "My pleasure. Though I do wish Patrick had come along, for the drama and for the ghosts. He's going to love this."

"Perfect! We'll switch houses," she said, hating the brittle humor verging on hysteria she heard in her own voice.

"I'm not sure he'll love it quite that much," Rohaan said.

Then they were on the Vespa, and he started it up.

Only when they were buzzing down the street on the little blue scooter, sun on her back, did Kate feel as if she had left the ghosts behind.

She had no idea what she would do when she had to go back.

6

Tommy walked up the length of Via Dionisio, barely aware of his feet moving. His world had shifted on its axis in the past hour, and it seemed to him that the town should have been affected. Instead, birds chirped from their perches on rooftops and old wires. The breeze carried the scent of flowers along the street. A sleek Maltese cat darted across the road, its paws soundless, a lithe gray ghost.

From the end of the street, the bench overlooking the valley beckoned to him. He wanted to sit there and look out at the world below, perhaps scream into the wind just to release the conflicting emotions that warred within him. Instinct drove him to seek out his wife—she was the only one he wanted to see right now—but things between them had developed a sharp edge since Nonno's stroke, especially after the fight they'd had over Kate's refusal to see the old man before he died. Tommy loved her so much, and they had always been open and honest. Even in disagreements, they had managed to get themselves on the same page eventually. This, too, would pass, he told himself.

But he couldn't wait for it to happen naturally. They had big decisions to make, and they had to make them together. Tommy only hoped she saw it his way.

When he saw the front of his house, the purple flowers, the tall double doors, he couldn't see the beauty of it anymore. It had been

meant to be an adventure as well as the foundation for a magnificent future for himself and Kate, and any children they might
have.

"What the hell did we do?" he asked himself quietly.

With a glance, he confirmed there was nobody around who
might have heard him. No one but the scrawny Maltese, who had
come back and crouched by an empty trash bin, watching him
with the disdain so common to cats.

Tommy laid a hand across his eyes and whispered sorrowful
profanity, blaming himself despite knowing none of this could
have been predicted or even imagined. *It's lunacy*, he thought. *This
is Dark Ages stuff. It doesn't belong to the world of today.*

"Fuck it." He went to the door, dreading the conversation waiting for him. Moving had cost them many thousands of dollars, but
if Kate felt the way he did about this morning's revelations, they
might need to just pack up and abandon this house, Becchina, even
his remaining family.

Not today, not with Nonna only beginning to grieve. But as
soon as possible.

He turned the knob and went into the cool quiet of the house,
shutting the door behind him. Adrift and in thought, he strode
down the hall to the kitchen.

"Babe, we need to talk," he said to the empty room.

Why had he thought Kate would be in the kitchen? The refrigerator hummed and he could smell coffee, but beyond that,
there was no sign of her. He walked back into the hallway, poked
his head into their sitting room, and then moved to the foyer and
called up the stairs but received no answer.

Tommy stood listening to the empty house.

His right hand prickled, and he glanced down at his palm as if
it meant to tell him something. Slowly, he turned to look back at
the front door. He opened it again, turned the knob. Kate had to
be home, or it would have been locked. It wouldn't be like her to go

out without leaving him a note, and certainly not without locking the door behind her. There might not be much crime in Becchina, but they had both grown up being taught to lock up.

"Kate?" he called as he started up the stairs.

At the second-floor landing, he saw that the door into the annex stood open. He looked up toward the third floor and called out again. It spoke of how silent the house remained that he thought he could hear the tick of the clock they had put on a decorative table in the third-floor hallway.

His palm tingled again, his subconscious reminding him that the door had been unlocked. The house creaked with the breeze, as always—breathed with it, as the air passed through open windows, changing the pressure inside—but he did not hear water moving through the pipes. She wasn't in the shower, and he doubted she would have gone down into the basement.

Tommy went into the annex.

In the former maid's quarters, he paused in the sunlight stream-ing through the windows. Noontime approached on what might have been the most magnificent day since they had arrived in Sic-ily, but the interior of the former chapel seemed gray, as if storm clouds had enveloped the town. Tommy shook his head, trying to clear his mind, but still the maid's quarters were awash in sunshine and on the other side of the threshold, the chapel remained gray and dark.

Impossible.

He crossed the threshold. It had been one thing to be told about impossible things as if they were true, but this he could not accept without explanation. The temperature dropped as he entered the chapel, but of course the sunlight in the other room accounted for that. What he couldn't account for here was the absence of that sunlight.

The windows looked out at blue skies.

"What the hell?" he said, pressing his palms against his eyes.

He blinked hard, then lowered his hands and looked again, but the view remained the same.

Everything on the other side of the glass looked precisely as it should. He had imagined Kate must have put up shades or covered the windows, but nothing blocked the sunlight from streaming in here the same way it did in the other room. Yet the light did not reach into the chapel, nor shine onto the floor.

Tommy felt weak. His left hand stretched out to grab the nearest support and found one of the chairs at the conference table. He dragged it toward him and sat down so haphazardly he nearly toppled out of the chair.

Impossible. He glanced around the room, thinking of the highest he had ever been, lying on a dock that jutted out into the Bass River on Cape Cod. There had been a meteor shower that night, but he'd also eaten mushrooms his ex-girlfriend had brought for their reunion, and the stars had painted the sky.

But there were no hallucinogens in his system today. Only grief, confusion, and a terrible dread.

"Kate!" he called, standing abruptly.

Still unsure of his footing, he held the back of the chair a moment, then pushed off, desperate to put this room behind him.

A scratching noise made him pause. Resting one hand on the doorframe, knowing he should at least go into the maid's quarters, he took a deep breath and turned again. Across the shadowy gulf of the chapel, he saw the door to the back stairs creak open slightly. He shivered, hating the squeak of the hinges. If he surrendered to the fear that crept along the back of his neck in that moment, he knew he would have to surrender to so many things in which he had never believed.

Tommy straightened up, then crossed the chapel. Something scratched at the tiles to his right, but he refused to let his focus be drawn away from the door to the back stairs. The room grew darker. The air pressure shifted—he felt it against his eardrums, as if the clouds were about to burst with rain—but outside the windows, he still saw blue sky.

He reached that narrow door at the back of the house, gripped the heavy wood.

The ground began to tremble.

7

Kate and Rohaan sat outside the gelato bar, ignoring the people passing on the street, caught up in conversation. Neither of them had wanted lunch, and Kate thought more coffee would only give her worse jitters than she already had, so Rohaan had gone inside and bought them each a lemon granita. Back in Boston, it would have been called a *slush*, usually consumed by kids at the beach or after a soccer game, but here, it was almost as ubiquitous as coffee. Kate could barely taste hers.

They were on the gelato bar's front patio. A decades-old delivery truck had stopped in the street, and the driver rattled out the ramp at the back of the truck, dropping it with a clang. Already, two cars had stopped behind him, one a sporty Fiat and the other a German touring car probably too big for Becchina's streets. If the Fiat couldn't squeeze through, the boxy German car had no chance. Rohaan's Vespa was parked beside the patio, and looking at the angry face of the Fiat driver and the nonplussed expression on the deliveryman, she knew the Vespa was the solution to a lot of headaches in town.

Of course, she had no intention of staying here long enough to find out.

"I don't know what to say to any of that," Rohaan told her, slumped in a white wrought iron chair.

Kate brought her attention back to him. "You think I imagined it?"

"Brought on by the recent revelations about your house? It definitely occurred to me."

"But it started before we knew any of that. Really, if I think back, it started the moment we opened the front door to move in."

Rohaan dug into his granita, then slid it disinterestedly onto the little, round wrought iron table. "You want me to believe in ghosts and demons?"

Kate felt panic gnawing at her, as if her composure had begun to fray and just a bit more stress would snap it entirely. "The opposite! I *don't* want to believe in ghosts and demons. And the more I see in this house, the more I hear, and the more I think the people around us believe, the more desperate I am for someone who can show me that it's all bullshit. So, by all means, Rohaan, if you can convince me that I'm letting my imagination run wild, I'm begging you to do it."

She had told him everything she could remember. Every creak, every glimpse of something in her peripheral vision, the rats, and the way Tommy's grandfather had behaved. Rohaan had listened in rapt fascination, eating his granita automatically, as if he had forgotten it was there. Now he really did seem to have forgotten it. Kate set hers on the table beside his cup, only a few spoonfuls missing from it.

"It's just too much," Rohaan said, dropping his gaze.

Kate felt sick. "You think I'm messing with you?"

Rohaan closed his eyes. "I don't know you very well, Kate. I barely know Tommy. We're friends, I think, but also virtually strangers. I don't know why you would invent stories as outrageous as these, or why—if you did invent them—you would bother to spin such fictions to someone you've known for so short a time. Especially when we've agreed to work together to make this community more prosperous. So, no, I don't think you're inventing this."

"So I'm crazy."

Rohaan's eyes opened. "I didn't say that."

She laughed. "Such an artful reply. You didn't say it, but you don't deny thinking it."

He slid his chair back. Its feet scraped on the patio. "Actually," he said as he stood, "I do indeed deny thinking you've lost your mind. I've considered it, and although it would be disturbing in one way and comforting in another, it doesn't seem likely. You don't behave the way I would expect a person who has had such a break with reality to behave. Which means, I'm afraid, that I'm going to have to find out for myself."

Kate didn't move from her chair. The relief she felt at not being thought a lunatic did not make her any less reluctant to go back to the house. "Do we really need to go back there right now?"

"I do," Rohaan said. "All my life, I've said I don't believe in ghosts, demons, angels, UFOs, or gods, but I want to believe in all of them. I just need to see one, to know it, to feel the tangible reality of being in the room with something beyond the natural world. So you can stay here and finish your granita if you'd like, but I am going back to your strange old house to search for something evil."

"Oh, I don't think the ghost was evil," she said quickly.

"I know. You said you thought it was trying to protect you. So I want to go and see if I can get a glimpse of it. Maybe take some video of the rats and find out where they're coming from."

Kate pondered. She looked at the clock on her phone screen and realized that Tommy should have arrived back at the house by now. She needed to see him, talk to him. He would not want to leave until after Nonno's funeral—hell, he wouldn't want to leave at all—but she would insist. At the very least, they had to move out of that house. She would not sleep there another night. There would be a hotel room for them, something dingy and small because no luxury chains had built hotels in Becchina and likely never would. But anywhere was better than home, tonight.

Rohaan studied her. "If you want to wait here, I don't mind. I can just walk through and see if anything seems strange, and then I'll come back for you."

"No. Tommy should be back." Kate stood. "I need to explain all of this to him. I hate to do it while he's supposed to be planning his grandfather's funeral, but I don't think I can sleep there tonight."

"If you feel that way at lunchtime, I can't imagine you'll change your mind when midnight rolls around," Rohaan said, "but let's go check out the spooks and see. If you're lucky, maybe you really are just crazy after all."

Kate shot him a dark look. "That's not funny."

"Sure it is!"

Rohaan went to his Vespa, straddled it, and started it up.

"Okay," Kate said as she climbed behind him. "Maybe a little."

Rohaan guided the little Vespa alongside the delivery truck. The driver gave them a small wave, causing the driver of the Fiat to shoot them a venomous glare. He would be stuck behind that truck for at least another ten minutes.

They rode along narrow streets, each turn taking them farther up the hill toward the center of Becchina. Shadows and sunlight took turns as Rohaan steered them upward. Kate caught a glimpse of the church's blue dome, and trepidation bloomed in her chest. The Vespa struggled both with the incline and the weight of two passengers, its engine groaning, and somehow the slower, labored progress toward home made it worse.

When Rohaan turned onto Via Dionisio, Kate wanted to tap his shoulder and ask him to stop. What if Tommy hadn't gotten home yet? She wondered if he might still be at the church with Marcello, talking to the priest, and if she ought to stop there first to avoid any chance of entering the house without her husband already there. The memory of her fear soaked into her, the malignance of the rats and the figure she had seen, the spirit of that priest—

The ghost, Kate. Fucking say it. The ghost.

But she wouldn't be alone. She would have Rohaan with her.

And maybe that would be better than Tommy, in a way. They had been living in the house together. He had heard some of the things she'd heard, and hadn't he been the one to spot someone moving inside their house on move-in day, even though the place had been empty?

Rohaan, though, was an objective observer. An outsider.

Now that she had told him everything, all her fears and suspicions, she realized she was eager to see the place through his eyes.

The Vespa juddered over the cobblestones, rattling her bones. She held on to Rohaan to make sure she didn't slide off. Ducking to the left, she looked up the street toward the dead end and at the façade of her house. With the wild, vivid colors of their flowers and the beauty of the windows and little balconies, it looked lovely and warm and entirely mundane.

Kate saw motion on her right and glanced over just as the sour-faced old woman they called Signora Housecoat came striding from her front door. She looked angry, as if the Vespa's growling motor had pissed her off, and she strode into the street right in front of them.

Rohaan swore loudly at her as he swerved to avoid hitting her. They passed so close by her that Kate could smell the garlic from whatever cooking she'd been doing that day. Signora Housecoat shouted at her, reaching out as if to snatch her off the back of the Vespa, but they had already passed the old woman by.

They were nearly at the house now. Kate spotted the car parked at the end of the road, blocking her view of the bench on which she and Tommy often sat to look out over the valley. She knew that car, but in the moment, she could not remember to whom it belonged.

Then the ground began to shake, and she forgot the car entirely.

Rohaan stiffened. She saw him use the brake.

The whole street seemed to rise and then fall hard. The cobblestones cracked open in front of them. Just as they braked, the front wheel went into a crack in the road. The wheel turned sideways, the whole Vespa upended, and Kate and Rohaan hit the cobblestones hard, tumbling, rolling.

The ground continued its upheaval.

The entire hill seemed to roar.

For a time, the house was forgotten.

8

Tommy braced himself, hoping the tremor would pass quickly.

The house swayed. The floor bucked, the back of the room rose and slammed down again. He clung to the door like a life preserver and shouted in fear as the whole world tried to shake him loose.

Beams cracked like gunshots.

Glass shattered.

The floor gave way, and Tommy fell.

Briefly, the abyss claimed him. Unconscious, he floated in shadow, until awareness slowly returned.

The first thing he heard was the rasping of his own breath. Something pressed into his ribs and thigh and hip, and forced his head down so his neck bent painfully. Bits of debris sifted and skittered nearby, like the sound of the last drops of rain on the rooftop at the end of a storm.

Tommy coughed, tasting dust and his own blood, but it served to clear his mind.

He had been unconscious, but he couldn't be sure for how long. He opened his eyes and was surprised to see a shaft of sunlight, enough for him to make out his position. A door lay atop him like a coffin lid, pressing him against the back stairs that had once led from the second floor to the first, at the rear of the annex. For several minutes, he lay there with only this information, numbly accepting, forcing it to make sense.

There had been an earthquake. Nothing unnatural in that—quite the opposite. Tommy and Kate had uprooted their lives and settled in a region where occasional earth tremors were not uncommon, not far from one of the world's most famous volcanoes. But an earthquake strong enough to collapse a portion of their new house—a house that had stood in the same spot for centuries? Well, that was pure bad luck.

He exhaled, his breath carrying a single word. "Fuuuuuuck."

Testing the weight on top of him, he found that he could shift the lower part of his body. The door pressed down on his head and shoulders, but the bottom of it must have caught on a beam or chunk of masonry, because from the hips down he had a bit of room to maneuver. Absurdly, even after the day he'd already had, it felt like good luck.

He paused to take inventory of his bones. His left knee throbbed. It felt warm and swollen, as if he had bashed it, which of course he had. But otherwise his legs were in working order, and though his arms had little space in which to move, they also seemed intact. Yes, good luck, indeed.

With a grunt, he twisted his upper body and forced his hands up beside his head. Using his back and shoulders to press upward, he pushed at the stairs below him. Had the weight of those upper floors been loaded onto the door, he would never have been able to free himself, but there was enough give for him to force the upper part of the door to rise an inch, perhaps two, and he managed to slide himself down the stairs.

Coughing, he extricated himself from beneath the door. His left knee had not broken but radiated pain, and when he coughed, his ribs pained him as well. He tasted blood, spit some of it onto the door, and reached up to massage his wrenched neck. Blood dripped down from a wound on his scalp, but even that seemed inconsequential. Tommy had survived with injuries that his body would forget mere weeks from now.

When he looked up, he saw blue sky, but the perspective felt wrong. It took him a moment to realize the trouble was the distance. The annex had no cellar, and only two stories, unlike the three in the main house. His current view should have been impossible. He looked up past more than two levels of destruction, which meant the back of the annex had been swallowed up by the ground.

Tommy looked down. The steps beneath him were stone. The back stairs had been made of wood, constructed when the annex had been built, which meant the stairs beneath him now were not the annex stairs at all. Glancing up again, he saw the wooden wreckage of those steps among the beams and boards and broken walls.

The stone steps beneath him had not been on the layout of the house, but he understood immediately that they must be the secret staircase Don Pino had talked about. Confused, bruised, and fascinated, Tommy wanted to see what awaited him below, but then he thought of Kate, and of Nonna. The quake had been powerful enough to collapse the rear half of the annex, which meant other structures had fallen. Maybe not many—Kate and Nonna might be perfectly fine—but he couldn't know that from down here. And he had to remember that aftershocks were a significant possibility, which meant that sitting in a hole in the ground with a dangerously damaged building leaning over his head was not the brightest idea.

Profanity issued from his lips as fundamentally as breathing.

He studied the wreckage above him. It looked as if it would be possible for him to climb up to the broken back stairs, and from there reach the door that led into what remained of the annex's first floor. It looked like only the rear half of the annex had collapsed—as if it had been sheared off—and the rest of the structure remained, although he feared it might all tumble down with the slightest new tremor.

Tommy glanced around, hoping for a less risky escape route. The door that had fallen on top of him had protected him from worse injury, and the opening at the top of the stone stairs had left the lower portion of those steps relatively clear of debris, which would make going down a lot simpler than going up. The shaft of sunlight that shone from where the roof used to be threw plenty of light and warmth on the rubble, but down the steps, into the ground, there was only shadow.

He took out his phone and checked the battery charge. Thirty-nine percent remaining. He thumbed on the flashlight function and began, carefully, to descend.

The stairs curved to the left. There were iron sconces affixed to the walls, but he had nothing with which to light them and no reason to think they still contained enough oil to burn. His phone's light revealed that a portion of the wall below had fallen in, granite sheared off by the violence of the quake. It might have been six feet square if it had not broken in half and fallen against the door at the bottom of the steps.

Either that iron door had already been slightly open or the broken wall had staved it in. Carefully, Tommy picked his way over the stone slabs and shone his phone's light into the two-foot gap between door and frame. He snapped a few photos, mostly by reflex, but then he hesitated. Upstairs, Kate might be searching for him, and he knew it would be smarter to come back down here when he could bring a structural engineer or at least someone could assure them the place would not crash down on top of him. But the same dangers awaited above, and this might be a quicker way out.

Kate. He'd been so frustrated with her, and so full of sorrow after Nonno's death, that he'd allowed a cold distance to accumulate between them. Now all he could think about was getting out of here, getting back to her.

Please be okay. God, please let her be okay.

"Listen to you," he said aloud. "Talking to God as if he's there. As if he's listening."

It felt like a sick joke as he stared down into the darkness. Tommy shivered, aware suddenly that the temperature had fallen. His stomach churned with the beginnings of nausea. Should he go up or down? How would he get back to Kate? If he went exploring, one more little tremor might bring the whole block down on his head. But climbing back up the rubble seemed a surefire way to end up falling and smashing open his skull or breaking his back.

Looking upward, he focused on the broken wooden stairs that had once connected the first and second floors of the annex. He and Kate had thought they were servants' stairs when they had first discovered them, but now he understood that they had been used by the exorcists to bring their . . . what, guests? Victims? Patients? The priests had brought them up to the chapel for the rites and then back down to be locked in their rooms.

He tried to imagine his nonno as a boy, dragged up those stairs by grim-faced old men. In the chapel, now half-destroyed, they had bound young Tommaso Puglisi to an altar or chair and prayed over him. The brown stains on the floor when Tommy and Kate had moved in could only have been blood. There would be no telling how many years they had been there, but some of those drops might have belonged to his grandfather.

Had the exorcists hurt him? Had he hurt himself, trying to escape?

Had he screamed and fought them, tried to break his bonds? Had he cursed and spat and pissed himself like something from a horror film, or had he just been a hateful child, angry at the world? Had it been some kind of mental breakdown, made worse by the priests' assumptions of evil and sin?

Or had it been real?

Tommy shuddered.

Whatever the case, this stone stairwell predated the annex, possibly even the main house, and it went deep beneath Becchina. He tried to picture the layout of this block in his mind, wondering where the tunnel down there might lead, but it was no use. He was just delaying the inevitable.

The caved-in door beckoned.

"If you're gonna do it, then do it, but hurry," he said.

Somewhere far away, emergency sirens wailed. He pushed himself through the door.

The phone flashlight seemed dimmer down here, but he could make out another flight of stone stairs. He went deeper. A dozen steps. Two dozen. His mind raced ahead into the darkness, and for the second time, he tried to match his location to the town overhead. By now, he was beneath the building behind their house, or farther. He gauged the direction he had been moving and pictured the town aboveground, and the realization struck him.

Tommy knew where he was going. It was the only answer. Combine the history of the House of Last Resort and the existence of the catacombs beneath La Chiesa San Domenico, and it only made sense that the exorcists had a way to get from the chapel to the catacombs without the rest of the town being able to observe them. This passageway had allowed them to move the bodies of the dead from the house in secret, so the town would not know every time they failed in an exorcism—every time one of the poor creatures they were trying to help died because of the torments inflicted upon them by their supposed saviors.

It made a hideous kind of sense.

He swept the phone's light back and forth. As he took the next step, his stomach convulsed. A wave of sickness swept through him, and he turned even as the bile rushed up his throat. A torrent of hot vomit erupted from his lips, but he managed to avoid getting it all over himself or the steps just below him.

"Jesus," he whispered, breathing through his mouth, hating the stink.

Shakily, shivering, he started to descend again. What had come over him? Could it have just been nerves? One moment, he'd been fine, just tense and on guard, and the next, that wave of nausea had racked his body. A queasy flutter remained in his guts, a sour twist, and he worried it would hit him again.

Off-balance, drained, and feeling weak, he missed the next step.

All he could do was shift his weight, pull his right leg up, and let himself fall. He pulled in his arms and legs, tucked his chin, cradled his phone against his body, and tumbled down those stone stairs. Tommy struck his head, heard the thunk inside his skull like a wooden baseball bat hitting a line drive. He rolled down the stairs, barely conscious, and when he reached the bottom, he lay on his side, head ringing.

Stupid, he thought. *So fucking stupid.*

But after that moment of regret, he felt grateful to be alive. He might have broken his leg, in a place where nobody would have found him for a long time. If he could get a phone signal down here, he might have been all right, but when they had been deep in the catacombs before, the phone had been useless.

Head still ringing, gut still sour, Tommy sat up. His neck hurt worse than before. He'd smashed his elbow and it bled freely, but it wouldn't kill him.

He turned the light on his phone to the darkness around him and found himself on another landing. A door awaited him, an iron thing that matched the one he had come through. This one had not been conveniently smashed in by falling slabs of rock, but when he rose and went to it, he found that the bar across it lifted easily enough. He gripped the iron ring set into the door and pulled, and despite the weight and age of the thing, it swung smoothly toward him.

Tommy went through and found what he had known would be there.

Catacombs.

And yet not the same. Not catacombs he had already explored.

The bodies in the wall niches here were dried and preserved much like the others, but there were men and women both, and there were children among them. Boys and girls of various ages.

The possessed. Of course.

His stomach convulsed again, and he went rigid, waiting to see if the vomit would win. After a moment, the feeling passed, but his skin prickled with a chill, and a film of sweat covered him in spite of the cold down here in the tunnel.

The neighborhood map he had drawn in his mind came together then. The catacombs beside and beneath the church were vast, long corridors and chambers that extended eastward, under the buildings that separated the rear of the church from the back of Tommy and Kate's new home. But not all the way—not this far.

Except in his mind, now, he pictured that dead end they had found, where a man-made wall of stones and mortar had been installed like some Edgar Allan Poe madman had bricked up his nemesis behind it. There had been thirteen crosses and crucifixes in that wall, certainly an effort to ward off evil—whatever evil the priests at the church thought they had built the wall to keep out. To separate the consecrated dead of the church's catacombs from those the exorcists had been unable to save, whose demons had ridden them down into death rather than surrender control of the flesh and bones of their hosts.

But you don't believe in any of that, Tommy thought.

He laughed dryly and spit a wad of sour phlegm onto the stone floor.

Never mind a Poe villain; he felt more than a little crazy himself.

He stared at the victims of the priests who had run his house. These were the remains of children whose minds had been so broken or who had proven themselves so difficult that no one could conceive of any explanation but demonic possession. He could almost hear what Rohaan and Patrick would say, the value this new section of catacombs would add to their ability to draw tourists. What had happened to these people was horrifying, and like the remains of Pompeii, the fascination with their ghastly deaths would lure many to bear witness.

Tommy brought the phone over to the nearest woman. He stood on the edge of her niche, knee aching, and shone his light on the tight skin of her mummified face, but he did not take a photograph. It would have felt obscene.

Her mouth remained open, teeth bared, lips pulled back in a rictus of emotion, as if she had died screaming or snarling. Her eyes had been sewn shut, but the lids were thin leather now, sunken and concave.

Down in her niche, in the dark place between her pelvis and the carved stone, little gray bodies writhed against one another.

"Jesus!" Tommy shouted, jerking backward.

He tripped over his own feet, stumbling back until he crashed into the niche behind him, into the lap of a cadaver. One of the dead. One of the demon-infested corpses of those the exorcists could not save. He did not believe it, would not allow himself to believe in any of it, and yet he let out a scream and hurled himself forward, crawling on the floor to escape the dry, sharp, papery remains.

Dust from the mummified corpse filled the air around him. He breathed it in.

The chamber around him came alive. It seethed with movement.

In the dark, they skittered toward him. Their claws scratched the stone.

Tommy breathed in the dust of the dead and knew what went into his lungs held the evil of the things that had never released their hold on the souls they had stolen. Suddenly, he believed it all, because the darkness scratched and whispered, and he shone his phone's light around him and saw them creeping nearer to him.

The rats.

The goddamned rats.

9

A single siren shattered the silence.

More likely, Kate realized, there had been no silence at all, only her own unconsciousness. She opened her eyes as a second siren joined the first, the strange, whining seesaw of European emergency vehicles. Kate had always loved those sirens in films and on television, an easy shorthand to establish verisimilitude. Now it helped root her. She came awake with full clarity of where she was and what had happened.

Another earthquake. Much worse.

Dogs were barking at each other. Or to one another, maybe each checking to see if the others were all right.

Like the dogs, people were shouting, screaming. Someone cried for help nearby. Her Italian might be limited, but she understood that much.

Her awareness of her own body came to her slowly. She lay on the road, something pinned under her back. Her right arm. God, she hoped it wasn't broken. The world telescoped down to just the space she occupied on the cracked cobblestone street.

Injuries. How bad?

Carefully, slowly, she arched her back and slid her right arm out from beneath her. It moved without making her want to scream or cry, so she assumed it wasn't broken. She brought that arm around in front of her, cradled it against her as she used her left hand to prop herself up into a sitting position.

Blinking, she stared at her feet. One of her shoes had vanished. The bare toes were scraped and bloody.

She took stock. Her arms were intact but scraped all to hell. No deep cuts, but abrasions welling with blood that would scab up nicely. *Vitamin E*, she thought. Promoted skin regrowth and helped prevent scarring.

The fourth and fifth fingers on her right hand were broken. She needed to wrap them. Probably needed splinting, but as more sirens and more terrified shouts rose around her, she knew the doctors would have greater worries than broken fingers. The right shoulder throbbed; something torn in there, but nothing broken as far as she could tell. Her shirt had ripped, bloody scrapes on that shoulder.

Kate reached up to touch her chin, suddenly aware of the breeze and the way the wind was enough to make her sting. She winced as her fingers touched her jaw and she knew her face had been scraped up as well. Searching her skull, she found no soft spots but an enormous lump where her scalp felt sticky. Her fingertips came away crimson.

All in all, lucky as hell.

Only then did she glance over at the Vespa. The front tire had plunged into the crack that had opened in the street and flipped the scooter over, but velocity had carried it forward. It lay on its side, front wheel slowly spinning. Dented and scraped all to hell, but intact.

"Kate?"

She turned toward the voice. Rohaan lay on the cobblestones a dozen feet away. Blood painted the left side of his face. His nose had been mashed on impact. He cradled his left arm just as she cradled her right, but from the pained pinch of his face and the awful angle of the arm, she knew Rohaan had not shared her good luck.

"Jesus," she said, forcing herself to rise, wincing and bleeding. "Let me look at your head."

Rohaan did not even try to get up. He lay on his back, protecting his broken arm, and his eyes could barely focus when she went down on one knee beside him and turned his head to see the wound there. Kate probed gently. She wasn't a doctor, but she knew there were all kinds of head wounds and that scalp wounds bled so copiously that it was easy to mistake them for more significant injuries. She thought this was superficial, but how could she really know? One thing was for certain: she didn't like the way his eyes seemed unable to focus.

"Stay here," she said. He didn't seem to hear her, so she moved her head to catch his attention. "Rohaan, do you hear me?"

He closed his eyes and rasped a yes.

"Don't try to move unless EMTs come," she said. "I'm going to get help."

Rohaan opened his eyes. She told herself that he had given her a small nod of acknowledgment, but she couldn't wait around for confirmation. There would be injuries all through town. If the main road had cracks like the one they'd driven right into, it was possible emergency vehicles would be unable to reach them.

A quick glance around showed damage to some buildings, while others were untouched. One house had halfway collapsed, while the one next door had a few shattered windows and nothing more. The old woman she thought of as Signora Housecoat was at the front door of a half-ruined home, helping a young mother carrying her infant escape danger. Over the rooftops, she could see black smoke rising in a couple of places, fires started by gas leaks or something. But most of what she saw seemed intact. The dome of the church remained in place, blue and gleaming in sunlight. She knew the story of the Italian hill town not unlike this one that had been shaken apart by a quake so that nothing remained standing.

They had been lucky.

Kate limped toward her house, just a few doors away. At first, she didn't understand what she was looking at, but when she came closer she could see that the back half of the annex had collapsed into the ground. The wreckage was all broken stone and jagged wood, loose wires, and one wall that seemed to have fallen over almost entirely intact.

She felt like throwing up.

Tommy.

She managed to pull out her cell phone. Holding the phone in her left hand, she tapped numbers with the unbroken fingers of her right. She tried to call 112, which was the emergency number in Sicily, but the result was an angry buzz even more strident than the sirens she could still hear. Quickly, she tried Tommy but only heard that buzz, and she knew cell towers must be overwhelmed. The same would be true of the regular phone lines.

"Fuck," she whispered, trying to hide the worst of her fears, even from herself. Rohaan did not look good, and finding help for him would not be easy.

She reached her house. On the front step, she jammed her phone back into her pocket. Shoulder swollen and throbbing, broken fingers sending sharp pain signals up her arm, she made it to the door. The knob turned, but the door stuck. She whispered curses at it, calling the door the worst profanity she knew. The quake had damaged the house enough that the door stuck in its frame.

"Tommy!" she shouted to the broken upstairs windows. "Tommy!"

Rohaan still lay bleeding back in the street with an unknown head injury and possibly worse, not to mention that broken arm. Maybe Tommy hadn't come home from church, and maybe that would be for the best, given that the church dome had been intact. If he had been there, at least he would be safe. But if he was home—if he was inside and not answering—suddenly Rohaan's injuries were secondary.

Kate looked at the door. Thick, heavy, hinges rusted.

She turned sideways and braced herself. As she did, she spotted the car still parked at the end of the road, right by the low fence and the bench overlooking the valley. She had come to think of that bench as their spot. Out there together, drinking coffee, looking over the edge of that cliff, was the closest they had come so far to making their dream of a new adventure come true.

Tommy.

Nothing mattered without him.

Left hand turning the knob, Kate hauled back and slammed her good shoulder against the door. To her shock, it gave way with a splintering of wood. She stumbled into the foyer, where the floor now tilted in a way it hadn't before. The floor was littered with broken glass, and the light fixture had fallen.

She called for her husband again. If he was here and conscious, he'd have shouted to her. Kate glanced left and right and knew he wasn't here on the first floor. She would have felt his presence.

"Are you here?" she shouted, and started for the stairs.

Out of the corner of her eye, she saw the figure move from the parlor, racing toward her from behind. *The ghost, the priest, oh my God,* she thought in the time it took to blink.

Then she heard glass breaking under someone else's solid step and knew it was no ghost, and it wasn't Tommy.

Tommy would never have taken a fistful of her hair and jerked her head back.

Tommy would never have held their serrated carving knife to her throat.

10

The rats followed him. As Tommy retraced his steps, pushed himself through the partly open metal door and crept along stone slabs, some of the rodents kept pace. They darted into crevices beneath fallen stones and scurried through narrow shadows as if trying to outrun him. Tommy resisted the urge to rush—if he put one foot wrong, he might bring rubble down on his head. He thought bitterly that the rats would find a way to escape while he bled to death or suffocated with ten tons of rubble crushing his chest.

But he climbed.

The beating of his heart felt like sandpaper in his chest, a painful rasp. Panic, he figured. Or something else, the same thing that made his skin crawl and prickle with chills, and made him feel so nauseous that he wanted to scream but feared he would be sick again if he opened his mouth that wide. A memory of this feeling flickered in the back of his mind, as if he had experienced dread like this, fear like this before, and it took a minute for him to realize he recognized these feelings not from real life but from nightmares. Dark, terrifying dreams that had driven him up out of sleep with a silent scream on his lips, back when he was a child, and more than once as a grown man.

Tommy thought he had mapped it out in his head now—that if he stayed down there, he could find his way to that Tell-Tale Heart wall, where the mortar was already loose, and if he could find a big-enough rock, he could probably smash it in, letting him into the main area of the catacombs on the other side. He could escape that way, he knew. But those thirteen crosses had not been planted in that wall without reason. It was to keep evil trapped inside the chamber that the earthquake had smashed open, and that he'd unwittingly entered.

Crazy, he knew. Completely absurd, small-minded, ignorant superstition. Minutes ago, he might have been able to tell himself that, but now images cascaded through his mind of the things he had seen since they'd arrived here, the sounds he'd heard, and the things he had felt. Now he'd breathed in the malignance in the air down here and been made sick by it. He'd seen the twisted corpses of the possessed and the dark intellect in the eyes of those rats, and he could not pretend to disbelieve it anymore. The darkness breathed down here. It had a heartbeat.

Tommy wouldn't spend a single moment down in those chambers than he didn't have to.

He escaped through the door that had been smashed open by falling rock. The stone stairs awaited. The bottom of the staircase was clear, but then he reached the place where he'd escaped from beneath the door that had fallen on top of him, and the debris of his house was everywhere. Spider-delicate, he scrambled over the rocks and slabs and fallen beams. A thick wooden beam balanced at the edge of the wreckage. He tested it first, gave it a shove, and discovered it was sturdy enough.

"Just go," he whispered to himself.

A scratching noise came from the stairs below and behind him, but he wouldn't turn around. He didn't want to look into the darkness of that chamber again.

Tommy made the climb quickly, moving on instinct, barely paying attention to where his hands and feet found purchase. Using solidly lodged debris for leverage, he kept most of his weight on the beam and he climbed, and before he knew it, he was even with the first floor of his house.

Through the wreckage, he could see part of the ruined hallway in the annex. The opening seemed large enough for him to crawl through—just barely—but the moment he took his weight from the beam and tried the rubble pile, things shifted dangerously. Portions of the second floor had crashed down all around this spot. He could picture himself trying to shimmy through the wreckage onto the first floor and the whole thing collapsing deeper into the hole, with him at the center.

Something scraped the beam behind him. Tommy didn't want to look back. A shaft of sunlight came from above, so he had been able to pocket his cell phone, but that did not stop the chill that danced along his spine.

To his left, a rat climbed silently from the gap between a chunk of stone and what seemed to be an intact section of the annex's first floor. It paused, turned its head, and watched him with yellow eyes. A bit of bile burned up the back of Tommy's throat. His stomach wanted to revolt again, sick with dread, disgusted by the rats.

They were following him. Kept moving into his field of vision as if they wanted him to know they were there, even as they watched him go. A smell wafted on the stale air that he thought must have come from the rats, but although it made him wrinkle his nose in distaste, he could not have said precisely what it smelled like—and then it hit him, and he wished it hadn't. When his mother was dying, every time she went to the toilet she would light a few matches to help disperse the smell. This stink reminded him of that—burnt matches and shit.

"Get the fuck away from me!" he snapped.

The rats froze, studying him, as if wondering what he would do next. When Tommy resumed climbing this time, they did not attempt to follow him any farther. The narrow gap into what remained of the first floor of the annex was too big a risk. Looking up, he could see that no such obstruction blocked the second floor. The chapel had broken in half like a calving iceberg, but he could see into the remaining portion of the room now.

He climbed, trying not to think about the rats or the danger or to worry about what might have happened to Kate. She should have been here when he got home. He was glad she had been out when the quake struck, but her absence frightened him.

A long electrical cable hung down from the second floor. Tommy wanted to use it to climb but feared a live wire, and so he stuck to climbing the debris instead. He reached the broken fringe of the second floor. The new tile they had put down in the chapel jutted out like shattered teeth. Tommy shifted to his right in search of a place he could drag himself up without ripping his abdomen open on the broken tiles. He thrust his right foot into what had once been a joist in the floor beams but now behaved like a stepladder. Dust showered below him. The joist creaked, gave way, and Tommy held on. His heart seemed to stop a moment, but then the joist caught on something that looked like a roof beam, and Tommy's heart started beating again, but more rapidly.

Raising his left hand, he grabbed hold of the floor's edge. The broken tile scraped at his palm, but he managed to grab hold with his right hand, too, and began to haul himself up. Leverage and determination did the rest. He held his breath, worried every moment that it would all give way, but he boosted himself up over the edge of the broken floor and slid on his belly, then turned on his side.

For a moment, he lay there, bruised and bloody and stunned to be alive.

Then he heard the muffled voice behind him and the sound of a struggle.

Tommy turned from the sheared edge of the floor and peered into the shadows of the remaining half of the chapel. The sun had been in his eyes a moment ago, and now he had to shade them to make out the two figures deeper in the room.

A muffled cry came from one of them. She shook herself free and called his name, just as he stepped out of the sun and into the remnant of that room where old men had once tormented young people until they died.

"Tom—" she managed, before her attacker clamped a hand across her mouth and yanked her backward.

"Kate," he said, his voice sounding hollow in his own ears. Shock had done something to him, but he did not have time to sort it out now.

As his eyes adjusted, he stared into the shadows at Franca and at the knife she held to Kate's throat. Even in the diffuse light of that half-room, Tommy could make out the blood on the blade and the scarlet tears that wept from the slightly pouting line of parted flesh on Kate's neck.

"You cut her," he said numbly. Frowning. Staring.

Tommy took a step toward them.

"I'll cut her again," Franca said. "I'll carve her head right off her body if you don't do as I say."

Tommy stared, trying to make sense of the scene. The fear in Kate's eyes—that much, he understood. But Franca had been their real estate agent. They had no other relationship with her except that she had come to the first meeting of the Becchina Tourism Board. Shock paralyzed him because he simply did not understand—but he understood that knife perfectly well. He saw the slice on Kate's neck and the blood on the knife very clearly.

"Anything you want," he said.

Franca bared her teeth, not in a grin but in some primal, feral hunger. "You're going back down there. Back into the hole, into the catacombs."

Kate blinked in surprise. "The catacombs?"

The knife jerked upward. Franca sliced the tip along Kate's cheek and had it back at her throat before she could hiss with the pain of that cut.

Tommy put his hands up. "Whatever you say. I'll climb back down."

The thought made him want to scream. The fear that had gotten into his gut and the primal part of his brain ran wild. But what choice did he have?

He glanced at the jagged broken tiles where the floor had given way. Without further instruction, Tommy sat on the floor, just a couple of feet from the edge. That shaft of sunlight illuminated the rubble and ruin below. He thought again of the rats down there, at their strange eyes and the way they had paced him, fascinated by him—and at the malign intelligence in those eyes.

A secret staircase had led to a hidden part of the catacombs—and yet . . .

"You know all about it," he said, staring at Franca.

The woman widened her feral grin and jabbed the tip of the knife into Kate's throat. Blood welled, dripped, as Kate winced in pain.

"I said I'm going!" Tommy snapped. "I just don't understand."

Franca narrowed her eyes. "You don't need to understand. Just do as I say."

"You showed us this house!" Kate hissed. "You never said anything about what was beneath it, but you *knew*—"

Franca pressed the blade against Kate's skin, drawing more blood.

Tommy seethed. "Kate's right. You timed it so we would see this place at the last minute. You knew we would jump at it—so much more impressive than the other houses that are part of the mayor's reclamation plan—and we wouldn't ask too many questions that way."

"You've been part of our plan all along, Tommaso," Franca said.

"What do you mean 'our plan'? Who the hell are you?"

Franca smiled. "I am who I am. There are many of us who pray to other gods. My gods are the *angeli della rottura*. You people spend your lives on your knees, bound in chains, puppets for your god. But the darker angels demand we break our chains, stand, and scream to heaven."

Kate struggled against her. "Demons. You're talking about demons. You're in some kind of cult."

"Not a cult," Franca replied. "A religion. Your church tries very hard to destroy the darker angels. My church gives them anything they need to live and be free."

"My nonno—" Tommy began.

"Your nonno was a strong man, but even a strong man can't live forever. Most of his life, he fought his demon—Alberith. Most of his life, he could bottle it inside. But it talked to him always, and it laughed at him. Alberith told him he would die one day, and the demon could wait forever. When he died, it would take his son—"

It clicked into place for Tommy then. "That's why Nonno drove my father away. To keep him safe."

Franca laughed. "Of course. But your father knew—"

"What? There's no way—"

"Your grandfather told him the truth. Your father said he was not afraid, that if his father could fight the demon, he could fight it, too."

Tommy felt sick. "But he was too weak. Nonno told him he was too weak."

Franca shrugged. "Did he? Or did the demon speak through him?"

It didn't matter. "My dad wanted to keep me away. Once he knew the truth, he didn't want me anywhere near Becchina. And my mother went along with him, so she had to know."

"She was so selfish. She cooperated while he was alive, but after he died, she convinced herself that your father had been the irrational one—the irresponsible one."

Tommy stared at her. "How the hell do you know so much about my family?"

Franca's grin faded. Now she looked like something old and rotten, brow tight with disdain. "I told you—you're part of the plan."

"To, what, set your fucking 'dark lord' free? How was he trapped inside my grandfather?"

"He's been waiting, Tommy."

"Waiting for what?"

Franca laughed softly. "For you, Tommy. He's been waiting for you. Only you could give him back his vitality. He's been inside your grandfather so long that the only suitable home for him now is inside you."

Nausea roiled in Tommy's gut. "Even if I'm willing to believe any of this, I'd never let that happen."

Franca marched Kate forward as if she were wrestling with a mannequin. Kate hissed as the knife bit into her. "You're gonna do exactly what I tell you."

Tommy stared into his wife's eyes. He saw such intelligence there, such love, such fear. But a low whisper slithered through the back of his mind, wondering how he could trust anyone now, even Kate. Franca had been nothing but the real estate agent, but stood revealed as a manipulator, a conspirator, a woman who served the needs of a demon—and Tommy did not believe in demons.

Never had.

Now, he wasn't sure. How else to explain the story unfolding as it was? The exorcists had been unable to drive the demon out of Nonno, but somehow—even as a young boy—Nonno had managed to subdue it, drive it down inside himself so that most of the time, the demon was caged. But someday he would die, and if the demon threatened his family, it made sense that he would drive his son away.

It made Tommy nauseous. All the times he had played with his nonno, gone for walks to the bakery, the demon had been looking out from behind his eyes. When he had met Nonna and been married . . . when their son, Tommy's father, had been born. Never mind born . . . *conceived.*

The demon had been there all along.

Tommy didn't want to believe—it all felt absurd—and yet how else to explain the presence of this madwoman with her bloody knife and the terror in his wife's eyes?

For only the second time, Tommy zeroed in on Kate. "You just do what she tells you. Whatever it is. I don't care about any of this—"

"Tommy, no!" Kate shouted.

"All I care about is you."

"*Bellissimo*," Franca said. "True love, so beautiful."

The woman whispered in Kate's ear, just loud enough for Tommy to hear. "Soon, he won't even know your name. But he'll be glad to take you to bed."

Tommy felt rage ignite, driving out his fear. If Franca would give him enough time, he knew he could figure all of this out—the puzzle, the purpose, the way to save Kate and himself. But he knew he would have to buy himself that time.

"What do you have to do with any of this?" he asked. "My grandfather—"

"Is nothing. And now he is dead," Franca said. "Alberith needs a home. You want me to tell you the truth? You do not need to be clever with me, Tommaso. I have nothing to hide. My lord loves this world, and he loves its people. He wants to stay here, but now your grandfather's corrupt old body has died, and there are rules that must be followed. Alberith needs a shell, a human costume, and the only way for him to take a fresh one without returning to hell and waiting for a fresh opportunity is if the new shell is the same blood as the first."

"Me," Tommy said.

Kate swore. "You planned this?" she said. "Lured us here?"

"Your husband's parents kept him away so long," Franca said. "Once both were dead, it wasn't difficult to persuade Mayor Brancati to seize abandon homes and offer them at the right price."

"But Kate is the one who convinced me to do this," Tommy said. "She saw it online somewhere."

"Yes," Franca replied. "An email, from me. That started it all. The rest was easy."

Tommy couldn't wrap his head around it. How could any of this be true, never mind all of it? He glanced down into the chasm at the back of his house, at the rubble there, and thought about how dangerous it had been down there. But Franca would kill Kate if he didn't descend once more, and that was far worse than anything else she might do.

"You'll let her go if I do this?" he asked.

"Probably?" Franca said. "I'm just being honest. Go through, search for another way out. And if you hear any voices calling out your name . . ."

"Yes?"

"Answer them," Franca said.

Kate called out to him again, but he couldn't listen to her now. If he did, he would never go, and Franca's patience would run out soon.

On his hands and knees, his wife shouting for him to stop, Tommy went back over the side of the shattered floor and began to descend into the wreckage and down into the catacombs again. Down with the dead men. Down with the demons, and the wild men and women the church had tried and failed to help.

He might have prayed, but where he was now, prayers seemed likely to go unheard.

11

Part of Kate—maybe the part ruled by a head injury—thought this must all be some kind of prank. The world had gone from boredom to wonder to absurdity to nightmare. The whole thing felt so ridiculous that of course it had to be a put-on. Tommy's grandfather had been part of it, that day when he had said those awful things to her, the things that had filled her with a chill she'd never felt in her life. All of this, it was some kind of bizarre joke.

Which was impossible, of course. Nobody could fake an earthquake. Tommy's family had not concocted some dramatic pretend death for their patriarch. And the cuts Franca had made on her throat and cheek—those were realer than anything she had ever felt. The pain seared her, somehow burning and icy at the same time. Blood drizzled down her face and neck, staining her shirt, dripping over her clavicle. She could smell it, and the smell of your own blood was never going to be part of a prank.

"Stand up straight!" Franca hissed in her ear, pricking her throat with the tip of the knife.

Kate's eyes filled with tears, but she fought them back with pain and bitter anger.

"Why?" she asked.

Franca uttered a dry laugh. "You heard why." She yanked at Kate's hair, tugged back her head to expose her neck further, and ran the flat of the bloody blade along the soft flesh of Kate's throat. "Tommy is doing what I tell him to save your life, but now that he's gone down into the tomb, I could cut you open, and it doesn't mean a thing. So be a good girl."

She used Kate's hair as a leash and forced her to kneel. Kate bared her teeth, breathing through them, stinging with pain and humiliation as she went to her knees.

"Why don't you, then?" she asked.

Franca gripped her hair, twisted her head to the side so she could look down into Kate's face. "When I know your husband has done his part, then I set you free."

Hope ignited in her. Could she really believe Franca intended to do that?

On her knees, she watched the edge of the broken tile floor, the spot where Tommy had scuffed himself down onto the rubble and vanished from sight. Franca released her hair and stepped away for just a moment, surprising Kate. It took her a moment to realize she ought to spring to her feet and make a run for it, but that moment was enough for Franca to grab a chair and drag it over.

"Sit," Franca said, holding the knife, eyeing her with such confidence that Kate did not dare try to take her one-on-one. Not while she had that knife, and Kate had broken fingers and aching ribs and probably a concussion. If it came to it, she would attack Franca head-on, but right now she knew the odds were badly against her.

She sat down. And when Franca produced a roll of duct tape from the jacket she'd dropped in a heap by the chapel door, and told her to bind her ankles with it, Kate obeyed her. When Franca stood behind her and told her to put both her arms back there, and then started wrapping duct tape around her wrists, Kate allowed it. Franca had already cut her, already made a slit in her throat that burned with exposure to the air. Kate had not the slightest doubt that Franca would kill her if necessary, so Kate decided not to make it necessary.

But she kept space between her ankles and her wrists, and she hoped she would find a chance to get free. She was grateful that

Franca hadn't decided to tape her to the chair itself, because that would have complicated things further.

Once the tape was in place, Franca left her sitting there and walked to the place where the chapel had sheared in half. She looked out over the edge, and Kate knew she must be checking to be sure that Tommy had not lingered. It was a good guess—she herself had been hoping he would try something like that, but from the way Franca's shoulders relaxed when she looked down into the rubble from the edge of that broken flooring, it was clear there was no sign of him.

Tommy, she thought. *Hurry.*

He would find a way to come for her. Kate knew that. That was the kind of husband—the kind of person—he had always been. But she also knew that she could not wait for him to free her, that whatever lunacy went on in Franca's mind, she was unhinged and more than willing to draw blood.

"All that shit you were saying," Kate began. "About getting Tommy here."

Franca turned to her, bathed in sunshine.

"You don't believe me?" Franca asked. "I sold this house to you, and that was not an accident. Oh, my acting that day—like a movie star, I think. 'Oh, Kate, I just remembered there is another house, I think you will love it.' So I bring you and Tommy here."

Kate stared. The article had first shown up in a thread she was following on Facebook, but then some travel company had sent it to her. It had prompted research, and conversations with both Tommy and his grandparents. Franca had been quoted in that article about the town selling homes for a single euro, and when Kate had started searching for real estate in Becchina online—just browsing—she had run across Franca's name two or three times in an hour. Total coincidence.

Unless it had been the power of suggestion.

"It was my decision," she said. "To buy this particular house."

Franca brushed her hair away from her eyes. "If you must think so. But you know this house is not . . ." She searched for the word but couldn't seem to find it. "You feel the pain here. The way they screamed. I know you can."

"You're delusional."

"Believe what you like." Franca shrugged. "Soon, it won't matter."

She walked back to where the quake had tipped over the rest of the chairs. The floor was cracked and covered in dust and debris. What remained of the house was clearly not safe, but Franca seemed entirely unconcerned as she picked up one of the chairs and sat. She had chosen a spot where she could watch Kate if she wished, but her focus remained on the broken edge of the floor, where the room had been ripped in two, and where Tommy had climbed down into whatever waited for him beneath the house—beneath the town.

Kate had spread her wrists as much as possible while Franca taped them, and that had given her a tiny bit of room to maneuver her hands—enough to twist them just slightly so that she could probe the duct tape with the tips of her fingers. She found the seam, the torn end of the tape, and began to pick at it with her nails.

A cold breeze caressed her, like a whisper in her ear. The house creaked worse than it ever had, and she tried not to think about what would become of her if the ground began to shake again.

She felt that whisper return, like cold breath on her neck, not far from all the slices and cuts Franca had made, drawing her blood.

The breeze spoke her name.

Kate froze. She glanced to her right. In the shadows stood a figure, a man she had seen before. A priest, barely there, like the image of a starburst on the inside of her eyelids after looking at the sun. Just the suggestion of a man, but she knew he was real. She had seen him, or another like him, before.

Behind him, in the shadows, there was another. And a third.

The three priests drifted out from the corner of the chapel toward Franca, who seemed not to notice them at all. She sat in the sunshine, but the afternoon sun had begun to creep across the sky, and the angle of its light would soon leave her in shadow.

The priests seemed to be waiting for her there.

Kate felt a flicker of hope, but she kept pulling and scratching at the edge of the tape around her wrists, because she had never believed in ghosts. She might be crazy. And if she was sane, there was no telling what they might do once they were finished with Franca.

12

The rats watched Tommy, but they kept their distance. He lunged at one, tried to stomp on it, but it eluded him easily, and the moment he took his attention away, it came nearer again. Close enough to watch him, just as the others did, but not close enough for him to lash out. Guided by the light from his cell phone, he could only illuminate one stretch of the tomb at a time, but as he moved the light around, he realized the rats surrounded him like escorts. Like prison guards. As if they were herding him deeper into the tomb.

His skin crawled. The sickness in his gut had returned. Every time he inhaled, he wanted to throw up, because he knew the evil still breathed down here. He could feel it, and see it in the strange angles of the dried husks of the mummified dead. The cadavers. The failures of the exorcists.

His body felt coiled, every muscle tensed to lunge forward, to rush through this cold stone hell until he reached that stone-and-mortar wall with its thirteen crosses . . . and yet he did not dare give in to the temptation to run. Tommy steadied his breathing and chose his steps carefully, and he tried not to look at the dead.

Yet how could he resist?

He breathed in the dry, heavy air of the tomb, and he stole at least a glance at every cadaver he passed. There were dozens. Some were adults, but there were at least twice as many bodies small enough to be children. Their faces were sunken and withered, dry skin pasted to bone. The eyes were vacant hollows, and yet some of those orbits seemed occupied, papery eyelids covering whatever remained beneath.

There were broken bones, strangely misshapen limbs, and each one of those cadavers told a story wrapped in mystery. How had their bones broken? Were those injuries self-inflicted from seizure or caused by violent ministrations from the exorcists? Those misshapen limbs . . . had those individuals been thought possessed because they were born with some physical handicap, an arm or leg too short, a hand without fingers? Were those signs of the devil, causing these poor souls to be turned over to the church by the superstitious?

Or had possession warped them?

Tommy didn't want to ask himself that question. Only days ago, he would never have allowed himself to think such thoughts. Even an hour ago, he would have pushed them away. But that was before . . . and now he was down here, in this hidden section of the catacombs of Becchina, among the dozens of people who had died in the care of the church—died, if he believed it, still possessed by the demons who had plagued them in life.

And where had those demons gone?

Every time he shone the light from his phone toward one of them, the shadows around them seemed wrong. Shifting. As if either the cadavers or the shadows themselves might stand up at any moment and slither toward him.

Something twitched in a niche to his left, down inside the mummified remains of a woman whose skull looked profoundly wrong. The right side had something like a horn jutting from the temple. The jaw had been distended, much too large, and the teeth . . .

Tommy turned the light of his phone away. He told himself it was because he needed to light the path ahead of him, and that was true. There were cracks in the stone floor, and places where cadavers had fallen from their niches and their bones stretched across the walkway as if they had been trying to escape this place. Dead, mummified, infested with demons, and trying to escape.

He turned the light back toward the mummified corpse of the woman with the horn and the distended jaws and those jagged teeth. Black teeth, sharp and gleaming, rows of them like a shark had.

A mutation, he told himself. *A birth defect.*

It had to be.

But he held his breath as he diverted the light again, hating to take his eyes off that corpse, hating to leave it in the darkness, where it might rise and come for him, crawling onto the walkway like these others he stepped over, even now. With those teeth.

Tommy inhaled, and he knew that he was breathing evil into his lungs.

The rats scurried along, keeping him company. They moved in and out of niches, never crawling over the bodies but racing alongside them as if these paths were always theirs. One rat did run up onto the chest of a cadaver—a thing with mushroom growth on its face, sprouting from its eyes and out of the spongy softness that its skull had become. The rat paused on its chest and looked at the dead thing's face as if waiting for something to happen. Then it nodded, approached, and entered the body through a hole in the papery skin of its neck, tail flicking behind it as the rat scurried down into the chest of the dead man.

He thought about Kate, not just of the knife Franca had held to her throat but of all the things he wished he could have said to her. God, he loved her, and he had turned his pain against her. This had been a dream shared between them, but he had let his own stress and the expectations of his family and his goddamned pride build up some ugly energy inside him—a bullet made from grief and resentment and guilt, anger at himself—and then he'd shot that bullet at the person he loved the most, because she was there. Because somehow, in some real but ridiculous way, life had led him to believe that your spouse was supposed to be able to heal you, to find the hurts in you and root them out, and if they didn't do that for you, that was just cruelty on their part. That if they couldn't make you feel better, that meant they didn't really love you, that they didn't want you to feel better.

He'd made his hurt into Kate's problem.

She wasn't innocent—she'd done much the same thing—but that didn't matter. He had been a bastard and a fool. If he could climb back up to the chapel now, he would tell Kate all of that— that he loved her and he was sorry he had resented her inability to fix him. But if he tried to go back up there now, he was confident that fucking lunatic Franca would cut her throat.

Franca.

Franca and Nonno.

Those were thoughts he'd been ignoring, too.

He didn't doubt that Nonno had been incarcerated in the House of Last Resort and subjected to the torment of exorcism before ultimately being released. Franca said the demon had never left him, that it had always been in him, and now that Nonno had died at last, the demon needed someone of the same blood to root it in this world.

Crazy. Crazy. Crazy.

But if it wasn't true, then how could he explain Franca? An attractive woman in her thirties, otherwise ordinary, who believed all of this enough to kill for it. How could he explain that?

Or the atmosphere down here in this tomb. Closing around him. Breathing with its own malevolent life. Inhale, exhale, aware of his passing through. How could he explain the rats who kept pace, their little yellow eyes the color of piss in the dark?

Tommy could barely breathe. If he could have caught a single decent breath, he thought he would have the energy to cry, but fear kept those tears inside. He passed more of the dead. Their empty eyes or pale eyelids seemed to track him as he went by, a terrible awareness. The tomb smelled of salt and flint and dust.

If the exorcists failed with these people, then where were their demons right now? In this moment, where were they?

The one blessing he had was the knowledge that Nonno had

not yet been buried here. His corpse would go through the process that these other cadavers had, dried and preserved and laid out in one of these niches. He had seen the rat that night Nonno died. At the time, it had horrified him, caused him to shudder with the primal disgust humanity had for vermin, but now he watched the rats around him and wondered what had become of *that* one.

His footfalls echoed off the walls, the sounds more claustrophobic than before. He thought the tomb had become narrower, and he rounded a corner and saw that the ceiling was lower here. There were shadows that suggested openings farther ahead, but he had the sudden certainty that he had come to a dead end.

A whisper rose in the tomb around him.

Tommy wanted to believe it was the echo of his own footfalls, but he knew it was not.

The dead, the still possessed, the corpses still filled with the echoes of the demons who had destroyed their lives . . . they seemed to breathe. To whisper.

It was an illusion.

From within each of the cadavers near him, a rat emerged. Big rats; small rats; skinny, filthy creatures, they emerged one by one and began to gather on the path ahead of him.

They averted their eyes. Lowered their heads.

Another rat emerged from the darkness of the path ahead. The others behaved as if their king had appeared.

Tommy wondered how far he was from the way out.

And if he could make it alive.

13

The chair trembled beneath her. Kate felt it shaking, but so slightly it might have been her imagination. Or the house settling after the quake, or a tiny aftershock, or just a tremor of fear that traveled through her bone and muscle and down into the chair. Maybe this little mini-quake had begun inside her instead of deep underground.

"Do you see them?" she rasped.

The ghosts.

They could be nothing else, now—unless they were entirely hallucinatory, and Kate felt sure they were not.

Franca turned toward her, smiling the smile of the cruel and the insane.

"What are you saying?"

Kate gnawed her lip, worried that Franca might not be the only crazy one. She watched the priests move through the room. Three of them, all old men, two in black suits with white collars and the third in a kind of robe—she couldn't remember what the church called them. They flickered as they moved, like watching one of the earliest silent films projected into life. No sound came from them, and she thought of whatever Tommy had seen on the day they arrived . . . and the locked doors that had opened . . . and the times she had felt not alone . . . and the night she had come sleepwalking into this room. Mostly, she thought of the rat that had come toward

234 · CHRISTOPHER GOLDEN

her the last time she had been here and the shadow that had seemed to step between her and that rat to keep it from following her.

The exorcists were so clear to her, but they were afterimages. Shadow puppets, as if on the other side of a veil, where sound did not reach, where she could not touch.

Franca didn't see them at all. But, watching the three shadows approach her, Kate knew she was not insane.

"They're here, Franca," Kate rasped. The bleeding slash on her throat stung.

"*Who's* here?"

"The exorcists."

Franca sneered at her and rattled off some profanity in Italian, or maybe in the dialect she'd grown up with. "They are all dead, idiot."

"Yes," Kate replied. "They are."

They were monsters, too, Kate thought. She pictured the rituals that had taken place in this room, all the blood that had been shed, the tears, and the screaming. Had every one of those men, women, and children been legitimately possessed, or had some been stricken with mental illness? The odds alone were enough to suggest more than one innocent had passed through this place. They were called holy men, yet Kate did not believe there had ever been such a thing.

But men who fought the darkness the best they could? People who took up the banner of all that was holy? Yes, they existed.

While they remained in the portion of the chapel that still had walls and a ceiling to keep them in shadow, they were silhouettes that flickered in the air. But as they moved toward Franca, they crossed into direct sunlight, where they became nearly invisible. If Kate had not seen them before, she doubted she would have been able to pick them out now. The exorcists were little more than the suggestion of a presence, a flicker when she blinked, as they approached Franca.

"They're all around you," Kate said.

Franca grew angry. She turned in a circle, arms out wide. "There is nothing here! No one but you and me, and down in the old tomb, your husband—but he will not be your husband when he comes out."

Kate barely listened. Hot wind gusted, blowing through the ruin of the house, but the air around Franca blurred and moved.

Then it began to speak.

Not in English, and not in Italian. Kate was sure the muffled voices that slid around them on the breeze were speaking Latin. She did not understand the language but recognized the cadence— they were prayers, of course.

Franca lowered her head, whipped around in search of the source of those voices. She had been predatory before, and now she looked like prey.

From downstairs, Kate heard the bang of the front door crashing open. Someone shouted her name. She blinked in surprise, wondering if this, too, was the voice of some ghost, but then she heard heavy footfalls mounting the stairs, and the voice called out again.

"Kate! Tommaso! *Sei qui?*"

"Marcello!" Kate shouted. "I'm in the chapel!"

Across the debris-strewn tile floor, Franca shot her a look of searing hatred. The quiet Latin prayers seemed to hush, carried off on the wind. She glanced at the bloodstained knife in her grip as if she had forgotten it was there—forgotten what it was for. Then she remembered, and she started toward Kate.

Marcello entered the room. She heard him dart through the maid's quarters and cross the threshold into the chapel, heard his footfalls come up short when he saw her in the chair, wrists and ankles bound.

"She has a knife," Kate said evenly. Almost calmly.

"Franca?" Marcello said. *"Cosa fai?" What are you doing?*

He seemed strangely calm, and the sound of his voice brought a waterfall of despair crashing down on top of Kate. Franca had lured them here. She had known about the house and the exorcisms and about the demons who had never been driven out. Was Marcello part of it as well?

But then Marcello moved around the chair to stand between Kate and Franca—between Kate and that knife—and she knew he was not.

"Where is Tommy?" Marcello asked.

Kate wasn't sure which of them he had spoken to, but she answered. "Down in the catacombs. The possessed—the ones who died here, the ones the priests couldn't help—their tomb is down there. She made him go back down with them."

"Why did you do that, Franca?" Marcello asked.

Franca smiled. "He belongs with them."

Kate's fingernails had peeled up a two-inch strip of the duct tape that bound her wrists. Now she worked faster. Stretching, pulling, peeling, using this finger on one side, twisting her wrists and going at it from the other side.

Franca inched toward Marcello with the knife.

"Kate?" Marcello said. "Do you see them?"

The same question she had asked Franca. Kate looked up and, yes, she could see the exorcists, the same silent-movie flicker as they surrounded Franca again. Their voices lifted, the Latin prayers louder, and she saw one of the ghosts move its hands as if in the sign of the cross.

"*Adjuro te, serpens antíque,*" came the voice on the wind, disconnected from the ghosts or any movement of their lips. Yet the voice belonged to one of them, she was sure. "*Per júdicem vivórum et mortuórum, per factórem tuum, per factórem mundi, per eum, qui habet potestátem mitténdi te in gehénnam—*"

"Marcello, help me!" Kate shouted.

Franca rushed at him, brandishing that knife. Marcello seemed to hesitate, ready for a fight. Kate swore under her breath, focused on the sting of the cuts in her face and throat, and she tipped herself out of the chair.

The ghosts were useless.

Just like the priests had been useless, at least for the people who had been brought to this house. They'd been exorcised, or they'd died here. The ghosts of these holy men were still trying their prayers and rituals, but whatever darkness had rooted in Franca's heart was not influenced by those prayers at all.

She thrust the knife at Marcello. He batted her hand away, then tried to grasp her wrist.

Franca turned the knife and jabbed at him, slicing his arm. Fresh blood spattered the floor. Ritual blood, in a room for rituals.

Kate lay on her side with her hands bound behind her. Her broken fingers sent sharp pain up her arms, spikes of agony strong enough to clear her head. As long as she was bound, she was helpless. From the corner of her eye, she saw Franca circling Marcello, looking for an opening so that she could stab him again, more effectively this time.

A soft caress touched her hands. Maybe the wind or maybe the ghosts—she didn't care. Neither of them would set her free. That was up to her.

Kate went fetal, knees tucked to her chin, and thrust her hands down. She brought her bound wrists under her butt, then her feet, and now her hands were in front of her. It was the work of only seconds to use her still-bound hands to unwrap the duct tape on her ankles.

Marcello cried out. Kate whipped around to see a bloodstain spreading on his left side, but he stayed on his feet. Franca wore a hyena's grin as she crept toward him, and for the first time, Kate wondered if that was really her smile at all—if something else might lurk behind those teeth, behind those eyes. Maybe the cruel madness inside Franca wasn't human at all.

It's real, she thought, though she had known it for a while now. *Evil*.

It's real.

Her heartbeat slowed. A chill rippled outward from her core.

The shadows of those long-dead exorcists lingered at the edges of the room, their prayers useless, nothing but observers now.

Despite the duct tape around her wrists, Kate picked up the chair she'd been sitting on and took three strides. Franca saw her coming and turned away from Marcello just as Kate swung the chair. Heavy wood cracked the bones in her face. Franca cried out and staggered backward, but her fingers only gripped the knife harder.

Kate followed. Her broken fingers throbbed and the chair felt twice as heavy now, but she swung it again. Blood and broken teeth flew from Franca's mouth. She staggered backward. Kate swung the chair once more, but this time, she released it mid-swing. The heavy chair collided with Franca, and both bitch and chair went off the edge of the broken tile floor, falling thirty feet onto the rubble below.

Franca didn't even scream.

A rush of emotion filled Kate. She ran to the edge, careful not to fall, and she called out for her husband.

"My God," Marcello said, moving up alongside her even as he investigated his knife wounds for severity.

"Tommy!" Kate screamed, as Marcello tore the duct tape from her wrists.

Out across Becchina, voices and sirens and sobs replied, the noises of the aftermath of that earthquake, but of Tommy, there was no sign. He was still down there.

Kate went down on her knees and began to turn around, thinking she could lower herself the way Tommy had. She could climb down the debris and go into that tomb, just as he had. Broken fingers and what was probably a concussion wouldn't stop her.

Marcello did.

"Hey," he said, grabbing her shoulder.

Kate glared at him. "He's down there with them."

She didn't explain who she meant. They both knew she was talking about demons. It didn't seem quite as insane anymore.

"It's all part of the catacombs. If he's looking for a way out down there, that's where he'll end up. There must be places that were closed up. We need to be there if he's looking for an exit."

Kate looked down into the darkness of the ruin below her, the deep hole where part of her home had been, the stone stairs that went into the ground, into the tomb where the church had buried the people the devil had claimed.

She wondered what the earthquake had done to the catacombs. In her mind's eye, she saw that crucifix-encrusted wall they had discovered with warnings etched into it, where the rats had scurried through a hole in the rock. If the tunnel hadn't collapsed, that would be the way.

"Let's hurry," Kate said, stumbling to her feet. "If there's not an exit, we may need to make one."

14

Tommy wondered if he would die down here.

The possibility had been in the back of his mind, but now it had come very much to the forefront. There had been tremors in the ground, in the stone beneath his feet and the walls around him. They seemed minor, barely noticeable, but with thousands of tons of rock and earth and a whole town over his head, he felt quite sensitive to the threat of another quake. More than that, the whole tomb seemed to thrum like a struck bell, but without the chime. A silent vibration that he felt in his skull and chest.

He didn't want to be crushed to death, but there were worse fates. The rats continued to keep pace with him. When he found himself in a dead end and retraced his steps, they followed. They scurried in and out of burial niches and vanished into the darkness of shelves where bodies had been stacked as if in childhood bunk beds. Tommy had lost count of the dead by now. There were enough of them to make him wonder how many exorcisms the church performed each year and how many of those had been sent off to the House of Last Resort as hopeless cases.

How long had they been coming here, these damned people? Dying here?

He had to get out of here, but which way?

Tommy held his phone out, but the flashlight seemed to have dimmed. He heard and felt the phone buzz, and he knew without looking at the screen that this was no text—not underground like this. It could only be bad news, and he confirmed it. The battery had dropped to 20 percent charge. That ought to have given him plenty of time if cell phone batteries operated like fuel tanks, but he knew it wasn't like that. The closer his phone got to a dead battery, the faster the juice seemed to drain from it.

His heart pounded hard enough to hurt. He glanced around, trying to imagine how he would find a way out of here without any source of light. In total darkness, he would be crawling over dried husks of dead people as the rats grew bolder.

It felt like he ought to have been spilling over with profanity, but instead he fell silent, numbed by his worst imaginings. No words would suffice.

Tommy had come to a junction in the crude tunnels. Going backward would only retrace his steps, which left three options. Two would likely be dead ends, and the path on the right seemed to curve away from what he believed was the direction of the church. Driven by urgency, terrified at the thought of being lost in the dark, he chose the center tunnel and started to hurry. He kept his focus on the path in front of him, not daring to look at the cadavers or the inscriptions in the walls. The rats scurried in the dark and rustled among the tattered clothing and funeral shrouds, but he ignored them, too. All that mattered was finding his way out.

The tunnel narrowed, and the height of the tunnel diminished, forcing him to stoop. He tried to shine his light farther ahead, and when he did, he saw three rats perched side by side in the middle of the tunnel as if they had been waiting for him. They might have been vermin he had seen before, up in the chapel, but he had no way to know. Their eyes were sickly yellow. The one in the middle stood on its hind legs and twitched its nose at him. It should have been comical, but Tommy took a step backward.

This time, when he heard rustling off to his left, he used his light to take a quick look. He hated taking the flashlight beam away from those three rats blocking his way, but now he felt cramped, even trapped, and he didn't like how much closer it all felt. Only careful footsteps kept him from twisting an ankle in one of the niches in the floor to either side. The cadavers were close enough for him to trip over.

The flashlight revealed the dried-out husk of a man. His lips had been pulled back, thin leather strips that revealed brown, broken teeth. His clothes looked stiff and dry, coated with dust, just trousers and a shirt that a farmer might have worn a century or two before. One of the dead man's eyes remained closed, the thin lid covering a sunken place beneath it, but the other eye had been removed—the whole orbit hollowed out—and as the light played over the dead man's face, something glinted back inside his skull.

It shifted back there in the darkness of that head. The skull shook just a little. A scratching noise came from inside, muffled but unmistakably the sound of one of these rats. Tommy moved the angle of his phone's flashlight beam, and now he saw the beady little yellow eyes looking out at him from inside the skull of the dead man.

And it spoke to him.

"*Tommaso.*"

His name, lingering and sibilant.

With tiny shrieks and the scratching of their claws, other rats chewed through chest cavities and burrowed through eye sockets. Skulls rocked side to side. Tommy backed away, shining his phone light around himself as if that might keep them at a distance. But they were too close already, close enough to reach out and grab hold of him with the spindly, mummified fingers of those dead people and their dead children.

The littlest corpse belonged to a girl no more than six. Her skull shifted forward. The nose of a rat pushed out a desiccated lump of something that might have been an eyeball. It looked out at Tommy from inside.

They all did.

Some spoke in Italian, but there were other languages. He picked up words, some meaning. Some were English.

"*Tu appartieni qui.*"

"*You're home, Tommy,*" one of them rasped. It sounded like his mother.

His feet were shuffling backward before he even realized he had begun to retreat. He gripped the phone too tightly, terrified he might drop it. The light flickered, and he cried out, his voice echoing off the tunnel walls and coming back to him as a kind of dry laughter. Or maybe that wasn't an echo at all.

"*You are your father's son,*" his mother's voice told him.

But he knew it was not his mother's voice at all.

The other voice, however—the first one that had spoken to him, that demon's voice—he knew that one. And it seemed more than real to him.

"*Tommaso!*" it said again, booming now, echoing along the tunnel, accompanied by the shrieks of hundreds of rats.

Tommy reached the opening where the tunnels had branched off. It occurred to him to run back the way he'd come, but if he showed his face there, Franca would cut Kate's throat. One of the other tunnels seemed open, but he shone his phone light in that direction and saw the tunnel floor undulating with a swarm of rats, slowly advancing, practically creeping toward him as if they thought he might not run if they were stealthy enough. A laugh escaped his lips, a bit of hysteria and something like madness. He felt like his mind had begun to fall apart.

The voices had fallen silent down in the tunnel he'd fled, but something moved down there now. Something heavy, and bigger than any rat. His breath caught in his throat. Whatever dragged itself along the stone floor of that tunnel now, it had not been there just moments ago.

Something scraped the floor. It exhaled, a long breath that rolled like invisible smoke up through the tunnel. Tommy stared into that darkness and could make out the shape of it, large and stooped, moving in strange, jerking steps, shoulders twitching, lurching forward.

He didn't want to see it.

But his hand moved, as if the oldest, most primitive part of his brain had taken control, and the fears of his earliest ancestors seized him. His subconscious knew that he had to look; he had to see it or he would never accept it.

He shone the phone's light down that tunnel and saw it lumbering toward him, its shadow distorted and hideous but not nearly as awful as the thing itself. This had been the cadaver in that niche along the tunnel, the man in a farmer's clothes with one eye missing, and the rat slithering around inside its skull, peering out with those piss-yellow eyes through the empty socket. Its body had been broken open like a piñata, its chest split and splayed wide, yellow ribs jutting out at all angles, trailing tatters of flesh and stained cloth. It surged toward him on an undulating tower of rats. They carried the head and upper body, arms limp at its sides, legs trailing behind the pack. As he watched, lost in nightmare, one of the legs tore off in a puff of dust and ancient decay and lay abandoned on the tunnel floor as the pile of rats swarmed toward him.

"*Tommaso*," it said in that same familiar voice. "*Figlio bello*."

What Nonno had always called him. In Nonno's voice.

Unless it had been the demon's voice all along.

He felt as if he might collapse, mind shutting down, body surrendering. But that primitive part of his brain knew better. Without any conscious decision to do so, he turned and ran, bolting down the single tunnel remaining to him, praying that this would lead to that man-made wall with its crumbling mortar. If the demon touched him, he knew he would die.

As he ran, he felt the phone buzz in his hand again and knew what it meant.

Ten percent battery life remaining.

Minutes.

The cadavers he passed in this tunnel did not stir, but he could hear the rats behind him, boxing him in. They had cut off the other routes, and he wondered why not this one.

Which was when he realized there could be only one logical reason.

They were herding him, driving him exactly where they wanted him.

15

The diminished population of Becchina likely lowered the number of casualties in the quake. Fewer people would have been caught in collapsed buildings or crushed beneath falling debris. But when Kate and Marcello rushed from the House of Last Resort, they still found chaos waiting for them. Sirens blared up and down the streets of the hill town. They started to run down Via Dionisio toward the center of town. The blue-sky perfection of the day felt jarring as a backdrop for such a catastrophe, interrupted by constant sirens and the screaming of mothers racked with irrevocable grief.

Kate coughed to clear some of the dust from her lungs. Even outside the house, the air was full of ash from crumbling buildings and the small fires burning around town. Marcello tried to talk to her, but Kate's entire focus was on Tommy now and what she believed must be keeping him company down in that subterranean tomb. And how she might get him out.

She spotted Rohaan's Vespa in the road, badly scraped, front wheel spinning, but otherwise intact. Rohaan lay where she had left him, give or take a few feet. Sweat beaded his face, and he had turned pale from the pain of his injuries.

Kate skidded down on her knees beside him, took his hand. "Rohaan, I know help will come. I'm so sorry I can't stay—"

"I'll be all right," he said, grimacing at the lie. He needed painkillers and a lot of rest, and someone to get him out of the street.

Marcello went down on one knee by Rohaan's head. "Do you want a blanket or something?" He glanced around at the shops and their broken windows. "I'm sure I could find something useful."

"No, please, just send someone." He looked at Kate, barely able to keep his eyes open. She imagined he must be badly concussed. "If you're going to the catacombs now, please make sure Patrick is safe. He was going to be working there today—"

Kate squeezed his hand with her uninjured one. "He's okay. I know he is. They were doing all of that work to brace the catacombs for something just like this. And I need him to be okay, because I'm going to need his help."

Rohaan frowned. "Where is Tommy?"

"Underground," she said, and then emotion closed her throat. She couldn't get the rest of the words out.

Marcello took Kate by the arm, supportive enough to hold her up while despair tried to destroy her, but tough enough to know they could not linger another moment here.

"You'll be all right," Marcello told Rohaan. "We'll see to Patrick."

Rohaan crumbled a bit, tears welling in his eyes. "I know you will. I need him to be all right. Him and Tommy, both."

Kate looked down the hill—another hundred yards or so, and they could turn into the intersection that curved around into the city center, where the church's blue dome towered over a fountain and a roundabout, a gelato shop, and a wine bar. There were cars stopped in the road and at least two places where the pavement had split, the ground opening beneath it.

Tommy. She tried not to think about what might have been waiting down in the tomb for him, focused only on keeping him alive and on making him an exit from the walled-off tomb.

Kate walked toward Rohaan's smashed-up Vespa. It didn't appear to be leaking gasoline. She grabbed it by the handlebars and hoisted it upright. Her broken fingers shot daggers up her arm, but this had to happen, and there had been far too much hesitation already. Pain cleared her mind, focused her thoughts.

"I need to borrow this," Kate said, not waiting for permission.

She turned the key, startled when the engine growled to life. "We will get you help. And we'll be back with news of Patrick."

Marcello hesitated, looking to Rohaan, who waved him away. "I'm not dying. Go check on my husband!"

Relieved, Marcello managed a laugh and ran to the Vespa. He straddled the seat behind Kate and put his arms around her waist. She revved the throttle, started them forward, guiding the Vespa slowly around the crack in the road that had caused Rohaan to crash in the first place.

Kate felt a spark of hope.

Signora Housecoat lunged from the shadows of her front door. She screamed, but it was more than a scream. The old woman moved like no old woman Kate had ever seen. She ran three steps, reached a two-foot crack in the road, and leaped across. House-coat landed badly, ankle breaking, but she tumbled into a somersault and came up with even more velocity, running toward them on one good ankle and one so broken that it must have torn and cracked further every time she tried to put her right foot down.

Marcello shouted something at Kate in Italian.

Kate didn't need a translation. She twisted the throttle. The Vespa leaped forward even as Signora Housecoat dove after them, arms outstretched.

The woman caught Marcello by his shirt and ripped him off the back of the Vespa. Kate cried out, and as she slowed, she glanced over her shoulder and saw Marcello strangling the woman with both hands, forcing her snapping teeth away from his face. Her speed and ferocity were not the only changes in the slouched old woman. Her teeth had been black and jagged when she leaped after them, and Kate had gotten a glimpse of her palms in the sunlight—where her skin was covered with little red thorns that had torn through from the bones of her hands.

Behind her, Kate heard Marcello roar in either pain or triumph, but she didn't want to see which. She twisted the throttle again, avoided a sinkhole in the street, steered around the rubble of a row house that had collapsed on the side of the road, and then reached the corner. She took it as fast as the Vespa could manage, afraid to look back, afraid of what might be following. Was Signora House-coat like Franca, serving the demons she believed had died in that house, or was she possessed by one of the demons herself, the thing lying dormant in her all these years, maybe waiting for the one inside Tommaso Puglisi to finally be free?

Kate thought it had to be that second one, actual possession, and somehow the image of Signora Housecoat in her mind, the sound of her screech as she attacked them, pushed Kate through all the doubts and presumptions she'd had throughout this ordeal. What she had just seen . . . that had not been an ordinary madwoman.

This felt like a nightmare, but it was not. This was the waking world, real and terrifying, and she had to face it head-on if she wanted to get out of this town with her life and the man she loved.

Sunshine warmed her. The wind dried beads of sweat on her back as she drove the Vespa. Anywhere else in the world, this weather would have been the perfect day, lifting hearts and spirits. Horror should not happen under gorgeous, sunny skies, she thought. But two kinds of horrors were unfolding today, one natural and one un-natural. One *evil*. She didn't have any difficulty thinking the word now and knowing its meaning. She had seen it.

Kate rocketed the Vespa across the town center, right for the front steps of the church. She steered to the left, passing the church, heading straight for the entrance to the catacombs. A worker's box truck had been pulled up near the entrance. The gates were wide open. Half a dozen people were milling about outside those gates, and as Kate pulled up on the Vespa, faces turned hopefully toward her. They were all waiting for help and answers, and she had nei-ther.

It surprised her to see Graham and Sue, the older couple from the north of England who had initially declined to help restore the catacombs. Once they realized it was really happening, that the dreams Tommy and Kate had for Becchina were sincere and would mean actual projects getting done, they had volunteered to help. Graham had injured his knee and had a purple bruise on his forehead, along with multiple scrapes. For her part, Sue seemed unscathed except for a coating of gray dust that could only have come from a collapse down in the catacombs.

As she hopped off the Vespa, Kate's heart froze to ice. She rushed toward the handful of people, dodged a man from the town engineer's office, and went straight to Graham and Sue.

"How much damage?" she asked. "Any fatalities?"

Sue brushed dust from her face. "We were lucky, Kate. Only one section collapsed as far as we can tell. A little side room—it might've been for storage or prayer. Some of the specimens are sure to be damaged, but I don't think it's very bad at all."

Kate squeezed Sue's hand in quiet gratitude. "How many still inside?"

"Eight or ten, just shoring up the danger spots," Graham rasped in that gruff northern voice. "Young Patrick's got them working. Trying to keep the whole place from falling in."

Patrick, she thought. He would help her.

"Thank you," Kate said, and she raced past the rest of them without pausing to talk. Down the stairs, to the open gates, and then through the main passage that led to the church's catacombs, where the wealthy and the holy had been buried. Away from the tainted ones, the ones the devils had claimed, the ones they couldn't save.

She'd be damned herself before she let Tommy become one of those.

Inside, a crack ran along one wall and small bits of debris had fallen, but the corridor leading down into the catacombs remained in good shape. The original lights had gone out—short-circuited or something—but the generator that powered the lights being used by the workers was still chugging, and though the lights flickered with the surges of electricity from the generator, the place was well lit.

She retraced the steps she had first taken with Tommy and Marcello and Don Pino until she got to the main door to the catacombs. It ought to have been propped open, but they had to be careful not to expose the cadavers down there to the outside air. A thick power cable prevented the door from closing all the way, so she knew it couldn't be locked.

Kate yanked the door open and hurried through. A bulb had burned out, and she started through the first section of the catacombs in near darkness. She could see light ahead, could make out the shapes of the notches in the floor and niches in the walls where the ancient dead lay, dried like salt pork on a sailing ship, saved up for another day. *Maybe the Rapture*, Kate thought with a sneer. Everything deserved a sneer from her today, she thought. Everything that didn't involve getting Tommy out of the goddamned hole in the ground.

A figure approached her through the darkness, silhouetted by the light that glowed deeper into the catacombs. For a moment, she felt a chill envelop her, certain this figure would be like the others she had seen, the flickering old-movie images of men long dead. But when she came nearer to him, she could make out his face.

"Don Pino," Kate said. "I need your help."

The old priest's English was limited, but he understood well enough to stop and nod and put one hand on her arm as if to comfort her.

"Yes? Tell me," he managed.

"Come with me," she said, taking his arm.

Kate hustled the old priest faster than was safe. He might stumble or trip on something, but she didn't care. She blamed him for some of this. He might have come to Becchina after the House of Last Resort had been closed up, but he had obviously known more

252 · CHRISTOPHER GOLDEN

than he initially let on. He might have saved them from some of this horror if he hadn't been so well trained to keep the church's secrets.

"Listen," she said as she rushed him past dried-out husks of the dead. "The woman who helped us buy our house here—Franca?"

Kate glanced at him to see if he was following her English, and it seemed he was. The old priest nodded.

"She wanted us here," Kate said. "Mostly, she wanted Tommy here. She worships a demon called Alberith—cannot even believe I'm saying these words, but Franca says that's the demon who was in Tommy's grandfather. His nonno? And with Nonno dead, Franca wanted to serve Tommy up to the demon to be his new home, or host, or whatever you have when you're an evil spirit and you need to live inside a human being to stay on earth."

Kate caught her foot on a pile of debris that had broken off the ceiling. She stumbled, nearly face-planting on top of a cadaver, dragging Don Pino after her. She laughed darkly at the irony. She had worried about the priest falling and nearly yanked him down herself.

She paused and looked around. Down along the tunnel and off to the left, she could hear voices, and the sound of a hammer clanging off metal. They were putting support beams in place— the same task they were doing when the earthquake struck, but probably a bit more hastily now. They should have evacuated and had an engineer come in to check for safety first, but this was Sicily, and corners were often cut. Kate thought the town engineer might be down there with them, so at least they had some expertise there.

Patrick's voice carried along the tunnel. Shouting at someone that a beam wasn't straight. She knew she ought to go and tell Patrick that Rohaan had been injured but that he was safe, though the truth was that she could not be sure of his safety—not after Signora Housecoat's attack on her and Marcello. Besides, she thought, Patrick would know that Rohaan had been overhead on the streets of Becchina when the quake hit. If he was willing to put his family's safety over the immediate need to shore up the ceiling in the catacombs, he would already have left.

Kate and Don Pino had reached the narrow little tunnel branch that went off to the right, the one that ended in that man-made wall with its thirteen crucifixes and the Latin scrawled on stone. It had to be this. She started down the branch, but Don Pino gripped her wrist.

Pissed off, she rounded on the priest. "Let go! This is the way!"

Don Pino shook his head. "*Non capisco.* Why you do?"

"I'm trying to tell you! The stairs you wanted to use to put Nonno's body in the tomb under our house? They collapsed. Franca made Tommy go down there . . . like the demon's waiting for him." She dropped her chin as she walked, laughing out loud. "Can you believe that? Like the fucking demons are just waiting."

Her laughter echoed back at her, shrill and frantic, and she realized she was on the verge of losing control. For Tommy's sake, she couldn't do that.

Don Pino pulled his hand away, staring at her as if he thought she might start barking like a dog or something. Kate stared at him, disgusted with his complacency, disgusted by the audacity of the men in the church who had thought themselves so fucking holy, so goddamned clever, that it was completely fine to drag troubled people away from their homes and families and lock them up in the cellar of a home in Becchina and torture them with prayers and rituals until they behaved themselves or died.

And if it was all true? All the possessions, all the exorcisms, that was nearly as bad. Because how many times had they failed? How many times had they assumed they were the only ones qualified to help, with the results the same? What torments had the possessed people endured? To them, the incompetent exorcists probably seemed as much like demons as the actual evil that had invaded their flesh.

Kate turned away from the priest. "Patrick!" she shouted, loud enough to strain her voice. "Patrick, it's Kate. I need you! Over by the crucifix wall!"

Don Pino seemed confused, even a bit alarmed, but then they heard Patrick shout a reply and the hurried tromping of his boots as he rushed to respond. Two other men had followed Patrick, locals she didn't recognize. All three men surveyed her for damage, trying to figure out the urgency in her voice.

Patrick shone his flashlight on her right hand and her broken fingers, then up to her face and neck. He looked shocked by the cuts Franca had made there and which Kate had now nearly forgotten. Adrenaline could get her through a lot.

"What's happened, Kate?" Patrick asked. "A cave-in? Is someone trapped?"

Kate didn't have time to take it gently. "Not the way you mean, but yes. The back of our house collapsed in the quake, and Tommy fell down into a tomb that had been walled off. Part of the catacombs we didn't know was there. We've got to get him out, and it has to happen now. I'm afraid he's hurt, or crushed, or worse."

"Christ, I'm not sure what's worse," Patrick said in his gentle brogue.

"How do we get to him?" another man said, his accent something other than Italian. Another one of the Imports, apparently, here to help Patrick try to make Becchina a thriving community. Kate felt a sick laugh bubbling in her gut. If they only knew.

She pointed down the short corridor. "The wall at the end there, with the stones built up to block off the way. The one with all those crosses in it. I'm certain that's the way in, that some superstition or other made them want to close it off, but he's trapped back there and—"

"Say no more," Patrick replied, pushing past her.

The two men followed him, one slipping a fat tool from his belt, something a cross between a hammer and a pickaxe.

Maybe it was the sight of that weapon, but Don Pino seemed

to finally understand what she intended. As Kate turned to follow Patrick and the others, the priest grabbed her arm.

"No!" he commanded, looking stern and fiery, like one of his own kind but from an earlier era, when she might have been afraid of a man of the cloth. *"Non devi farlo! Il male deve restare sepolto!"*

Kate's Italian was weak, but she got the basic gist of that. Something about not letting the evil out. Anger had been simmering within her, side by side with her fear. Now it boiled up, and she leaned in close, eye to eye with the old man.

"So you do know what's down there," she said. "But as long as it stays locked up, you don't care what happens to my family and me, right?" She spit on the ground at his feet. "Fuck you, Padre."

Kate hurried down the short, narrow side tunnel. One of the men with Patrick stood back, holding an industrial flashlight so the others could see what they were doing. Patrick had a short shovel, and he jammed the blade into the crumbly mortar between two stones. Sparks flew, and mortar scraped and cascaded to the floor. When he stepped back, the man with the axe-hammer tool started chipping away at the same spot.

He paused long enough to slam his shoulder against the crevice they'd been working on. Stone scraped against stone. Patrick and the other man paused and looked at each other.

"Did that shift a little?" Patrick asked.

"I think so."

They went at it again, faster now, more urgently, taking turns digging between the stones, putting weight on them, trying to loosen up the wall. Kate thought to mention the place in the bottom corner where the rats had scurried through, but she doubted that would give them much better luck than they were already having.

This time, Patrick smashed his shoulder into the wall.

Two of the largest stones shifted, scraping, pushing inward.

Patrick had a smile of satisfaction on his lips.

"No!" a voice shouted, and Kate turned in time to see Don Pino coming at her.

The old priest had no weapons, but he had strength enough to shove her out of the way. She careened into the man holding the flashlight, and the light wavered as they collided with the tunnel wall together. Don Pino grabbed Patrick and tried to rip the shovel from his hands, cursing him in Italian, or Latin, or in some kind of primal language that gave voice to the panic in the old man's eyes.

"Fecksake, Father, get off me!" Patrick shouted, and he shoved the old man backward.

Don Pino's arms pinwheeled a bit, and then he fell on his ass on the stone floor. He grimaced in pain and then lay on his side, defeated, surrendering. The priest crossed himself and began to pray quietly.

"What in the hell's got into him?" Patrick demanded, staring at Kate.

Before she could answer, the tunnel filled with a resounding clang. The man with the flashlight turned it around in search of the source of that noise, and the light found the largest of the crucifixes had fallen from the wall. The place where it had once hung had started to push inward as well.

Patrick and his coworkers wore doubtful expressions now. Seeing the cross there on the ground, it suddenly didn't sit right with them.

"Please," Kate said. "Keep going."

The men hesitated.

Which was when someone else began to smash against the wall, but from the other side.

All of them flinched. Patrick took a step back from the wall, staring at it, at the damage they'd already done and the crucifix that had fallen. As they stared, a second cross fell off the wall. It stabbed into the stone floor and stayed upright, swaying slightly.

Then, from the other side of that weakened wall, Kate heard her husband begin to scream.

THE HOUSE OF LAST RESORT · 257

"Tommy?" She hurled herself against the wall. Felt some of the mortar give way and one of the largest stones shift. "Tommy!" she screamed.

In reply, he screamed again, but his screams sounded like pain instead of urgency.

They sounded like terror.

16

The rats were on him. Tommy screamed as they dragged at him, climbing him. He screamed as he stepped backward and hurled himself at the wall again. His shoulder cracked, but the stones shifted a bit. Was it bone or tendon, that crack? Pain shot along his arm and up the back of his neck, but he barely noticed. Pain was nothing, even the rats were nothing, compared to the dread that crawled on him, the fear that churned inside him. Because he *felt* it . . .

All through his childhood, he'd heard people say they could feel the presence of God. First, he had envied them, and then he didn't believe them. He still couldn't feel anything divine in the world. But *this*—the way his skin crawled, the suffocating pressure in the air, the quickening of his pulse—he felt all of that and no longer hesitated to put a name to it. There could be only one word—*evil*.

Terror blossomed from the base of his skull, that primal place where ancestral memory had passed down the fear of this feeling. He had never imagined himself a man who would scream, and yet screams ripped from his lungs as he twisted sideways and bashed himself against the wall again as a rat bit his neck and another scrabbled into his hair, tearing at his scalp. Blood dripped on his forehead.

The light from his phone flickered once.

Tommy turned to look back the way he'd come, and he saw it, looming in the tunnel behind him. In silhouette, it almost seemed as if the thing had a real body, but another step and he saw the truth of this abomination. It was a moving sculpture made of the churning bodies of rats and the corpse of some poor dead bastard whom the exorcists couldn't save. The teeth gleamed, sharp and black, and they gnashed together with a hunger undefined. Tommy had no memories before the second grade, but now images flooded his mind from his earliest life, and he thought of the darkness beneath his childhood bed, the three-inch gap between his closet door and the wooden frame that hinted at things lurking inside, and the way those dark places seethed with the promise of malevolence. He thought of an older boy in his neighborhood, Benny, and the day his parents told him Benny didn't want to hurt him, that bullies just wanted attention, but his parents hadn't seen the gleam in Benny's eye, the way that hurting Tommy seemed the most delicious thing Benny had ever tasted. They didn't know the things Benny whispered to him at the playground when he pushed Tommy down.

Whispers filled the tunnel around him. Voices came from the other side of the wall, urgent and terrified, but these whispers were something else. The whispers came from the rats and from the dead, and though he did not know the language, he understood their desires. They were hungry, and they wanted to be free. They had been caged in this place, and in these corpses, for a very long time.

Good boy, a voice whispered. Nonno's voice, in the back of his skull.

"I'm not helping you!" Tommy screamed.

His cell phone died.

The light went out.

Trapped in darkness, he felt his heart smashing against the inside of his chest as if it were trying to escape. It thundered in his ears, blood pumping, as if to shout that he still lived, that he should run, but where could he run when he couldn't see anything?

From the other side of the wall, Kate shouted his name. Blinded by the dark, Tommy heard people smashing at stone and mortar, trying to break through. He felt the rats swarming around his legs.

A rat dug into his shoulder and whispered in his ear, *"You've always been mine."*

Tommy hurled himself against the wall. His skull struck stone. Delirious, he slid down the wall, and the rats were all over him in the dark. They squealed and whispered and scratched, so many of them it felt as if they were an ocean, the tide rising to drown him.

"Tommaso," the dark whispered to him.

His heart beat a deafening crescendo in his ears. He forced himself to his feet and tried to smash himself against the stone wall again.

From the squirming, squealing darkness, something wrapped long, thin, dry fingers around his wrist. It yanked him backward, into the mass. Its fingers dug into his flesh, drawing blood that trickled hot rivulets along the unnaturally cold skin of his arm. He thought of the walks he had taken with his nonno as a small boy and the songs they had sung, and how it had made him feel loved—and he yearned for that.

Yes.

The word was in his heart. It dripped from him with every sluice of his blood.

He thought of his father, who had thrown him in the air and laughed with him, who had bounced little Tommy on his knee, and who had grown distant and sometimes cold around the same time he had fallen out with his own father and declared they would never return to Becchina.

Oh, how Tommy longed for him now. His father had loved him, had tried to protect him the best he could, and had fucked it up as so many did, by keeping secrets it would have been safer to share.

Teeth tore through cloth and skin and muscle. Ice entered his veins, raced through him. In the dark, he heard nothing but his heart thumping inside his head. No more clangs of metal against the other side of the wall. No more shouts from her . . . his person . . . his Kate. Whispers slid into his brain as if someone had upended a basket of snakes there, and they coiled and snapped at each other, hissing in chorus.

Tommy bent his legs.

He lifted his arms to protect his head.

He didn't know he was doing either of these things.

He screamed one last time as he drove his body straight at the wall.

17

The stone wall collapsed toward them in a rumble of rock and mortar, crucifixes swallowed by the rubble. Kate let go of her shovel and jumped backward just in time to see the tool cracked in half. A massive, egg-shaped rock spilled down from the upper part of the wall and struck the side of her leg. If she hadn't already been moving, it might have broken bone.

Men shouted around her. Patrick dove out of the way of the falling wall, but an older man named Gaetano did not move back in time. The rocks struck Gaetano's legs, and he fell backward, crying out in pain, hands flapping around as he stared down at the rubble that had trapped him. Gaetano hadn't been as lucky as Kate, and he looked too frightened to even attempt to dig himself out.

Not that the rats would let him.

They came pouring through the wall as it came down, along with her husband.

Kate called his name, limping toward him. As he crashed through the wall, several rocks had come down on top of him, but they had been a cascade—all together—and she hoped he was safe. Several rats rushed at her. Kate kicked one away and leaped over the other two, and then she was beside him.

Someone's flashlight went out.

Another flickered and grew dim.

"Tommy!" she shouted, grabbing him by the shoulders. "Are you okay?"

THE HOUSE OF LAST RESORT · 263

It seemed such a hideous question. So stupid. Of course he wasn't okay. But then Patrick was beside her, and together, they pushed rocks off Tommy and dragged him away from the rubble and the rats, and kept going because those rats were squealing.

Legs smashed under the rubble, Gaetano began to scream. "Jesus, get them off! They're biting! Fuck, someone . . . they're biting me!"

Kate felt for him, but there were others in the tunnel, and she had come here for her husband. She and Patrick half dragged, half carried Tommy until they were clear of the worst of it, closer to the lights in the main tunnel.

"Together, come on," she said, shooting a hard look at Patrick. "Get him to his feet, or we'll never get out of here."

"Where would we go?" Patrick demanded. "Let's wait for help!"

Kate shook her head. "I need him out of here. Out in the sun, right now."

Patrick frowned in confusion, but when Kate started to hoist Tommy to his feet without his help, he started to do his part. Kate knew she should have told him about his husband, but Rohaan's injuries weren't life-threatening, and right now she needed Patrick's help.

"Kate . . ." Tommy's voice sounded like stones grinding together. He had to be injured, but now wasn't the time to assess.

She turned to get him out of there and nearly ran into Don Pino.

The priest paled, standing in the main tunnel, wan yellow light turning him into some kind of specter. She thought about the priests in the chapel at her house, the ghosts that had haunted her but had also tried to keep her safe from much darker things. Did she really believe that?

She found that she did.

"Kate," the old priest said. "*Per favore.* No—"

"Get out of the way, goddamn it. Give us some blessings, not your fucking cowardice!"

The priest stepped aside. Kate and Patrick practically dragged

Tommy into the main corridor, and Don Pino glanced nervously back the way they had come and then started to follow.

Tommy kept staggering along with them, but he glanced back down that dark tunnel, and then he halted, trying to turn back. He began to make ugly, grunting noises in his chest, huffing like some animal about to charge.

"We need to go, Tommy. Come on," Kate pleaded, trying to propel him toward the exit.

Back down that side tunnel, where all the crucifixes had fallen, the man whose legs were trapped began to scream. In a moment, others started to shout. Kate peered back that way and, in the dim light of the one remaining flashlight, she saw the rats swarming. Biting.

Gaetano went silent as he pulled his legs free. The pain must have been blinding, but his screams were finished. Leveraging himself on the rubble, he stood up in a single fluid motion. One of his legs bent inward at the knee, the wrong direction, broken and misshapen. Limping, he shoved another man aside and started down the dark tunnel, toward the light.

A woman with rats in her hair stopped trying to pull them out, dropped her hands, and followed.

A horrible knowledge nested in Kate's gut. A brand-new faith that she wished she'd never had.

"Patrick, hurry. We have to go, right now!"

They started to drag Tommy, against his will, but after a moment or two, his feet started moving again, and at last, they left that side tunnel behind and hurried along through the catacombs. Kate ignored the mummified cadavers in the walls. These people were long gone. They were dust.

There were other things to fear.

18

As a little boy, when Tommy felt scared . . . when he wanted to cry because the darkness under the bed or in his closet seemed to breathe . . . when he knew each corner of the ceiling held something his eyes could not see but that yearned to take him, to snatch him, to have him forever . . . when he felt those things, he would draw up his covers and put his pillow over his head. He would make himself as small as he could, just a lump under a pile of sheets and blankets, and he would be quiet as a mouse, eyes open, praying that somehow his blankets and pillow would be enough to fool the darkness, to keep him safe.

He did that now.

Down inside himself, he curled up as small as he could be, hiding from the darkness that watched from every corner.

Through his eyes, he had seen the people scream as the rats swarmed and bit them. And he had watched those people *change*— seen the demons show their faces. In the tomb, they had whispered to him so many things he wished he had never heard, secrets and horrors. The things the exorcists had done to the boys and girls, and to women and men, who had been shipped there by the Vatican. The hopeless ones, the ones with devils inside them. So few had been saved, so many had died with those devils still inside them.

Caged inside the corpses of the damned.

Dried cadavers. Silent as dust.

They could travel in the rats. See through their eyes. But they could never do more than look, like tourists, as long as the wards in that wall remained in place. The crucifix wall, that sealed them inside the tomb built by the exorcists.

And then Tommy had come, and he had saved them. Just as Alberith had promised.

While Kate and Patrick dragged and pushed at him, tried to force him out of the catacombs, he had glanced back and seen what happened when the devils went free, when they left the bones of the damned behind and rode inside the rats, and infected by their evil, those rats began to bite.

Coiled up inside himself, Tommy had seen them begin to change—the ones who had been bitten. Their eyes were massive and oily black, their bodies bursting with scarlet thorns that broke the skin from within. Their chests split open, each revealing a rib cage like a jail cell, and behind the bars, the eyes of evil stared out from an infinite void of cold blue stars. Those stars were screaming. Their teeth blackened and fell out, replaced by rows of bruise-purple points like sharks' teeth.

He wanted to scream, but his voice was no longer his own.

Don Pino seemed to notice. The priest started to run and stumble. Kate and Patrick had forced Tommy to move and hustled him through the catacombs, and it was only as they neared the exit that he finally understood that he had been privy to insight that the others had not—that he had seen the effect the bites of those infected rats had on the people down in the catacombs.

"You don't see their real faces," he said to his wife. "Why don't you see them?"

Were they even there? Had his mind invented those devils? Was any of it real?

Kate said nothing. Just refreshed her grip on his arm and half dragged and half carried him, urging Patrick to hurry.

He wondered if Kate had even heard his question.

Tommy curled more tightly inside himself, thinking of the little boy he'd been, and the closet and under the bed, and he wished he had blankets and sheets and a pillow to hide beneath. But he only had himself.

Then they were outside, in the chaos after the quake, in the sunlight.

And he screamed.

19

Hearing Tommy scream, Kate felt her heart break. He had his moods like anyone else, but he was a good man, full of empathy and humor. Hearing him scream froze her. She wanted to comfort him, hold him until he could explain what he felt, but he tore away from her and Patrick and tried to retreat into the darkness of the catacombs.

Patrick snagged him by the back of his shirt. Tommy tried to rip free, but Patrick wrapped an arm around him from behind.

"Tommy, you're all right now! No fuckin' rats out here," Patrick said.

Kate started to go to Tommy, but Don Pino took her wrist to stop her. She spun to face him, but he looked right past her, staring at Tommy and Patrick. He tried to say something to her in Italian, but Kate scowled and pulled away. As she rushed to her husband, she heard Don Pino praying loudly behind her.

Just before Kate could reach them, Tommy struggled with Patrick, cried out, and smashed an elbow into his gut.

Released from Patrick's grip, Tommy made for the catacombs again, but Kate ran ahead of him and stood in his path. He hung his head, stooped over like a scolded child. She took him by the shoulders and gave him a hard shake.

"Snap out of it, for God's sake! You can't go back there!"

Tommy snapped upright, teeth bared, eyes the same putrid

yellow she had seen on the rats down in the tomb. When he spoke, it was a voice she knew, but not her husband's voice.

"*Always poking your nose in where it doesn't belong,*" Tommy said.

She'd heard that voice from Nonno, right before his stroke. It had ice in it, and venom, and the kind of cruel laughter only sadists and psychopaths could muster.

Tommy shook her loose and tried to grab her face—maybe to hurt her or just move her out of the way. Reflex kicked in, and she slapped him hard enough to rock his head back. The impact echoed all around them, even with the alarms and emergency vehicles still crying out across Becchina. People began to emerge from the catacombs, just a few, and they were terrified, some injured.

Tommy's eyes cleared. He touched his cheek where she'd slapped him. The skin had turned red.

"Kate," he rasped, with a gaze of bottomless sorrow. "Help me."

She didn't spend time trying to make sense of it or lying to herself about what she believed was happening to him. Kate knew that even a moment spent in denial might be the end of her husband.

So she slapped him again. His eyes narrowed in pain. Kate grabbed his hand, squeezed him tight. "Focus! Stay with me!"

They ran. Tommy kept moaning in pain, bending over to clutch at his chest and gut. He spoke to himself, arguing in undecipherable mutterings.

Patrick and Don Pino followed as quickly as the old priest could manage. There were screams and cries from inside the catacombs, and others began to emerge, but once Kate propelled Tommy around the corner, away from the church and up the cobblestoned street toward their wounded home, what happened behind them no longer mattered.

"Kate," Patrick called, trying to keep the priest moving. "What are we doing? What's going on?"

Tommy caught his foot on a cobblestone and went down. He smashed his knees on the stones and snarled in pain, remaining on all fours. Kate grabbed him under one arm and tried to haul him up.

Patrick kept talking to her, but she barely heard him. Her mind blazed with the truth she could no longer even pretend to deny. The way her husband had looked at her, spoken to her, she knew the same evil that had been in his grandfather now infected him. Frantic, desperate, she cast around in her mind for any information that might help, anything she'd ever heard or assumed, but everything she understood about the diabolical, she had learned from fiction.

"Kate!" Patrick said.

She spun on him. "Look up the street there," she said, pointing toward the house and the place where she and Rohaan had crashed the Vespa. "Your husband's up there. We had an accident when the quake hit."

"What?" Patrick gaped at her, shocked and angry. "Why didn't you—"

"Rohaan will be fine. And I needed you. But go to him now. I'm putting my husband first, and it's not fair for me to want you to do anything different."

Patrick glared at her, then looked at Tommy, hesitant to leave her in the midst of this—whatever he thought this really was.

Kate turned from him to glare at Don Pino. The old priest took a step backward as if he meant to flee from her. With Patrick looking on, she pulled Tommy to his feet and marched him toward the priest.

"You know what this is!" she told him. "Do something!"

Don Pino opened his hands and spread his arms as if he might start a sermon, but he shook his head as he did so. He began speaking Italian, apologizing to her with a shrug that looked as if it might go on forever.

"He's saying—" Patrick began, starting to translate.

"I know what he's fucking saying. He's copping out. His bosses put him in charge of this church, practically right on top of the

tomb where they buried a couple of hundred corpses in secret—
dead people they believed had been possessed when they were alive,
and that maybe still had demons in their goddamn bones when
they went into that tomb. They wouldn't have assigned him to a
church right around the corner from the House of Last Resort if
they—"

Don Pino clapped his hands together to interrupt her. "I am not
un esorcista!"

"And I'm not a fucking child," Kate snapped. "Don't clap your
hands in my face. You knew more than you said. You could have
helped us! Now—"

Tommy began to breathe hard, like someone trying not to
vomit. With an anguished cry, he pulled his T-shirt over his head,
hiding beneath the fabric, keeping as much of himself as he could
out of the direct sunlight. The day had begun to wane, but the sun
remained hot overhead. It was Sicily, after all.

The sun hurt the thing inside him, the thing he was fighting.
Kate could see it so clearly, and she knew the others could as well.
She whipped around to look at the old priest, needing his help and
wanting to strangle him at the same time.

"What do I do?" she asked, hating the pleading tone in her voice.

"*Dire le preghiera!*" the priest cried, forlorn, still looking as if he
might run.

"Say the prayers," Patrick said.

He hadn't run to help Rohaan yet. Kate felt gratitude so powerful it nearly brought her to her knees.

"Then say them!" Kate shouted.

But the expression on Don Pino's face told her what she needed
to know. Whatever these rituals were, he either did not know
them or did not have faith in them. But she had nothing else to
believe in.

"Useless asshole," she spat.

Don Pino started to reply.

Patrick quickly translated. "Hurry. Or it's going to be—"

"Too late!" Tommy rumbled. He looked over at Kate. His eyes had a yellow film. For a second, she thought he meant it was already too late, but she could still see the humanity in his eyes.

They started up the street toward number seventeen, Patrick under one of Tommy's arms and Kate beneath the other. They escorted him, half carried him, but when Patrick saw Rohaan and Marcello sitting on a curb, tending their injuries, he broke off from their trio and ran to his husband.

Kate shot a frightened glance at Tommy. She was relieved to see Marcello alive but fearful that she would not be able to get her husband into the car on her own.

That was her goal now. Get him into the Fiat and take him down from the hill, away from Becchina, away from Sicily. She warred with herself over this idea. The malevolent thing that had spoken to her with her husband's mouth, looked at her through Tommy's eyes . . . she had no reason to believe they could outrun it. But it had been here so long, and she thought maybe, just maybe, if the sun kept beating down on them and she could get Tommy away from this place, they could leave the demon behind.

As if it could read her mind, Tommy began to laugh. The sound slithered under her skin.

"Tommy," she said, trying to keep him moving toward the car.

Don Pino followed. He looked scared enough to piss himself again. Every part of his body made it clear how desperately he wanted to run, but when they came to the house, with its beautiful bougainvillea making it look as if nothing at all had happened here, as if peace and tranquility were the foundation of this house . . . she steeled herself.

Tommy had begged for her help.

Don Pino stepped between her and the Fiat that sat by the curb.

Kate took out her keys and clicked the fob. The car chirped to tell her the doors were unlocked.

Don Pino pleaded with his eyes. He pointed to the front door of 17 Via Dionisio. *"Dentro,"* he said, brushing the air to get his point across.

Every part of Kate longed to get in that car and get out of Becchina, to take Tommy away from here. She felt sick to think that she had urged him to move here, to connect to his family here, but how could she have known?

The old priest straightened up, a grim set to his features and a new vigor in his bearing. For the past few minutes, he had seemed like a rabbit about to bolt, but that had changed, as if being on the threshold of this house had made him surrender to fate or to the courage demanded by his calling.

Don Pino took Tommy's other arm and tried to move him to the front door.

Tommy twisted around and tried to bite him. The old priest moved his hand, but only for a moment. He began a quiet prayer and reached into his pocket, pulling out a rosary, which he wrapped around the hand that held Tommy's arm.

"What are you doing?" Tommy asked, his face blank, ordinary. Just her husband.

Kate stared at him.

"Katie?" he said. He so rarely called her that. "Are we leaving?"

The Fiat. His gaze ticked toward the car. Did she see a hint of that sickly yellow? Either way, she could feel how much he wanted to be in that car, to be away from Becchina. Kate shared his desire to get into that car and get out of here, to navigate around cracks in the road and debris, to find ways around emergency vehicles . . . to be as far from Becchina as possible by the time the sun went down . . . it was the most powerful yearning she had ever felt.

But the thing trying to keep control of her husband, to sink itself down into his heart and root itself in his bones—that thing wanted to leave even more than she did.

Which meant they had to go inside the house.

Her home. Tommy's home.

"Come on, babe," she said, taking his other arm. She glanced at Don Pino, and a silent understanding passed between them.

The priest kept praying. His voice grew louder. Tommy's head began to loll from side to side, like a snake being charmed by the music from a gourd flute. As if mesmerized, he went along with them as they walked him across the threshold and into the house.

Tommy snapped up as if an alarm had gone off. He ripped away from them and cracked the priest across the face with the back of his hand. Blood flew from Don Pino's mouth, and he staggered backward, crashing into a little side table, knocking over framed photos that the earthquake had somehow spared. They shattered as they hit the floor.

Kate tried to reach for him.

Tommy lunged for the door.

It swung shut of its own accord, slamming hard enough to add more cracks to the wall around it. Tommy grabbed the knob, tried to twist it, to yank it open, but the door would not budge.

"Tommy?" Kate ventured, scared more for him than herself. Terrified of what would become of him now. Only hours ago, all of this had seemed ridiculous, and now it had come true in the worst-possible way.

He dropped into a crouch, glaring at shadowed corners. Red spots appeared on his hands and arms and face—every part of his skin that was exposed—and they began to drip blood, staining his clothes, spattering the floor.

"Oh my God," Kate whispered as she watched sharp points push out through Tommy's skin. They looked like inch-long thorns, and the bleeding grew worse.

Tommy's lips parted, but the voice that came out didn't belong to him. It seethed with disdain and malice.

"*Come, then, and let us begin,*" the demon said, with the lips she had kissed on her wedding day. "*You were never able to drive me out before. This will be no different.*"

Kate saw the first priest emerge from the wall to her left.

Another came from behind her, and a third from the shadows along the ceiling. The ghosts of the exorcists had haunted this house for many long years. They had shown themselves to her but never to Tommy. Was this moment the reason? Had they known something about Alberith, something about Nonno and his family? Had they been waiting here, in this house, all those years, for this?

"You are less than nothing now, priests. Only phantoms, less than souls," the thing in Tommy said. *"I may simply eat you."*

The ghosts surrounded him, five in total. In the gloom of the foyer, they were like heat haze over pavement. They made the sign of the cross in unison, and although they uttered no sound that Kate could hear, their lips began to move, and the ghosts of the exorcists began to pray.

The demon in Tommy hissed. He gnashed his teeth.

"Fuck you!" it shouted, and it turned to the nearest ghost, trying to claw at its gossamer shape in the air.

Which was when Don Pino picked up that small side table and swung it into the side of Tommy's head.

Tommy went down hard. His cheek bounced off the floor.

"What the hell are you doing?" Kate screamed. Had he gone insane? Was he possessed, too? There had been others down in the catacombs—she knew that. Other demons who had remained steeping in the dried-out cadavers of their hosts, their victims, and who'd gotten inside those rats and escaped when the wall came down. Had Don Pino been bitten by one of those things, passing its evil infection to him?

But the old priest staggered. The effort had taken a toll on him. He dropped the table and massaged his arm, and she wondered if he'd given himself a heart attack or only torn a muscle.

The ghosts surrounded Tommy, who had crumpled to the floor.

Don Pino opened the front door—it gave way to him without resistance—and he shouted in Italian, calling back down the street for help.

Kate knelt there, hands in her lap, not knowing what to do.

These were ghosts. Acceptance had been forced on her, and now she had precious seconds to stare at them, to know without doubt that what she saw was real, and to think about demons. Cold crept along her spine, but she also felt a warm ember inside her chest, because if this evil existed and the ghosts of these priests lingered to fight against it, then the opposite of evil existed, too.

For the first time in a very long time, she prayed. For Tommy and for herself.

Don Pino stepped back from the door, and Kate looked up to see Marcello cross the threshold. He looked at Tommy on the floor—Tommy, whose head was bleeding, but whose skin was still torn up by those inch-long black thorns.

"It's real," Marcello said, looking to Kate.

Don Pino gestured to the unconscious Tommy. Kate and Marcello exchanged a look, both understanding what came next.

"You get his arms; I'll get his feet," Kate said, wiping away tears she'd only just realized were there.

They moved to lift Tommy, to carry him up the stairs.

Though insubstantial, the ghosts moved aside.

In and out of the light, barely visible, they followed Kate and Marcello up the stairs like a funeral procession. Don Pino came the last of all, leaning on the banister, his pallor gray and worsening.

The time for the last resort had arrived.

20

Tommy felt sicker than he had ever imagined possible. He lay on a hard surface, stretched out. His guts were on fire, boiling with the need to vomit, and yet he felt no urge to retch. It was as if the sickness in him did not want to come out. Pain surrounded him, the sting of wounds and the warm trickle of blood covering his body. It was his own blood, but it felt greasy, filthy, and the stink that filled his nostrils and created a disgusting film inside his mouth was the most repulsive stench he'd ever encountered, worse than the stink rising from a dying homeless man he'd discovered in a parking garage stairwell years before. He'd called 911 and stayed with the man until paramedics arrived, and it had taken all his empathy to hide his response to the smell of filth, shit, and infection.

This smell was worse, and it was all around him. Inside him.

Tommy would have cried, but he could not muster tears.

He tried to speak, but his mouth would not open for him. It opened and closed, and words came from his lips, but he could not control any of that. His eyes had a film over them, blurring everything, and the sounds in the room were muffled, as if he had fallen down a well. All noises and voices drifted to him from somewhere out of reach.

His vision rippled and bled as if he were underwater, looking up at the surface and trying to make sense of the warped shapes and patterns of light that waited for him there.

Someone spoke, but the syllables stretched and twisted, as if slurred by the world's drunkest man. The liquid shapes moved above him, and one came nearer—bent over him—and Marcello's face came into focus. His cousin, his family.

Tommy tried to lift his hand, to reach out to Marcello, but his body would not cooperate.

God, he felt so sick.

Kate, he tried to say, but his voice would not come.

Pain erupted all over his skin. He managed to glance down at his arm and saw that his skin was covered with red sores, with sharp points that pushed up through his flesh and looked like teeth.

Tommy tried to scream. He didn't reach for Marcello. He didn't grab his cousin's neck with a hand that had thorns protruding from the palms. But *someone* did.

With Tommy's hand.

Marcello unleashed a torrent of Italian profanity as he skirted backward and nearly fell over a chair.

"Fuck yourself!" Tommy's mouth roared. *"I will rip out the throat of anyone who comes near me!"*

His thoughts had been muddy, as if fresh from sleep, but now all that uncertainty burned away and he *knew*.

Inside his head, the voice spoke again. This time not with his lips or his breath but just down inside, where only Tommy could hear it.

Hello, Tommaso. We are going to be such good friends.

Panic. Terror. Hysteria. He felt all of that and more, enough to make his heart explode.

Let me out, let me out, let me out!

Those were his thoughts, not the demon's. The devil's. Whatever it was. The sickness that churned inside him . . . that *was* the demon. It hadn't made him feel sick, it was that feeling, the nausea and revulsion, the temptation to smash his own head into the wall, to crush his skull so this would be over. Anything so he would not have to feel this anymore. Whatever it took to get the sickness out of him, he would pay that price and more.

His own death. Someone else's death. The implosion of the whole fucking universe.

Whatever it took.

Laughter slithered in his skull. Sick as he was, Tommy felt overwhelmed by claustrophobia. He had been trapped, stuffed down inside his own body, suffocated by the sickness. And it mocked him. No words were needed—he could feel the derision in its presence, in the way his lungs filled and emptied. He could feel it sneer, using his own face to do it.

Marcello grabbed his left wrist. A piece of cloth had been wrapped around his arm, blood soaking through from the wounds Tommy had given him.

On his other side, another figure pushed through the milky veil across his vision. She grabbed his right wrist and pinned it to the table.

Kate.

Crying.

Her tears dripped onto his face. One landed on his cheek. Another splashed onto his nose and then dribbled up toward his right eye, and into the corner of his eye as if it had come from his own ducts. Tommy inhaled sharply. More tears splashed him, but that right eye stung as if he'd rubbed some peppery spice into it.

The left eye remained blurred, seeing through a greasy film created by the presence of Alberith. But the right eye began to clear. He blinked several times—only that one eye able to close—and the whole room came into sharp clarity. It felt like surfacing from a lake in the last moment before his lungs would have failed.

They were in the chapel.

Now that he knew, he could feel the table beneath him and realized he lay atop the lava table with its painted flowers.

"Kate?" he managed with his own lips.

For a moment he doubted the word had come from his mouth, but he saw the surprise and spark of hope in her.

"Tommy? Can you hear me?"

His stomach churned, and he felt a chill through his body. The sickness might abate for a minute or two, but it hadn't left him. Of course it hadn't. For more than seventy years, it had waited inside his nonno, and now it had him.

"It's never going to let me go," he rasped.

"We are here, cousin," Marcello said. "We won't leave you."

But while Kate looked hopeful, her eyes wide with determined love, Marcello looked as if he would need only the slightest provocation to flee—and Tommy would not have blamed him.

Another figure approached on his left, where the film still covered his eye. Even before the old priest began to pray, Tommy knew it was Don Pino just from the stoop of his back and the smell of cigarettes that wafted off him, which Tommy had barely noticed until today, though it had always been there.

The prayers began, in Latin. An invocation that Tommy realized had been there all along, in multiple voices as steady as the tides crashing on the shore.

While he had been drowning inside himself, the priest had been praying for him. Conducting the rite of exorcism. But it wasn't only his voice. There were others, all in Latin. Some were barely a whisper, a rasp, the creak of the boards and beams of this house when the wind blew. His right eye might see Kate clearly, but now that he heard those voices, it was through the milky left eye that he could make out the gossamer images of other priests.

Kate noticed the line of his gaze.

"You see them," she said.

Tommy did. They were barely there, just hints of things, and he would have thought them an illusion if not for their voices. If not for their prayers, intoned in ragged whispers. He knew who they were, these ghosts. Kate had said she had seen one, but even before then, she'd heard them in the house, had known they were there even before she could admit it.

"Tommy? You *do* see them?" Kate asked.

Marcello glanced at her, confused, but it was clear he only saw

Don Pino. He heard only the voice of the old priest who had never been an exorcist, who had been left to watch over this abandoned place like a security guard.

Kate looked to the ghosts. "He knows you're here. He wants your help. Please—"

The sickness seized Tommy again. His stomach convulsed. He shuddered and began to sweat, and fresh blood wept from the wounds all over his body. The demon remained, and the thorns in his flesh were evidence, if any had been needed.

The ghosts of the exorcists lifted their voices, echoing from shadows and in corners only they could see. Tommy caught a glimpse, with his one good eye, of the other side of the chapel, where half the room had collapsed into the ground. The house ended there in a sawtooth line of broken tile, where he'd climbed up from the rubble and then back down into the catacombs.

The sun had sunk lower in the sky.

Tommy realized he had been unconscious for a while. He vaguely remembered that someone had struck him in the head when the demon had evicted him from his own mind. He had lost time. Dusk was not more than an hour away, which meant he had been imprisoned down inside himself for hours while the demon did whatever it felt like doing. With his one good eye, he studied Kate's face, saw the blood spattered there, saw her exhaustion, and wondered how bad the demon had been, what it might have said or done while he had been unconscious.

Shame flooded him. He knew there was no reason for it, that whatever the demon had said or done, they would know it wasn't him—but he felt that shame nevertheless.

How long had the ritual gone on? How many prayers had been said over him, just to allow him a chance to struggle with the sickness, to make room for himself in his own mind?

Tommy opened his mouth to speak again and found he could not.

No, no, no, no, he thought as the thick, greasy film began to cover his eye again.

He thought that this time it might trap him down inside himself for good, but before that happened, he wanted to tell Kate it had been her tears that had let him break through. Had it been love, like some fairy-tale magic? Tommy thought it was something more, that what Kate had given him was the pure expression of the connection between them, the humanity and empathy they shared, all their hope. Somehow that purity had given him a window back into his own life. A periscope, giving him a view of the world above the place where the demon had tried to drown him forever.

As the window closed, as the milky blur occluded his vision again, Tommy discovered that he was still there. He couldn't really see, or hear, or feel much of anything, but he was still there.

Kate.

It wasn't as simple as love. As wonderful as love could be. This was trust, and partnership, and hope for the future. They were in this together, whatever might come, and they both knew it.

Kate.

Tommy's right hand twitched. And he felt it.

And he felt her grip on his wrist, that contact with his wife.

He realized that there was still a little spot on his right eye that remained clear. Just a tiny aperture that the demon had not been able to close.

Hope is such a fragile thing, the thing infecting him whispered. *Watching it die is perhaps the most delicious taste there is.*

That voice. Nonno's voice, but not really Nonno. That voice belonged to the thing that had poisoned Tommy's grandfather, tainted him all his life, and now would taint every memory Tommy had of him. *Figlio bello.* Nonno singing to him and holding his hand. Those precious moments could not have been shared with the demon. Nonno had kept the evil inside, caged within himself, held on to it all his life and been its master until his mind and memory unraveled, and then he died.

Did Tommy have that strength?

He didn't think so. And the demon didn't think so, either.

But Tommy had Kate and the little bit of control remaining to him.

He found he could feel his lips and make them move.

"Kate," he rasped.

"He's still in there!" she cried.

Marcello turned to Don Pino, urging him to be louder, as if only the old man's prayers were giving Tommy this last moment of strength.

And it *was* a last moment. Tommy knew that. It felt as if he hung from a cliff over the abyss, just by his fingers, and though he had found a better grip, it would not last very long.

Kate bent over him, looking into his eyes. Through that tiny pinprick of vision remaining to him, Tommy saw the little spot of blue in her left eye, and the slashing angle of her left eyebrow, and the little spray of freckles across her nose that only came out in the sun. He wished that she would kiss him, but there were sharp points pushed up out of his skin, and he didn't want to hurt her.

She let go of his wrist so that she could reach up and touch his face.

The ghosts of the exorcists prayed louder.

You misunderstand all of this, the demon whispered in his mind. *This may be your world, but in here, with me, I am your personal hell. This is why we do it, poison you inside. There is no suffering as sweet for us as this.*

His free hand shot up and grabbed Kate by the side of her face, raked thorns across her cheek and jaw and nose. Blood flew, and she screamed.

It should have destroyed Tommy, seeing his own hand used to hurt her that way.

But her blood splashed his face, his lips, his eyes.

His vision cleared.

He roared and sat up.

Don Pino shouted to Marcello in Italian, but Tommy did not

need a translation. The old priest thought the demon had completely taken over. Of course he did. In that moment, Marcello would have believed it, too. Even Kate, staggering away in shock with blood streaming through the fingers she splayed over her injured face, would have assumed it.

But the ghosts saw *Tommy*. Their prayers changed.

The exorcists lunged for him, and their hands passed within him. They grabbed hold of something, and he felt as if they were tugging at his insides. The sickness remained, but the ghosts of the exorcists weakened it, confused it, allowing Tommy to solidify control of his own body, just briefly. Bile burned up the back of Tommy's throat, and he turned and threw up the contents of his stomach.

Marcello tried to hold on to him, but Tommy tore free.

In seconds, the clarity of his vision began to fade. The greasy film began to slide over his eyes. He went to wipe it with his fingers and knew he would have control of them for only a moment or two as the demon reasserted its vileness.

"Tommy," Kate said, through her pain. "I know it isn't you. Fight this."

She was on her knees, speaking into her hands as her blood spattered the floor. She wanted him to know, down inside wherever he was, that she knew he would never hurt her. That she knew it was the demon.

He could feel his clarity waning. Only moments of control remained.

Maybe his last moments. The last time he would ever be able to use his own mouth. He should have used those moments to tell Kate that he loved her, that he was sorry.

Instead, Tommy kept silent. With all the control left to him, he twisted around to face the dying sunlight. Don Pino and Marcello stayed back, fearful of the demon.

The first step, Tommy dragged his foot on the tiles, but the next step came easier.

Inside him, the demon sneered and spat and swaggered.

Then Tommy ran across the tiles, out into the long shadows and golden light of the impending dusk, toward the jagged edge where the earthquake had sheared off the rest of the house. He would not be climbing down this time.

Under blue sky and hot Sicilian sun, he leaped.

And he fell.

His left leg struck the broken stairwell on the way down, and he felt bones snap.

Inside him, the sickness roared its fury.

Tommy wondered how long the demon would stay trapped in the bones of his corpse, down in that tomb, before it finally went back to hell.

21

The aroma of fresh coffee woke him. It might have been the greatest smell the world had to offer. For a time, that scent was all he knew and all he wanted to know. His eyes remained closed, but he could feel the sun on his face, and he knew from the angle of its warmth and the birds singing outside the window that it must be early morning. It felt as if he were waking into a beautiful dream instead of rising out of one.

Pain told him this was no dream. In spite of the sunshine and birdsong and the softness of the sheets and blanket, and the tantalizing aroma of coffee, the pain remained. It ebbed and flowed like the bass line running beneath a song. The cast on his left leg felt too tight, the skin beneath it sweaty and itchy. The side of his skull throbbed with a sharp line of pain that felt unnatural, as if something had cracked inside his head. His whole body hurt.

"Coffee," he whispered, just the exhalation of the word, the way a tired man might speak his lover's name while lying beside her in the morning.

"Tommaso," a woman's voice said, cracking with emotion.

He opened his eyes.

Nonna sat in a chair beside the bed, on the edge of her seat, her eyes red from crying. She stared at him with such sadness and hope that he nearly wept himself. She dabbed her eyes with a tissue, trying to master her emotions. What must she feel? he wondered. Grief, certainly. And relief. Probably regret. Tommy thought Nonna must have had plenty of that.

A tall figure stood behind her chair, swaddled in sunlight so that for a moment he was just a shadow. It might have been anyone, but then he moved to stand beside Nonna's chair, and Tommy saw it was Marcello, with a fresh haircut and a healthy, glistening tan. Marcello looked like a new man, entirely different from the frightened, battered cousin he had been . . . how long ago?

"Marcello," Tommy said, his voice rusty, but still his own. "What day is it?"

With a shake of his head, Marcello went toward the door. "Just a moment."

The door opened and shut with the shush of freshly oiled hinges. The lack of sound made Tommy frown, and he glanced around the room. His neck hurt—his everything hurt—and little jolts of pain jabbed into his back and spine and ribs. What the hell room was he in? The view from the window, at least from his supine perspective, offered only blue sky and the corner of some roof or another. Was he in Palermo, or Rome, or somehow still in Becchina? How badly had he been injured?

He remembered falling and the sharp pain of the impact. He recalled the feeling of bones breaking and being unable to draw a breath.

And rats in the darkness, watching.

And a whisper as he slept.

The malignance that had gotten inside him could not continue to possess someone, corrupt them body and soul, if that someone was dead, and Tommy might have been dead. He thought he had been, briefly. He had launched himself off the broken edge of his broken home, thirty feet above jagged stone and shattered beams, and in that moment, death had been his fondest wish.

Now he smelled coffee, and his nonna sat at his bedside, and it was a beautiful day. He was grateful that his wish had not come true.

"Nonna," he said, reaching out to take her hand.

His grandmother flinched from his touch, drew back, pushed up from her chair. She hung her head, facing away from him.

The door opened again, and Marcello reappeared. He stepped into the room with someone following right behind him.

Kate.

Tommy grinned. She had cuts and bruises and bandages, but she was healing. She looked weighed down with worry. Of course she had been worried. Their lives had exploded, and if he had been unconscious for weeks or perhaps longer, she had been in limbo, waiting to see where life would take them next.

Her face lit up when she saw him awake, head propped on the pillow. Kate hurried to him, ignoring Nonna and Marcello entirely.

"Babe," he rasped, and she sat on the edge of the bed and wrapped her arms around him.

Pain radiated through his body from that embrace and the jostling of the bed, but it made him feel alive to hurt. He inhaled her smell, so familiar—her shampoo, the salt of her sweat—and this was better than coffee. Tommy felt safe in spite of his pain. He felt protected.

Kate kissed him, gently, and took both his hands in hers.

"I wasn't sure if you'd ever open your eyes again," she said.

Something about the way she said those words troubled him. "I was pretty banged up."

"Banged up? You broke your left leg in three places. Four ribs. Punctured a lung. You had a pretty serious concussion—and you know head wounds bleed so badly; the blood was everywhere. I couldn't believe you were still breathing."

Kate watched him while she spoke, as if her surprise at finding him still alive had not faded.

"You smashed up your right elbow pretty badly, too," she went on. When she smiled, it seemed bittersweet. "But here you are. Back among the living at last."

Tommy heard her voice, but he lost the thread of her thoughts. Something was not right. He started glancing around the room again—pain be damned. An IV unit hung from a post beside the bed. A muted monitor blipped silently, presumably his life signs. On a side table was an array of medications. Marcello looked on, and Nonna sat in an uncomfortable-looking chair. But they were not in a hospital.

"Where are we?" he asked.

For the first time, he noticed Kate's eyes had begun to well up. She blinked and wiped at them, as if the unborn tears had betrayed her.

She kissed his forehead. "Of course you're confused. I should've realized. But you're just across the hall from our room, babe."

"Our room?"

Kate squeezed his hands. "You're *home*, Tommy."

For a split second, he thought she meant Boston. But of course this wasn't that at all. He glanced at Nonna and Marcello, and suddenly, he could hear the ruckus of workers hammering. The whine of a power saw kicked in.

He stared at Kate as his throat went dry and a little knot of sickness formed in his gut. Contractors were at work repairing the house. Their house.

Tommy felt a scream building in his throat. How could Kate have let this happen? How could she have stayed here?

And what of the others? When the wall between the exorcists' tomb and catacombs had come down, the rats had swarmed out—dozens, maybe hundreds of them. Some carried unimaginable sickness, evil that had been waiting down there for generations. They'd bitten people, and those people had been infected . . . inhabited. What had become of them?

"I don't understand," he said quietly, wondering if Kate would hear him over the sound of rebuilding.

Gaze full of love and regret, Kate glanced at Marcello and nodded. In response, Marcello crossed the bedroom and opened the door, as if he had been waiting for her signal to do so. Tommy heard a scream echoing from another room or another story. Before he could even try to understand, Marcello moved aside to allow two men into the room. One was slender and deeply dark-skinned with three matching scars on his throat, while the other was older and white, short and squat, with round little glasses that sat on the bridge of his nose.

They were priests, armed with Bibles and crucifixes and white collars, and each carried a small censer on a chain. They swung the chains on long arcs, incense spreading around the room, eddying in the breeze from the window. The smell made Tommy retch. The coffee aroma had spoiled him. This stink was its opposite in every way. It made his stomach churn in revulsion. Anger flared inside him. They were hurting him. Tommy didn't know why, but these priests were here to hurt him.

Tommy tried to tell them to leave, that the incense was making him sick. A string of vomit bubbled up the back of his throat and spilled from his lips. The priests began to pray, and Tommy found that he could not speak a word.

Fuckers, a voice said inside his head, full of loathing. *I'm going to skin them alive.*

Marcello escorted a weeping Nonna from the room, but Kate stayed behind with the two priests as they began the ritual.

Tommy saw the sorrow in Kate's eyes and he shared it. He understood now.

He wished he could put his faith in these priests, but he did not know how much experience they had. Were they up to the challenge of this assignment? They were new here, and this was—after all—the House of Last Resort.

Reopened at last, Tommy thought, hysteria building.

Under new management.

Acknowledgments

Over the years, I've had occasion to put my gratitude in writing many times. It's never easy, because you always leave out people who deserve your thanks. So, first and foremost, my deepest gratitude to the friends and family who've calmed me, listened to my rambling, and cheered and championed me. Thanks to the readers, especially those who've come back time and again, and who've shared their enthusiasm with me. You keep me going.

I'm especially grateful to my editor, Michael Homler, and the entire St. Martin's team, including Cassidy Graham, Allison Ziegler, and Hector DeJean. Special thanks go to Jonathan Bush, the gent responsible for the best book covers an author could hope for.

Thanks, always, to my agent, Howard Morhaim, and my manager, Pete Donaldson. I feel so fortunate to have you both in my corner.

And, forever, to my wife and partner, Connie Golden, and our squad. You're the reason.